THE BY
CORRUPTED
Union

JILL RAMSOWER

❀ Created with Vellum

Books by Jill Ramsower

The Byrne Brothers Series
Silent Vows
Secret Sin (Novella)
Corrupted Union
Ruthless Salvation

The Five Families Series
Forever Lies
Never Truth
Blood Always
Where Loyalties Lie
Impossible Odds
Absolute Silence
Perfect Enemies

The Savage Pride Duet
Savage Pride
Silent Prejudice

The Of Myth & Man Series
Curse & Craving
Venom & Vice
Blood & Breath
Siege & Seduction

CORRUPTED UNION

JILL RAMSOWER

ONE

Humans hadn't been hunted as prey for thousands of years, yet something in our DNA still remembered. An instinctive sense of survival. Even when the conscious mind hadn't detected danger, the senses knew.

For example, the prickling sensation of unease that crept across the back of my neck after letting myself inside my parents' house. The place was supposed to be empty. Mom and Dad hadn't come home yet. The lights were off. The house was quiet save for the soft humming of appliances filling the sunlit silence.

I'd started to rummage through the fridge when I felt it—a burning awareness heating my back.

Someone was behind me. Watching.

A thousand thoughts flashed through my mind in an instant. Mom and Dad would have said something rather than skulk in the shadows, so it wasn't one of them. Dad's security? As the governor of New York, he always had a bodyguard nearby. Could one have returned to the house for something?

And decided to stalk you instead?

Not likely. I knew most of the team he worked with, and they were all good guys. Who did that leave? The alarm was still activated when I'd come in. Either the person had the code or had somehow broken in without triggering the alarm. So which was it? Only one way to find out.

My heart rate kicked up another notch.

I grabbed the milk and closed the fridge without turning around, stepping to the side and reaching into the cabinet above for a glass. At the same time, I slipped my other hand into the drawer at my waist to where the steak knives were kept and set one on the counter. Only then did I turn around.

How did the senses know? They'd been spot-on. I couldn't help but be impressed by evolution, though that wasn't where my thoughts should have taken me. The unfamiliar man leaning against the doorframe across the room was the very definition of intimidating. His muscular frame dwarfed my own, and tattoos peeked above the collar of his snug Henley. But it was more than that—his presence radiated a savage calm, as though the world was meant to lay at his feet because if it didn't, he'd burn the whole damn thing to ash.

I should have been terrified. That was how a normal woman would react when confronted by such an unapologetic predator. But I wasn't normal. I was only afraid of one thing in life, and this man wasn't it.

"Are you lost?" I asked in a steady voice. Adrenaline filtered into my bloodstream, a purely physiological response that couldn't be helped. Fear was a different monster. True fear was a tar-like quicksand that suffocated a person from the inside. I knew fear, and this wasn't it.

The man tilted his head a fraction. Maybe only a single degree, but I noticed, and I could have sworn it denoted curiosity. He found me amusing.

I found his interest irrelevant.

"Not lost, just waiting," he eventually answered. His voice was rugged yet soft, like the vibrating rumble of a hungry jungle cat.

"For my father?"

"Yes."

"People usually make an appointment. Tends to go over better than breaking in."

"People are *usually* frightened when they encounter a strange man in their house." He began to inch closer.

"Not my house." I leaned my elbows on the counter behind me, getting my hands as close to the hidden knife as I could allow without revealing my weapon.

"Your parents' house, close enough."

As he neared, I could see the rich turquoise shade of his eyes. He was beautiful for a criminal—well-defined jawline, thick sand-colored hair, and a rare facial symmetry that Hollywood would envy. He had to know that with his looks, breaking and entering was pointless. He could probably charm his way inside the White House. Why had he felt the need to seek out my father this way?

"What's your name?" My curiosity got the better of me.

His lips twitched in the corners. "Keir."

I didn't offer my name, and he didn't ask. I got the impression he already knew. "If you're here for my dad, then you must want something from him. You have to know this won't help your cause. And if you're here to hurt him, then you should know he always has security with him."

"I'm only here to talk."

"About what?"

"Business."

A man of many words, I see.

He made it to the large marble-top island only a dozen feet from me. My jaw clenched. Something about this man piqued my curiosity, and I sensed the intrigue was mutual. Dragging out information annoyed me, however. Why wouldn't he just tell me what this was all about? My father wasn't the secretive type and couldn't be bought, so what could this *Keir* need to discuss that warranted the cloak-and-dagger charade?

"Why aren't you afraid?" he asked in an even,

deliberate tone. Taking one step, then another, he started to round the island.

"Do you want me to be? Is that what gets you off?" I shot back, keeping my voice as level as his.

"You don't like to answer questions."

Step.

"Neither do you."

Step.

His eyes, as bright as the Caribbean Sea, trailed over my face as though memorizing my features. His scrutiny made me uncomfortable.

"You shouldn't come any closer," I finally warned, a breathiness seeping into my voice.

Step.

"Why not?"

He was now only a couple of feet away from me. He seemed even larger up close. I wasn't exactly petite at five feet five, but he towered over me. Had to be six feet three or four. And it wasn't just his height. He was broad like a professional athlete, thick with mature muscle. Probably somewhere close to thirty years old. Confident. Calculating. Deadly. Pure predator.

I pulled the knife from behind my back in one quick motion and held it securely in my fist. "Because I have this, and I'll use it."

Keir's eyes seemed to brighten further. "Now, why would you go and do a thing like that?" He inched forward.

"Protect myself?"

Completely ignoring the knife, he eased forward

until the blade touched his chest. "Take out a weapon when you don't plan on using it."

"What says I'm not?" I swiftly raised the knife to his throat, the tip pressing against his skin.

He leaned forward just enough for the blade to draw a prick of blood. "Because I'm still breathing," he murmured.

I never had a chance to respond.

One second, I had the knife at him, and the next, he'd grabbed my hand, spun me around toward the counter, and forced my hand to hold the blade at *my* throat instead of his. I couldn't move an inch. His arms were steel beams wrapped around me while his solid body pressed against my back. I was at his mercy.

"If you don't use the weapon, you run the risk of your opponent using it against you." His lips were so close to my ear, each softly spoken word felt like a caress. A shiver glided along my skin and rattled my insides to the point of chaos. It was the only explanation for how wires could be so crossed that a bolt of lust struck deep in my core. How could this situation possibly turn me on? It didn't. My brain had to be misfiring.

He is incredibly hot, Ro.

And dangerous! I shot back at the whimsical voice in my head, disgusted.

"I never claimed to be a fighter," I said with an edge. "Just that I wouldn't run crying." I held still. Partly because the knife tip was teasing at breaking my skin, but also because there was no point in fighting

6

him. I wasn't going anywhere if he didn't want to release me.

Outwardly, I reflected perfect calm, but on the inside, an intoxicating sense of exhilaration flooded my veins. Like Frankenstein's monster struck by that first lightning bolt, I felt my body come alive. The situation was dangerous. I shouldn't have enjoyed what was happening, yet a part of me wanted to seize the feeling with both hands and never let go.

"I don't believe much of anything would bring you to tears," Keir mused as if to himself.

The blade drifted gently down my neck, slowing at my fluttering pulse point. My breaths grew shallow and more frequent, each one drawing in more of his intoxicating scent—old leather and motor oil wrapped in a trace of expensive cologne. It was an odd assortment of flavors that somehow complemented one another perfectly.

"I'm sure you could manage, but I'd prefer if you didn't."

He made a curious rumbling sound in his chest, then slowly shifted his hand, releasing mine and moving to gingerly grasp the blade. He disarmed me in a way that requested my surrender rather than forced my submission. I could lash out and cut his fingers since the knife handle was still firmly in my grip. But his actions seemed to convey that he wasn't there to hurt me, so I followed his lead and released the weapon.

He tossed the utensil on the counter, then slowly released me, making sure to position himself between me and the knife. Cold air circled me at the loss of his touch.

"If you didn't want to hurt me, why didn't you just stay back? Or do you enjoy tormenting people?"

Keir stared at me. I used the opportunity to do the same, trying to figure out the unnerving man across from me.

"I could have done a lot worse if I'd wanted to torment you."

"Then why?"

Silence.

"Because I could." His delayed responses were a strategic power play. I got the sense he was used to a position of control, even lording over the pace of a conversation.

I refused to play by his rules.

"No." I shook my head. "You did it to show me that you could. There's a difference."

He gave a slight nod. "Then you have your answer."

Maybe, but it offered no clarity. Everything about this man was shrouded in mystery. I wanted to take the knife and slice away his mask to unveil what lay beneath.

My curiosity pissed me off.

It meant I felt some vested interest in what I learned, and that would be pointless. Keir clearly lived in a universe beyond my own—somewhere seedy and reckless and poised for devastation. I wanted no part of it, and therefore, should want no part of him.

"I think it's best if you wait outside," I blurted, crossing my arms over my chest.

Keir's narrowed stare seemed to twist me around like a Rubik's Cube, searching for a solution. However, his efforts were cut short by the sound of the front door opening. We turned our attention to the entry, but no one appeared. It suddenly occurred to me that they expected the alarm to be armed and didn't know I had stopped by. His security officer was likely launching into some practiced emergency protocol.

"Dad, it's me!" I called out. "I'm in the kitchen."

Muffled voices filtered into the house before my dad stepped into view. "Hey, Ro! We weren't expecting you." His movement faltered when he caught sight of our visitor.

"Yeah, sorry about that. I forgot to text." I looked at Keir, who now stood beside me. "Um, this is Keir. He came by to see you." I hadn't had time to think about what I'd tell Dad when he got home. I could have run to his side and told him how the man had been waiting inside the house when I arrived, but I didn't, and I wasn't sure why. To keep from making a scene? Maybe. To prevent Keir from getting arrested? That seemed to resonate louder than the other possibility, which only irritated me more.

Dad slipped off his suit jacket and draped it on a kitchen bar chair, his eyes never leaving Keir. "Why don't you head upstairs, sweetie, while I have a word with Mr. Byrne."

"No reason for her to leave," Keir offered, to my

surprise. "I'm only here for a friendly conversation, and after the short time I've spent with Rowan, I'd say her female sensibilities aren't at risk." His eyes cut to me, glinting with humor.

Was he ... teasing me? What strange upside down world had I fallen into?

I appreciated that he was mocking the archaic masculine need to shelter innocent females, but it set me off balance. He acted as though we knew one another. As though we'd shared an understanding substantial enough upon which to base a private joke. Granted, I hadn't ratted him out, but that didn't make us friends.

I did my best to school my reaction when I realized my father was searching my face for insight into what had passed between Keir and me.

"My daughter's sensibilities are none of your business. As far as you're concerned, she doesn't exist." My father's harsh retort surprised me. He was protective, but his status as a public figure meant he was rarely aggressive.

Hoping to defuse the situation, I poured myself a glass of milk from the jug I'd almost forgotten about and prayed Dad didn't notice the knife half hidden behind a jar of utensils. "Mom at one of her meetings?" I asked casually.

"She is, though she should be home any minute, so it'd be best if we could move this along. What brings you so far from the Moxy, Mr. Byrne?"

The Moxy? What was that? I made a mental note to look it up.

The two men stood across from one another, the white marble island between them, with me stationed like a referee off to one side. Of course, we also had the presence of Dad's security chief lurking at a distance, but that didn't seem to change anything. These two were ready to go head-to-head.

"I see you've been doing your research," Keir said evenly.

"I had a feeling you wouldn't be dismissed so easily, though I already told you I wasn't interested in doing business with your ... organization."

"Very presumptive of you to dismiss us without hearing me out. Thought you were known to be one of the *good ones*—levelheaded and open-minded."

"Say what you came to say." Dad's command hung in the air.

"As you're aware, the mayor is close to announcing his appointment to replace the retiring police commissioner. The man he plans to put in power is even more corrupt than the mayor himself, which isn't saying much."

The shadow of a grimace darkened my father's face. "You know as well as I do that as the governor, I have no control over who is appointed to that position."

"Come on now, Alexander." Keir tilted his head. "You've been in the game long enough to know how it works. Just because it's not in your job description doesn't mean you don't have any influence."

"I've built my career on integrity." Dad glared. "I don't intend to throw that away now."

"You don't have to cross any lines to cast your influence. Say you had some very private information about the mayor—information he'd prefer to keep out of the press. That knowledge might give him reason to rethink his decision."

Dad glowered. "That's blackmail."

"It's politics, and you know it." Keir maintained his unflappable tranquility throughout the conversation, as though plagued by perpetual boredom. He was fascinating to watch.

"And you would provide me with this information in order to help install who? Someone equally as corrupt but more in line with your way of thinking?"

Keir tipped his chin. "Men as upstanding as yourself are hard to come by, but that doesn't mean we couldn't find someone better suited for the job. Someone we could both agree upon."

Dad shook his head, his lips pursed. "I have no plans to interject my authority over the mayor. So if that was all ..." Dad crossed his arms and stepped back to clear the path toward the front door.

I could have told Keir that would be my father's answer. His standard of ethics was unimpeachable, which was one of the reasons I worked so hard to measure up.

As though he'd only been trying to help for my father's benefit, Keir slowly bobbed his head. "Don't say I didn't warn you." His eyes lifted to mine, deflating all the air from my lungs like a leaky balloon.

"Is that a threat?"

I shook loose of Keir's thrall to look at my father. I'd never heard such violence in his voice.

Keir lifted his hands in surrender. "Just reminding you that once a new commissioner is named, it'll be that much harder to get rid of him. Government red tape and all that bullshit."

"Again, not my problem."

"Now, that doesn't sound like the city's renowned savior." Keir wasn't ready to give up. I wasn't sure if I was impressed or annoyed.

Dad glared at him. The air grew saturated with a suffocating display of power, neither man willing to back down.

Keir finally conceded with a smirk. "I suppose I'll see myself out." His eyes caught mine one last time before he turned for the door.

Watching his retreating form was like watching the shoreline disappear as I drifted out to sea. I wanted to call him back and make him stay so I didn't lose that feeling of breathlessness he had created. But I knew that yearning was reckless and counterproductive to everything I'd worked toward—like bingeing an entire pizza after a week of clean eating—only so much more catastrophic. Someone like Keir Byrne would decimate the landscape of my life. Why was I even thinking about him?

I shook my head, hoping to rattle lose some sanity, then went to give my dad a hug.

"Sorry about that," I murmured. "I shouldn't have let him in."

"I'm surprised you did. He doesn't exactly give off neighborly vibes."

I raised my brows with a touch of levity. "I was trying not to judge."

Dad huffed out a laugh and kissed my forehead. "It's good to see you, Ro. I can always count on you to brighten my day."

I wished the sentiment brought me joy rather than a tightening of the vise around my rib cage. "Bad one?" I asked.

"Nah, just long. You staying for dinner?"

I shot him a calculating look. "Depends. What are you having?"

"I do believe Melody has a lasagna ready to go in the oven."

Licking my lips, I closed my eyes in savory anticipation.

"I take it that's a yes?"

"I suppose I can work it into my schedule," I teased.

"As if you'd pop in all the way up here for anything else."

"Ouch!" I grinned, knowing my smiles never fully reached my eyes and wondering not for the first time if my parents could tell or if they'd forgotten the difference.

TWO

"I WAS STARTIN' TO THINK YOU'D BEEN HIT BY A BUS. T'was the only explanation I could figure that would keep ye away." My grandmother's penciled-in eyebrow arched high on her forehead.

My paternal grandmother had trouble getting around but was still as sharp as a tack. If I was scared of anyone in my family, it was her. I'd be better off letting down my own mother than disappointing Nana Byrne. Where my mother, Brenna, was firm but understanding, Nana's authority was absolute.

"No buses, Nana. Just running a bit behind." I kissed her cheek, earning myself a reluctant smile. If only she knew how much worse it was. I hadn't forgotten or even accidentally run late. I'd sat outside the governor's place in my car and debated intentionally skipping dinner to stalk Rowan Alexander.

I'd known the governor had a daughter, though I hadn't anticipated running into her. I'd read about her as part of my research on her father. Twenty-two. Rich. Flawless face full of makeup in every single picture of her. I wondered if she slept in the damn stuff. Probably in a sorority and never been told no in her life. Finishing her final year at NYU with a political science degree with pretty dreams of following in her father's footsteps, no doubt.

Or at least, that was what I'd envisioned.

I'd been wrong.

She wasn't anything like I'd expected, and the disparity gnawed at me. Who was this girl, and why was she so damn ... controlled? Her reaction resonated with me in a way I couldn't ignore. It was a forced calm I knew all too well. Through the years, I'd been told by more than one person that I was dead inside. Too detached. Too unfeeling. I knew that wasn't the case. I had my reasons for the way I was, which made me endlessly curious about Rowan.

What made her stone cold enough to face an intruder twice her size without so much as a tremor in her voice? I'd sat in my car and done more research into her without finding anything remarkable other than a pencil-dick boyfriend who probably didn't know what a clit was, let alone where to find it.

I'd had to battle the urge to follow her home and learn everything I could about her. Did she tuck her head and hurry along the sidewalk or keep her chin raised, daring anyone to meet her eyes? Would she take a cab or slum with the rest of the city down in the subway? The only black SUV out front was her father's. Why didn't he insist on her using a private driver? They had the means.

I had so many damn questions and knew that if I waited until she left her parents' three-story mansion on the Upper East Side, I could learn a wealth of information by following her home. The compulsion to do it was almost insatiable. Almost.

If it hadn't been for the fact that the female contingency of the Byrne family had scheduled a dinner at Paddy and Nana's house that evening, I wouldn't have fought the urge to follow Rowan. Instead, I tethered together my tattered self-control and drove to my grandparents' house. If I had skipped the dinner, I'd have never heard the end of it. We only had these dinners once a month. As the eldest son of the eldest son, the family expected me to set an example.

Nana waved an arm toward the kitchen. "I think the girls have it about ready. You can sit next to me tonight and tell me what ye've been up to." Nana and Paddy had come over from Dublin when they were teens and still carried remnants of their native accent. They probably could have worked to drop the accent had they wanted to, but my proud Irish grandparents would never have considered such blasphemy. I'm glad they didn't.

Hearing the lyrical quality of her words brought back fond memories of time spent at their home.

She led us to the dining room, and I followed for fear of further reprimand. Paddy had been the leader of our business for decades, but it was Nana who ran the family. No one crossed Nana Byrne. If it wasn't for her, my dislike of social gatherings would have likely kept me from attending these dinners, but with her around, that wasn't an option. Fortunately, I'd trained the people around me not to expect much in the way of conversation from me.

The Byrne clan had grown to nearly three dozen, and that was just those branching from Paddy and Nana Byrne. Paddy had four brothers and three sisters. All five brothers had gone into business with him back in the day, but two had been killed, one followed his wife back to Ireland, and the other had been sent to prison.

Our family was the only remaining pillar of the Byrne legacy, and one of a select few Irish families to have survived the organized crime shakedown in the seventies and eighties. Paddy was shrewd. He'd adapted and kept the family afloat. Now, we were on the brink of a new era of prosperity. Wealth had come in spades, but we were still considered one of the weaker underworld groups. That was changing.

My cousin Conner had come to dinner with his new Italian bride, Noemi. Their marriage solidified an unprecedented alliance between the Irish and Italians. And a year earlier, Oran, the eldest of the Byrne grandchildren, had married a Donovan girl to unite what was left of their dying clan with ours. The next key maneuver was to give us a better grip on law enforcement, thus my visit to Evan Alexander. With a little more finesse, all the stars would be fully aligned, and we'd be untouchable.

I couldn't think of anything more important than providing a good life for the people surrounding me— my siblings and cousins, their children, and the generations to come. Family was everything to me, even if I preferred not to talk to them. For Nana's sake, however, I forced myself to converse over the chaos of dinner.

My grandparents' house no longer fit the family, but Paddy and Nana had refused to move, so we made do. The kids clustered in circles to eat picnic style on the floor while the adults used every chair available. It was loud, packed, and made my skin crawl. I ate fast, then excused myself to the back garden for air. It wasn't long before my father joined me.

"How did your visit with Alexander go?" he asked, his breath a white cloud in the crisp evening air.

"He held firm."

His lips thinned. "That's what I suspected." Jimmy Byrne was getting older at sixty-two but had been the de facto leader of the family business for decades. He'd done well over the years, and I respected his insight, though we didn't always see eye to eye.

"I still say we'll have to go at this from a different direction. He isn't the sort to respond to being threatened, and while we could try to lean on the mayor, we'd end up stirring up trouble with the Greeks. They've owned him for years."

Pop frowned as if considering, his arms crossed thoughtfully over his chest. "Sometimes it's better to creep in the back rather than bust down the front door." His eyes cut to me. "He has a daughter, you know."

"Alexander? Yeah, I'm familiar," I said warily. I couldn't see any way in which my father's mention of her was a good thing.

He shrugged. "We need someone on the inside. A seat at the table. What better way to do that than actually sit at the governor's family table?"

Shit. I wasn't sure what I would have disliked more— him suggesting I pursue Rowan Alexander or that we threaten her. It had been a toss-up which way he'd lean. A kidnapping would be more direct and a hell of a lot easier. Considering she was his only kid, all I'd have to do was lean into the threat I'd already presented. He wouldn't like it, but he'd give eventually. But a marriage? I hadn't signed up for that. Rowan was more intriguing than I'd expected, but that didn't mean I wanted to marry the woman. Jesus.

"We're in a good spot, Pop. Don't think this is necessary."

"You seen her?" he continued pushing.

"I have, and she's hardly more than a kid," I said more forcefully than I should have.

Pop eyed me, then shrugged, though I didn't buy it. "Maybe you're right. Maybe it would be better if Tor got to know her. They're closer in age."

I knew I wasn't going to like what he said.

The youngest son of my uncle Tully was a professional fighter. He was ambitious but surly on the best of days. The thought of him pursuing Rowan made me irrationally angry.

"I'll work on convincing Alexander," I said through clenched teeth. "Leave Tor out of it."

My father's keen eyes studied me. "I trust your judgment, son." He patted my shoulder and nodded. "It's gettin' fuckin' cold out here. I'm going back in."

"I'll be there in a second."

"Take your time." He knocked his knuckles against the vinyl siding and let the storm door slam shut behind him.

I blew out a long, steamy breath, but it didn't ease the tension coiled in my neck and shoulders. I needed a drink. A tall one. Instead, the back door opened again, signaling I had company. I looked back to see my cousin Oran's wife.

"Oh, sorry. Didn't realize anyone was out here."

"You're welcome to stay," I said, halting her retreat. "There's room for both of us."

Caitlin was a lovely young woman—quiet but perceptive with an easygoing demeanor and a smile that didn't quite reach her eyes. Back when marriage between our families had first been brought up, Oran and I as the two eldest grandsons had been offered as options. My cousin quickly volunteered himself for the match. He was eager to situate himself at the head of the family, and the two seemed to get along well. It hadn't bothered me until the recent death of his father, Brody Byrne. That was when my suspicions set in.

Oran had been the only one to know Brody changed his plans that day. It could have been a coincidence that the Albanians happened upon him leaving the club, but my gut told me it had been a setup. When I'd mentioned my concern to my father, he'd been so overwhelmed with grief that he immediately dismissed the notion. He didn't even want to entertain the possibility. Three months later, we still hadn't spoken of it. He might have forgotten, but I hadn't.

Caitlin wrapped her arms around her middle and leaned against the stair rail. "I'm still not used to so many people in one house. I had to take a breather."

"I'm used to it and still have to take a breather."

She hadn't been gifted an easy road in life. Mother died when she was young, and her father was killed not five years ago. Their family business had dwindled, and she'd had to sacrifice herself in marriage to unite what was left of her family with ours. It wasn't a pretty business, but she'd handled it admirably.

"How's your brother?" I asked.

She nodded, the first hint at a real smile ghosting her lips. "He's good. Working hard, as always."

"Yeah?" I encouraged, hoping she'd hint at what he'd been up to. I was curious how the Donovans were surviving at this point.

"Yeah, Oran's really been helpful with contacts and giving Flynn direction. I see good things for him in the future."

Interesting. It sounded like Oran had embraced the alliance, which I'd been doubtful about, considering I'd seen him not six months ago sneaking around with another woman at our club. It seemed with each passing day my perception of my cousin was dwindling for one reason or another.

"That's good to hear."

She smiled, her teeth clenching to fight back a shiver. I shrugged off my jacket and wrapped it around her shoulders.

"You'll need this if you're going to stay out here any longer."

"You going back in?"

"If I don't, Nana will come looking for me," I said wryly.

Caitlin chuckled. "I'll be in shortly."

I squeezed her arm. "No rush." If I were her, I wouldn't want to hurry back to Oran's side either. I had a really fuckin' bad feeling things with him were going to get ugly ... sooner rather than later.

THREE

"I DIDN'T REALIZE YOU'D COME UP HERE YESTERDAY. WE could have made the trip together." I tried not to sound annoyed as I followed Stetson up the stairs of his father's ten-thousand-square-foot brownstone. The place wasn't five minutes from where my parents lived, which meant I'd made the trek two days in a row from the West Village to the Upper East Side. It was only a half hour, but still. The travel time had eaten up a chunk of my weekend.

"It was a last-minute thing. Dad got back from a trip and asked if I'd stop by for dinner. It was just easier to stay here." He turned around at the top of the stairs and pulled me into a hug. "I'm glad you came, though. Our schedules haven't meshed up well lately."

He was right. Though, to be honest, neither of us had made much of an effort to align our busy schedules. We'd known each other so long that it made our relationship different from other people's. Even though we'd only started officially dating a year ago, we weren't ridiculously obsessed with spending every minute together. I'd known Stetson since middle school. Our fathers were longtime friends, so we saw each other regularly growing up. Dating had felt like the natural progression of our relationship, and our fathers hadn't exactly been shy in their hopes that we'd get together. When I told Dad that Stetson had asked me out, his smile could have turned night to day.

"I had hoped to do some studying today, but I figure I can squeeze in a few hours in the morning before class." I gave a hint of coyness to my smile, peering up at him through my lashes.

Stetson was cute in a boy-next-door sort of way. His light-brown hair was thick with short curls, and his golden-brown eyes lit with a mischievous glint I found endearing. Tall and lean, he was surprisingly athletic for his height. After being on his varsity team all four years of high school, he now played field hockey for a club team. More than anything, though, Stetson was comfortable. Easy. We both knew what to expect from one another and seemed to like it that way.

"You always ace your classes," he teased. "One night off won't hurt anything." He gave one last squeeze, then released me to walk down the hallway. "Come on, Duke is about to play. Preseason starts tonight," he called back to me.

I stood for a second and glanced down at the outfit I'd spent too much time picking out. A forest-green cashmere sweater that accented my hazel eyes, cut short to hint at an exposed midriff above skinny jeans that were damn near painted on. Stetson hadn't even noticed.

Sex wasn't exactly the cornerstone of our relationship, but it had been a week, and I'd at least hoped to catch his eye. After my run-in with Keir the night before, I'd been so strangely turned on that I couldn't sleep until I'd relieved the aching need pulsing between my thighs.

Adrenaline did funny things to the body, or so I told myself. It was the only logical explanation.

I shook myself out of the memory and followed Stetson to the swanky TV room. The three-story home, plus the basement, was opulent in every way. My parents' house was just as old as this one, but they'd updated to a modern design that was light, open, and inviting. Stetson's father insisted on keeping the austere feel of the traditional decor in his home. Black-and-white checkerboard marble floors ran throughout the main level with wainscoting, dark paneled wood, or richly colored fabric lining the walls. The crown molding was ornate, the fixtures an ostentatious gold, and the furnishings could have come straight from a palace. Not exactly my idea of homey.

At least the second floor was a bit more updated since that was Stetson's domain. He had the entire west end of the second floor to himself, which was why he frequently came home. His place wasn't bad, but he definitely preferred the lush Upper East Side to campus.

I was surprised to see several soda cans on the coffee table and the normally neatly folded blanket wadded into a ball instead. The house was always immaculate, which meant that even a few out-of-place items seemed odd.

Stetson saw me eyeing the uncharacteristic disorder. "Dad told Hannah not to mess with my wing. Something about her getting older and me being too spoiled."

"You do something to piss him off?" I teased.

"Who knows with that man," he grumbled playfully, settling into the large gray sectional.

We watched the start of preseason basketball for a half hour before I had to get up and relieve my boredom with a trip to the bathroom.

"While you're up, can you grab me a beer?" Stetson asked, eyes trained on the TV.

A frown tugged my mouth. "Yeah, sure."

This was not how I'd envisioned spending my evening. At least dinner would be soon, and then we could spend a little time together.

"Hold up," Stetson called. "I forgot that the bathroom in here is having issues. Use mine or the one off the guest room."

I rerouted to the hallway, rolling my eyes as Stetson

whooped at the television. The guest room was closest, so I let myself inside. The drawn drapes and the navy-themed decor made the room feel eerily solemn, like one of those old Victorian-era movies when a room was boarded up after its occupant had died of some contagious disease. I couldn't imagine why his father didn't update things, except that the place sort of suited his personality. I'd never felt comfortable around Lawrence Wellington. I didn't know what it was, but my skin itched with the need to escape when he was nearby.

That was how I should have felt when Keir held that knife to my throat.

Your intuition told you he wouldn't hurt you, and he didn't. That's not so strange.

I rolled my eyes. *Right. And you're not remotely biased.*

Crossing the room to the en suite bathroom, I turned on the light and paused in front of the gilded mirror for half a second—just the briefest glance. That was all I ever allowed. Only long enough to check that my heavy cat-eye liner was on point, black mascara fully coated my blond lashes, and a flawless layer of foundation made every last freckle invisible. I performed the spot-check in a blink but otherwise avoided mirrors whenever I encountered them. I didn't like to see what stared back at me. *Who* stared back at me.

While I couldn't totally escape the truth, I could avoid summoning the resulting dark emotions by removing mirrors from the equation. I wasn't a fan of emotions in general. I'd always been able to keep mine in check, which was the reason my response to Keir had been so unsettling. What kind of person was aroused by a man holding a knife to their throat? It was a question I didn't want to answer.

I shook my head to clear the intrusive thoughts and finished doing my business. After washing my hands, I reached for the door when an odd sound caught my ear. Was that … crying?

I looked up and studied the antique vent cover on the ceiling as another feminine wail drifted down, no mistaking it. No animal or inanimate object made sounds so saturated with emotion. The soul-crushing despair reached inside my chest and clutched my heart with rabid desperation until I could hardly breathe.

Who could the sounds be coming from? Stetson's parents were divorced. No other woman lived in the house, though the housekeeper, Hannah, worked at the house full-time. The old row-style homes were built without space between them, but I didn't think it was possible to hear the neighbors. Could it be a television?

I listened for another solid minute. The sobbing continued without interruption, and my gut told me this was real. Someone was in horrible distress, and every fiber of my being ached with the need to help.

I left the bathroom and returned to Stetson, making sure to grab him a beer from the mini fridge on my way.

"Thanks, babe." He popped the top and continued watching the game.

"Your dad's housekeeper isn't a live-in, is she?"

"No, why?"

"Does she work on the weekends?" Hannah would be

the most logical answer, though I couldn't imagine the demur older woman making such sounds.

"Nope." He finally turned to look at me. "What's up?"

"I know this sounds strange, but I could have sworn I heard crying from upstairs."

His brow furrowed. "Crying? Like a baby crying?"

"No, it was a woman."

"That's strange." He shrugged. "There's no one here except Dad and us. Last I saw, he was in his office, but he's been up on the third floor a bunch lately working on some project. It could be him or even just the old pipes whining or something. You know how ancient this place is."

I thought of Stetson's father and internally shivered. I might have been sparring with my emotions, but that man was a machine. Could he have a woman up there? Maybe he'd had a date that had gone badly. But why would she be upstairs? None of it seemed to fit, but I felt awkward pressing Stetson about it. His father was a sensitive subject. I could understand. If Lawrence Wellington were my father, I'd have issues too.

I kept my worries to myself and nodded. "You're probably right." I smiled weakly, hating the helplessness that filled my veins with lead, weighing down my entire body.

You're overreacting. You don't even know if someone's actually up there.

I know what I heard.

You know what you think *you heard.*

Whose side are you on?

I made a mental promise to the wailing phantom that I wouldn't forget her and tried to carry on with our evening.

An hour later, we sat at the dining table with Stetson's father as we finished eating dinner. I'd hoped Stetson and I would have dinner alone, but that wasn't to be. Instead, the three of us sat at a table for twelve beneath a crystal chandelier and a blanket of silence.

"I'll be back in Norfolk this week," Mr. Wellington said, placing his napkin on the table. "I told Hannah not to worry about coming over until Thursday. I wasn't sure what your plans were."

He didn't usually tell the housekeeper to stay away when he was gone, which was often. Had something happened between them, and he was giving her time away as an apology? It was a possibility.

Stetson took one more sip of wine before setting down his glass. "That works for me. I don't think I'll have any need of her while you're gone."

Lawrence Wellington nodded, his gaze shifting to me. "So, Rowan, are you still planning to graduate in December?"

"Yes, sir."

"And then you'll join your father's campaign staff?"

"That's the plan."

"You'd do well handling the press. Not sure what Evan thinks, but a girl as pretty as you would be an asset in front of the cameras. Everyone loves a pretty face, and when you smile, they'll forget whatever they meant to ask."

Damn, this was awkward. I wanted to shove his chauvinism up his ass but knew he thought he was relaying a compliment, so I just smiled thinly.

"Dad, come on. Ro is way more than a pretty face," Stetson chided. "One of these days, she'll be the queen of New York society."

All my gratitude toward my would-be champion soured. The last thing I wanted for myself was to be the ringleader of a bunch of socialite housewives. I knew I'd signed up for that by dating one of the richest men in the city, but I didn't have to like it.

"She's certainly suited to the role." Mr. Wellington raised his glass toward me and winked. I suddenly felt the need for a scalding-hot shower. "You two both have class in the morning?"

"Yeah," Stetson answered. "But my first class doesn't start until nine, so I think I'll stay here one more night."

I set down my napkin and stared at him. "You're not going back with me?"

"Nah, I'm already here, so I might as well stay another night. You okay going back alone?"

"Of course." Getting around the city at night didn't scare me. I was more bothered by Stetson's lack of interest in joining me than anything.

"I can always have my driver take you back to campus, if you'd like," his father offered.

I'd rather have walked the entire distance than sit in a car with his creepy driver for half an hour. "That's not necessary, but thank you." I forced a smile. "And I actually think I'll head on out now. I still have some studying to do."

"I'll walk you out." Stetson placed his white linen napkin on the table and joined me with his hand at my lower back. "Shoot me a text when you get home," he said when we reached the front door.

"I will." I grabbed my purse from the entry table and gave him an uncertain smile.

Stetson cupped my jaw, angling my face to his, and placed a quick kiss on my lips. I was out the door and two houses down before I realized two things. One, I was headed north to my parents' house rather than south to my apartment, and two, I felt absolutely nothing when Stetson kissed me.

Granted, it wasn't a passionate kiss, but Keir hadn't kissed me at all, and my insides had swum with feeling.

That's how you wanted it, remember?

Yes. This was the path I'd chosen for myself, and I'd done so intentionally. I needed to remember that feelings weren't supposed to play into the equation.

♦

MY PARENTS LIVED a short ten-minute walk from the Wellington mansion. When I rounded the corner onto their block, I realized I was scanning the area for a short-haired, tattooed version of Thor lurking in the shadows. Even more unexpected was the disappointment that tugged at my shoulders when I reached the front entrance without any sightings.

Had I honestly expected him to be chilling on the sidewalk outside the house? Of course not. That would have been ridiculous. Why would he show up again one day later?

I took a deep breath and rang the bell. The security guard on duty answered, greeting me with a smile.

"Hello, ma'am. Come on in. I believe your father's in his office, and last I saw your mother, she was cleaning up in the kitchen."

"Thanks. I'm just popping in to talk to my dad for a minute." I smiled and made my way upstairs to the room Dad used as his office. The governor's title came with a home we could have moved into when he was first elected, but my parents had declined. They insisted on staying for the same reasons I couldn't wait to leave. Too many memories.

"Well, isn't this an honor," Dad beamed. "Two visits in a row. What did we do to earn such a treat?"

I crossed the room to hug him, not entirely sure how to answer the question. "I was over at the Wellingtons with Stetson and thought I'd stop by."

"Works for me. Have you eaten?"

"Yeah. We had dinner with his dad."

"How's Larry doing?" Dad sat on the corner of his desk, motioning for me to take one of the chairs.

"That's actually who I wanted to talk to you about."

His brow furrowed with concern.

"Nothing bad, I don't think. I mean ... I heard something strange at his house and wanted to run it by you."

"What did you hear?"

"I would swear I heard a woman crying. Stetson said the three of us were the only ones home, but I would bet my life that the crying I heard came from the third floor of the house."

Dad's brows slowly rose to peak in the middle of his forehead. "And...?"

"And I don't know. It felt ... off. I've always gotten a strange vibe from him. I thought I'd ask if he was into anything ... nefarious."

Dad choked on a laugh. "Nefarious? I think your imagination has run away with you."

I frowned, fighting back frustration. "I'm telling you, my gut says something's not right."

"If he was into anything bad, sweetheart, I would have cut ties long ago. My career is too important to associate with anyone questionable, even an old friend. And I certainly wouldn't have encouraged you to go out with Stetson if I didn't think highly of their family."

I knew that's what Dad would say. I wasn't sure why I'd even brought it up. He genuinely trusted Lawrence Wellington, but I wasn't sure that trust was well-placed. Though the two were friends in college, they hadn't been close in a long time. Not like when they were younger.

"Okay," I conceded, knowing I was fighting a losing battle. "Can I ask you something else?"

"Always." He wouldn't be so obliging when he heard who I wanted to talk about.

"Who was the man here last night?"

Dad stiffened. "That was Keir Byrne. His father runs one of the largest Irish crime families in the city."

Oh *shit*. That explained a lot. Keir wasn't just a thug —he was the real deal. A modern-day mobster. I knew that stuff still existed, but it was so much more discreet than it was in the movies or in the past when the Italian Mafia ruled the city. I wondered how much had changed from their perspective.

"Are they dangerous?" I would figure they were, though I'd never heard reports of assassinations or other gruesome crimes associated with organized criminals from the past.

"Absolutely, though times are different now. The internet especially has changed the nature of criminal activities. People can obscure themselves and make evidence tracing a nightmare."

"Do people like that come to you often?" If so, that was one part of his job he had kept from me.

Dad's head tilted a fraction. "Is that what this is? Are you worried about me? Because you shouldn't be. I'm not scared of him or any others." He stood and pulled me into his chest, holding me tight. "They try to intimidate on occasion, but they're just posturing. I've faced far more dangerous men over at the capital, I'm sorry to say."

"Is that my Ro?" Mom's voice carried up the stairs before she came into view. "Two nights in a row. This is a pleasant surprise."

"I just stopped in for a second," I explained. "I have an early class in the morning."

"My driver can take you back—and don't even try to argue," Dad insisted. "It's dark out, and I'm already paying him to be on call. Might as well make use of him."

I smiled and shook my head. Dad knew me too well. I hated having people do things for me when I was capable of doing stuff myself, but in this instance, a quiet ride home hidden behind tinted windows sounded like a welcome reprieve.

I said my goodbyes and slipped into the back of the governor's official black Escalade. Thirty minutes later, I was in the elevator on my way to my apartment, eyes on my feet to avoid the mirrored walls. One mirror tonight was enough.

Once in my apartment, the quiet seemed to amplify the sound of sobs in my head. Why the hell couldn't I let it go?

You know why.

I groaned aloud and flopped back onto my bed. Just because someone was crying didn't mean anything. People cried all the time.

But what if she needs help?

My gut twisted, igniting a spark of anger. What was I supposed to do? Call the cops and tell them I thought I heard someone crying? They'd tell me just how ridiculous I was being.

Wouldn't you rather look ridiculous than risk knowing you could have prevented something awful?

"You're being insane!" My hollered words rang in my

ears long after the walls absorbed the sound. "That could have been a damn TV playing for all you know."

I desperately tried to quiet the maddening inner voice only to leave room for the haunting sight of Lawrance Wellington winking at me. Something was off about him. Always had been. If he hadn't gone to college with my dad, I couldn't imagine the two being friends, but Dad was loyal to his past. It was what made him such an excellent politician. I was far more suspicious by nature.

Who was Lawrence Wellington? Had I ever truly asked that question? His presence in my life had always been a given, so I'd never thought to look beyond what I'd learned growing up.

I went back into my living room and grabbed my laptop out of my backpack. Once it was booted up, I typed Lawrence Wellington into the Google search bar. The first search result was a Wikipedia page, followed by an article in *Business Insider*.

Ex-Banker Builds $10 Billion Fortune from Shipping Boom

LAWRENCE WELLINGTON LEFT *his job in venture capital to buy out a failing shipping business. Decades later, he has one of the world's largest maritime fortunes thanks to his company, Atlantic International Shipping (AIS).*

Wellington's savvy financial background enabled him to restructure the company in a way that kept business afloat.

And after a twenty-million-dollar investment in rapid growth strategies, he soon forged one of the world's largest container lines.

"The company grew like wildfire," said Marshall Cranston, a London-based cargo analyst at research firm Venture Vessel. "AIS took decisive action in executing its growth strategies."

A representative for New York-based AIS didn't respond to a request for comment.

THE ARTICLE CONTINUED with details about the size of the company and outlined its recent endeavors. The Wellingtons were obnoxiously wealthy. I'd always known that—it was a big part of why Stetson didn't take school seriously. I came from money as well, but I had decided on working with my father years ago, and that necessitated an exemplary school record. Stetson didn't have any particular ambition. He didn't see the point in school, but his father had been adamant that Stetson get his degree.

I didn't necessarily learn anything new from the article, but it did make me wonder about Wellington's initial move into shipping. I couldn't recall if he'd come from money, and if so, how much. Had he invested his own money for the project, or had a bank been involved? Or maybe private investors? Dad might be more open to telling me what he knew about Wellington's background than he had been in discussing possible criminal activities.

I skimmed a few more articles before abandoning that line of inquiry to pursue one I had even less business looking into. I typed the name Keir Byrne into the Google search bar. Nothing. This time, I entered Byrne family Irish Mafia. Was that what it was called? Wasn't the Mafia an Italian thing? I had no idea, but the internet seemed to understand. The first result was an article dated only a few months ago titled "Coincidence or Assassination?" It had my attention.

ONE OF THE *leaders of the powerful Byrne family was shot and killed last night outside a club owned by his Irish family, a known faction of organized crime in the city. Brody Byrne, one of three sons to the notorious Patrick Byrne, was fifty-eight when bullets from a passing car ended his life.*

While Mafia-type criminal activity hasn't been in the forefront of the news in recent decades, the death certainly has all the hallmark indications of a hit. Byrne left behind a wife and three grown children. Authorities are looking into the death, but according to Police Commissioner Paul Cooke, drive-by shootings have one of the lowest rates of prosecution due to the evidentiary challenges.

THE MAN PICTURED BORE a striking resemblance to Keir. Similar blue eyes. Same ruthless glint. Would that be Keir's fate one day? How dangerous was the life he led?

Dad said he wasn't scared of the Byrnes, but I wondered if that wasn't bravado talking. Keir and his family were unquestionably dangerous. It was only logical to fear them.

You didn't fear Keir.

Yeah, but I'm different. Broken.

Or ... hear me out ... maybe your intuition told you he wouldn't hurt you. Remember that whole survival instincts, hunter and prey monologue? If you could tell he was watching, maybe you could intuit that he wasn't dangerous.

You're awfully opinionated.

I rolled my eyes and continued to scour the internet for information on the man who had jump-started my pulse after years of flatline. My curiosity was insatiable, and that wasn't the only thing. For the second night in a row, the thought of turquoise eyes and the unrelenting dominance of an iron will had me coming within minutes of touching myself. Faster than I'd ever climaxed before and hard enough that I successfully avoided thinking about his effect on me before falling blissfully asleep.

FOUR

STICKY CLUMPS OF BLOOD MATTED HER HAIR. IT WASN'T A ton of blood, but her white-blond hair made the deep crimson that much more obvious.

The sight turned my stomach inside out. What terrified me the most was how perfectly still she lay. Time froze as thoroughly as the body at my feet. The wind didn't blow. The birds didn't chirp. All but my thundering heart had stopped—it pounded as though trying to jump-start the world around me, but it was no good. Nothing moved. Not even me.

I stood paralyzed and helpless, unable to move or cry for help, though my mind screamed from behind its iron bars to do *something*. The only thing I managed was to peer down in shock at my open hands, palms up and covered in blood.

My stomach revolted, panic burning its way up my throat.

The girl had hardly bled—where had it all come from? My hands were coated in sticky crimson. My clothes were splattered and smeared. I was covered from head to toe.

Agonizing terror refused to be contained any longer, bursting from my lungs in the form of a horrific wail. The sound caught in my ears as I lurched upward in bed, a hand slapping over my mouth as I raced for the bathroom.

I made it to the toilet in time to spew an acidic cocktail of bile and dinner remnants. Tears poured down my cheeks, which was almost as unsettling as the nightmare. I didn't cry. Hadn't since I was a child. Yet rivulets of salty sadness streaked down my face.

It was just a dream, Ro.

You know it was more than that.

No. It was a dream.

I might have felt concerned about whoever had been crying, but that didn't change the fact that what I'd just seen was a dream. I wouldn't let my subconscious color my waking thoughts.

So you're going to let it go?

I didn't say that. I only meant that I won't go off half-cocked.

I splashed my face with water and took several deep breaths.

Then what are you going to do?

I need more information.

And where will you find it? You couldn't come up with anything on Google, and Dad wasn't any help. If you go to the authorities, anything they find could end up hurting Dad.

It was true. Dad and Lawrence Wellington had been friends for too long to avoid a controversy. Any questioning I did would need to be behind the scenes. Maybe a private investigator? That might work, but who? And did they have an obligation to report crimes to the authorities?

I couldn't let this touch my father, but I also didn't think I could ignore the crying woman. Something deep in my bones told me Stetson's father was bad news. I just needed proof.

What will you do once you get that proof?

I'll tell Dad, and he can handle it privately.

And Stetson?

I bent at the hips and lowered my head between my arm, my hands propping me against the bathroom vanity. Everything was so confusing where Stetson was concerned. How would his father's actions impact my view of him? Should I tell him about my suspicions? If so, when? How would he respond?

I hated uncertainty. I liked plans and order and knowing exactly what to expect.

An echo of the woman's cry drifted through my

mind like a chilling gust of wind. She needed me, and when it came down to it, that was all that mattered.

Okay, Wonder Woman, how do you plan to accomplish this great rescue?

I rolled my eyes and plodded back to my bedroom.

Don't be dramatic. All I want right now is more information.

Who can get that to you without raising any red flags?

Someone good with technology. Someone who didn't mind bending the rules and who was used to getting information on people. I didn't know anyone like that personally, but a pair of turbulent ocean eyes flashed in my mind.

Keir Byrne had managed to break into the governor's home and offered dirt on the mayor for blackmail purposes. He was exactly the sort of man who could dig up information on Lawrence Wellington.

A seductive tendril of excitement, the same as I'd felt in my parents' kitchen, coiled tight in my belly. I couldn't deny that I wanted to see him again. Was I letting my intrigue cloud my judgment? Possibly. Keir didn't strike me as the type to play nice. If he found a skeleton in Wellington's closet, would he use it against my father? He wanted something from Dad, and Wellington's indiscretions could be used as leverage against my father.

But wouldn't it be better to deal with whatever was happening behind closed doors than have the press blast the information on every news channel? Whatever we uncovered could be a ticking time bomb.

Or it could be absolutely nothing.

And if that's the case, no harm, no foul.

What a clusterfuck. I plopped back onto my bed and stared at the ceiling.

How about this? What if we just go talk to him and see how it goes?

I raised my hands, half expecting to see red crusted beneath my fingernails.

She needs you.

I know.

That meant there was only one option.

Tomorrow, I go to the Moxy.

🔥

I WAS aware of each agonizing second that ticked by as I sat through my classes the following day. The anticipation was a never-ending electrical current running through my veins. I considered skipping class since my thoughts were too distracted to listen to a lecture, but I refused to give in to the pull. Logic controlled my actions, not my curiosity or libido.

And there was a significant chance Keir didn't even work until later in the day. I'd looked up the Moxy and discovered it was the sort of establishment that did most of its business at night. A strip club buried in the middle of the Garment District. Not the best place to be at night, but if I went in the late afternoon, I had a decent chance of catching Keir and still getting home before it got too late. I preferred not to be wandering that area well after dark.

I had no idea where else I might find the Irishman, so it would have to do.

I arrived just after four o'clock. The area was relatively quiet at that hour. While the late September sun had already hidden itself behind a wall of city buildings, the bustling chaos of night hadn't quite kicked into gear.

The painted black exterior of the building boasted no windows, effectively communicating the explicit nature of the club within. However, the paint was kept fresh, and the decently new awning was lit from within by green neon lights. The effect was sharp and even a little enticing.

I'd never been inside a strip club, though I'd looked up the place online to have some idea of what to expect. The images showed leather booths for private pole dances and classy chandeliers lighting rich wood paneling on the walls. It was a mix of between a sports bar and a gentlemen's club. When I walked inside, I was relieved to see the photos had been an accurate depiction. I didn't have to frequent strip clubs to know they could be a lot seedier than the Moxy.

Girls danced, even at this early hour, and sensual music pulsed in the air. A dozen patrons were sprinkled throughout the place, along with cocktail servers in skimpy dresses and several intimidating men dressed all in black like the one stationed at the front door. His face was striking, save for the scowl carved into his lips.

"If you're lookin' for Jolly, he's not here," the man said as though giving me the time of day had physically pained him.

"Jolly? Uh, no. I was looking for Keir."

The man's dagger-like stare narrowed as he looked me up and down. "What do you want with him?"

"He came by my place a couple of nights ago asking some questions. I wanted to follow up with him." Somewhat true yet sufficiently vague to muster scrutiny. Hopefully. I used every ounce of my unearned privilege to sound confident enough to overcome any remaining doubts. It seemed to work.

"How about you give me your number, and I'll have him call you." It wasn't a question.

Before I could decide if it was best to argue or tuck and run, a gorgeous server with blond curls approached.

"Tor, you givin' this sweet thing a hard time?" She had a Southern drawl that made her instantly likable. I wasn't sure I understood the effect, but it was the same with puppies. Only sociopaths could look at a puppy and not get a hit of dopamine straight to the bloodstream.

The man she'd called Tor grimaced.

Okaaay. So ... sociopath?

Probably.

"Doesn't involve you, Stormy," he grumbled.

"I was just here to talk to Keir," I blurted, hoping Stormy, as he'd called her, might be more helpful.

She flashed a brilliant smile. "Well, that's easy

enough." She shifted and peered over her shoulder. "He's right back there."

"Fuck, Storm. Maybe she didn't need to know that." The man groused at her.

Stormy was totally unfazed. She winked at me, then flitted away, giving me the impression these two quipped like that on the regular. I probably would have laughed if my nerves didn't have my entire body in a stranglehold.

I stepped around Tor and spotted Keir sitting with his back to me at a table, watching a woman dance on a small raised platform. I took her in as I approached. She was lean and toned, but her movements were too exaggerated for my taste. Too intentionally erotic. She wasn't capitalizing on the seductive possibilities of the music playing. Considering the purpose and her audience, that might have been best, but it seemed a shame.

There you go again, analyzing everything.

Yeah, well. What else am I supposed to do?

The voices quieted the second Keir's piercing stare met mine.

There it was again. Exhilaration, like epinephrine straight to the heart. How did the sight of him tangle my thoughts while unraveling my insides? I wasn't scared of him. If it wasn't fear bubbling up inside me, then what? I couldn't deny the answer blaring in my head as I closed the distance between us.

Attraction—a primal, magnetic pull that hooked me at the molecular level. And it wasn't just his rugged good looks that drew me in; it was the effortless way he emanated power, as if born with an abundance of self-possessed confidence so natural to him that boasting was unnecessary. Keir Byrne knew his strengths and saw no need to flaunt them. The mere scent of such surety was intoxicating.

"If it isn't Little Miss Alexander. You've managed to surprise me—not an easy feat." Somehow, he knew exactly how loud to speak so that he could be heard above the music, but just barely. It forced me to give every ounce of my attention to each word he spoke.

"Glad I could add a little amusement to your day, though it looks like you're plenty entertained." My eyes cut over to the woman who continued to gyrate on the private stage.

"You've mistaken concentration for entertainment. I'm working," he said dryly. "Madison here is auditioning, so if you don't mind…" He reached for the bottle of water on the table and returned his gaze to the stage. Had I irritated him? I had a feeling he'd gone from amused to insulted, and I needed to fix things quickly.

"I just need a minute to talk with you, Keir. Please, just one minute."

Hell if my entire body didn't warm every time his eyes touched me.

"I told you, I'm auditioning right now, so unless you want to dance, *leave*," he ordered in an arctic tone wrought with challenge. If he thought throwing down the gauntlet would send me running, he was mistaken.

I walked right up to him, flung my purse at his chest,

and slipped off my shoes, not allowing my stare to waiver for a second. Rowan Alexander didn't cower for anyone. No matter the outcome, what I was about to do would be worth the spark of fascinated surprise that flashed behind those tropical eyes of his. He never moved or spoke, but I could see it there in the Caribbean depths. I had his attention.

"I dance, then you listen. Agreed?"

He stared at me for ten solid seconds before his chin dipped.

Seizing my moment, I stepped on stage. The current occupant looked from me to Keir, then reluctantly backed away.

Don't worry, honey, I'm not after your job.

I tried to clear my head and allow the music to filter into my body. I wasn't familiar with the song, but it had a sultry beat and grinding bass making movement come easily. What Keir hadn't known was that I was at home on the stage probably more than anywhere else. Dance was my therapy. My one true love.

I no longer took lessons, but I tried to find time to dance most days. I did it for myself. Performing for others wasn't my favorite, so I tuned out the flashing television screens and other dancers. I ignored the covetous stares of the men around me and let the music take hold.

The jeans I'd worn had enough stretch to allow movement—not ideal, but sufficient. And my short sweater with a scooped neckline was perfect to add a tease of skin. I wasn't about to get naked, but I wanted to make sure Keir knew I wasn't embarrassed to be seen, and more importantly, that his attempt at intimidation had failed.

I began to sway and arch and roll my body in perfect harmony with the music. Up on that stage with the seductive pull of an electric guitar filling the air, it was easy to summon my sexiest moves. I simply imagined that Keir was the only other person in the room. That I was dancing for him alone—to tease him to the brink of madness.

My hands trailed over my body as I moved, as though I was deep in a session of pleasuring myself, delighting in the feel of my own touch. I bit my bottom lip like I might if I was straining to keep myself quiet, and I moved seamlessly from one inviting position to the next, a symphony of carnal seduction.

When I finally permitted myself to peek at my adversary, my veins flooded with elation. Keir's entire body had gone rigid with tension, an enormous bulge tenting his pants.

I'd gotten to him. The unflappable Keir Byrne was on edge. I'd pushed him to the limits of his perfectly honed control, and I wanted more.

I wanted to see him snap.

Already on my knees, I arched my back until the top of my head gently met the floor. I pressed my chest upward, allowing my sweater to fully expose my bra, and brought my hands to my breasts, then slowly trailed down my front toward the apex of my thighs.

Two other men edged closer to the stage on the

opposite side where Keir was sitting. I could feel their eyes on me, but they were inconsequential compared to the blazing touch of Keir's stare. He branded me with those ocean eyes of his.

"*Enough.*" The savage growl ripped through the air, halting my movements.

Keir was on his feet. I lifted upright, though still on my knees, and watched him grab my purse and charge toward me. My eyes rounded as he grabbed my wrist and hauled me from the stage toward a dark hallway.

"What is it you want from me, Miss Alexander?" he bit out.

"*Rowan,*" I shot back. "My name is Rowan." I wasn't sure why I cared what he called me, but I did. I wanted to hear the guttural purr of my name on his lips.

"I know your name," he said dismissively. "Tell me why the fuck you're here."

Stubborn asshole. Fine. I'd get to the point. "I have a job for you."

The tension surrounding him slowly melted as a devious smile teased at his lips. "This gets more interesting by the minute. Go on."

"I want someone investigated without the information going public."

"Seems like something your father should be capable of doing."

My spine stiffened. "I brought up the matter with him. He declined."

"And I was the next person who came to mind?" he asked condescendingly.

"Hardly. But it's a delicate matter. I need someone to get me answers discreetly. I'll pay you."

He studied me, growing more intrigued by the second. Good. I'd use whatever I could to my advantage. "Who is it you want to look into?"

"Lawrence Wellington."

His eyes narrowed. "The shipping mogul?"

I nodded.

Keir's head fell back as a rumble of masculine laughter filled the air. I wasn't sure how I knew, but I got the sense this man didn't laugh often, and the effect was mesmerizing. Even though it came at my expense, I could see myself doing terrible things to hear that sound again.

Once he regained himself, he stalked closer, a sharp edge returning to his features. "That man practically owns the entire Red Hook shipping terminal. Why the fuck are you wanting to look into Lawrence Wellington?" His words were harsh, but his tone was somehow still calm and steady. His ability to stay composed was impressive.

"My reasons have no bearing on an investigation."

"They do when I'm the one investigating."

Shit. I hadn't considered him asking me why. It was a reckless oversight, but I didn't let it thwart me. "His son is my boyfriend. Before going any further into the relationship, I'd like to make sure his father won't be a detriment to my father's career."

Well done, Ro! He can hardly argue with that logic.

"Seems like something your father would be happy to do to protect you both."

"They're longtime friends. Dad wouldn't even entertain the notion." *Please, stop asking questions!*

Keir continued to study me. "Yet, for some reason, you feel compelled enough to seek me out."

"Why not? You had no problem breaking into my parents' house. Surely digging into someone's background is hardly an imposition, especially if you're being paid."

"I want to know why," he persisted.

"Why what?"

"Why you even suspect something's off."

I resisted the urge to grind my teeth in frustration and smiled instead. "I told you, I'm just being cautious."

He shrugged. "Then the answer is no." He turned to walk away.

My mouth fell open. "What? Why?" I hurried after him.

"Because I said so."

"I told you, I'll pay you."

He turned and spread his arms wide. "As if I need your money, Miss Alexander." He stared at me, a glint of smug satisfaction in his eyes.

I stretched my spine as tall as possible, bristling against what I was about to do. "*Please.*"

He took a step closer. "As much as I love seeing your pretty lips beg, it's not enough, so unless you give me a reason"—he moved close enough that I could feel the heat radiating off him—"to motivate me, then the answer ... is still ... no." The menacing vibrations of his voice feathered across my skin.

I inhaled, breathing him in. Intentionally intoxicating myself with his scent.

I need him to help me.

No, you want *his help. You could do this on your own.*

Shut up.

"I think he hurt someone. A woman." The rushed words hung between us, dangling precariously on a knife's edge.

Keir's nostrils flared despite the preternatural calm that settled back in place like a well-worn coat.

"Explain."

"I was at his house with my boyfriend. I heard a woman crying—not just crying. The sounds were ... soul-crushing. When I asked Stetson who else was there, he said his father was the only other person in the house. And before you say I was just hearing things or it was a television or a neighbor, it wasn't. I know what I heard."

Keir pulled away from me. "I don't like it."

"Don't like what?" I balked.

"Any of it. That man is immensely powerful. You need to leave it the fuck alone."

I gaped at him. "Just *leave* it? Forget that some poor woman may be chained in that man's house?"

"You don't honestly believe that's what's happening," he challenged.

I paused, unsure what to say. It was an egregious accusation. If I'd felt certain about it, I would have gone to the authorities. "It's just a little digging into his background," I pleaded one last time.

He shook his head. "You're in over your head. Walk away, Miss Alexander."

A woman's angry voice carried over the music in the club behind him. We both turned to see a bouncer approach a man and give a menacing warning, inches from his face. The unruly customer seemed to back down, palms up placatingly, but spat at the bouncer's feet as soon as he turned his back. The music was loud enough that the large man in black couldn't hear it, but I saw it, and so did Keir.

He sighed. "Your time is up," he shot over his shoulder before weaving his way around tables to where the man sat back down.

I watched in fascination as Keir calmly spoke to the man, his head motioning for the door. He was kicking him out. The man grew irritated, eventually grabbing his glass and swinging as though to hit Keir over the head with it, but the Irishman was too fast. Displaying speed I wouldn't have thought someone so large could possess, he blocked the man's strike, pinned the arm behind him, then gripped the back of his neck to slam the man's head into the solid wood table three times in quick succession with such force, I cringed.

When he straightened, hardly a hair was out of place. More than that, it was as if the violent outburst had never happened. His adversary, if he could be called that, crumpled to the floor in an unconscious heap. Keir was unmoved, walking over to the woman who'd first caught our attention with her cry.

They exchanged a few words before he nodded once and turned back to me. His now empty stare collided with mine before he shot a look at the bouncer nearby. The next thing I knew, I was escorted outside, my shoes dropped at my feet, and the door slammed behind me.

FIVE

I'D SPENT YEARS OF MY LIFE LEARNING TO READ PEOPLE. The skill was an essential component of my line of work, but it also helped me keep my cool. If people didn't catch me off guard, I didn't get upset, and no one got hurt. My childhood was spent trapped in that series of cascading events. I refused to succumb as an adult.

So why the fuck couldn't I get a proper read on Rowan Alexander? Never in a million years had I anticipated her walking into Moxy, let alone accepting the challenge I'd thrown down. I fully expected her to tuck tail and run. Not only did that not happen, but she owned that fucking stage. She looked like a goddamn fantasy without even taking off a scrap of clothing, and I wasn't the only dick in the room standing salute.

Knowing everyone in the club could see her dance sent me closer than I'd been in years to losing my shit. What she did on that stage wasn't meant for anyone but me. I wanted to plunge my thumbs straight into their eye sockets, and that was a bad fucking sign.

If I'd been thinking logically, I would have listened to her request from the beginning and avoided the entire scene. We needed her father's cooperation. Helping her would be just another foot in the door with her father. But somehow, I'd known. Deep in my gut, I'd known that Rowan Alexander was trouble.

Now, not only did I have images of her seductive dance seared into the back of my retinas, I was also sitting outside Lawrence Wellington's house when I had a shit ton of better things to do with my time.

I'd told her that I wouldn't help. I'd told her to let it go, but a woman who would seek out someone like myself in a strip club wasn't about to back down. I knew it better than I knew myself. I'd gnawed on that information for two days before I'd finally caved and done a cursory search on the man.

He was powerful enough to be familiar, but I'd never interacted with him personally. Information on him was surprisingly hard to come by, and that, more than anything, made me suspicious. People in high places with an impeccable public persona were often the worst of the lot.

Who was Lawrence Wellington?

I was on my second night of surveillance trying to find out. I'd also assigned our resident techie to do a deep dive on the web, but that would take time. Besides, plenty could be learned simply by observing. And one of the great things about living in the city was easy viewing.

Men like Wellington could tuck themselves away in a high-rise, but that was as secluded as he could get. And he hadn't even gone to that extent. The shipping mogul must have valued prestige over privacy because he lived in a single-family mansion in the exclusive Lennox Hill neighborhood, his movements just as traceable as any other schmo on the street.

I tried to assure myself that looking into the man was strategic and had nothing to do with Rowan. Information on him might mean leverage over the governor. It was a lead worth following up. I told myself that Rowan was simply the source of my information and played no other part in my decision, but deep down, I knew that was bullshit. Her involvement created a sense of urgency inside me that I couldn't ignore. She thought something shady was going on, and I had a feeling she would end up tangled in whatever web lay waiting.

Two hours into my night, a black Mercedes sedan pulled up in front of the house. I immediately started recording on my phone. The sun had set, but the ambient city lights were enough to keep me from needing more sophisticated recording equipment.

The driver popped the trunk, then stepped from the

vehicle. I watched with an unobstructed view as he opened the back seat, pulled out two short-barreled SIG 550s, and quickly placed them in the trunk.

And just like that, everything changed.

I didn't even breathe as the passenger exited the car. He never turned in my direction, preventing me from seeing his face. The two men went up the front steps to the Wellington family home and were welcomed inside.

Jesus fucking Christ. Tell me I'm wrong.

I pulled up the recording on my phone and zoomed in on the guns. Blood pulsed like bass drums inside my head as I verified my suspicion. The two guns were both authentic, possessing the select fire switch only found on military-grade Swiss-made SIGs. They weren't easy to find. We were the only black-market dealers I knew of locally who had access, and even then, it didn't happen often. We'd only had one shipment in the past six months, and Oran had reported them stolen within days of their arrival.

What kind of monumental coincidence would it take for those two weapons to have been sourced outside of that stolen shipment?

I studied the car and saw no indications of diplomatic immunity that would suggest a connection to the Swiss Embassy. The presence of men dealing in illegal guns supported Rowan's theory that Wellington was into more than shipping. This shit just kept getting worse.

A wary unease scratched at my skin with jagged claws.

I needed a drink.

Thirty minutes later, I was at the Moxy sipping the Redbreast whiskey I kept on hand for days like this. I stayed in the club for the distraction, though I hardly noticed the people around me. It was late enough that the place was packed. I sat at the end of the bar, my back to the room in an attempt to dissuade conversation, which worked until Torin showed up. My cousin wasn't intimidated by anything, least of all me.

"You gonna tell me what's going on?" he asked under his breath while signaling the bartender. He wasn't purposely being discreet. That was just Tor. He seemed to save all his energy for the boxing ring where he went nuclear on his opponents.

"Is something going on?" I swirled the amber liquid in my glass.

Tor shot me a look that said don't be a dumbass. "You forget that I saw you here with that girl last week? Don't even pretend nothing is going on there. You've been on edge ever since."

"She's Evan Alexander's daughter," I said with a sigh.

"No shit." He huffed. "Girl can dance."

I had to grind my teeth against the surge of rage that overtook me. "Watch it." A promise of brutality roughened my voice.

"Oh yeah?" he asked with a genuine note of surprise. "Didn't expect that from you."

I shook my head. "There is no *that*. I've just got a lot of shit going on."

He did a slow nod that told me he didn't buy it for a second. Whatever. He could think what he liked.

"Need a hand with anything?" he asked.

"Not at the moment." I downed the rest of my drink in one swallow, relishing the burn that filled my chest. "I'll let you know if things change." I stood, bumping my fist into his before leaving. I had work to do, and it was getting late.

♦

I WALKED through the NYU campus the following morning with purposeful strides. It seemed empty for a college campus, not that I was one to know. School was never my scene. Fortunately, my family wasn't the sort to carry academic expectations. I'd graduated from high school and never looked back.

Eventually, I found my way to 19 West 4th Street, room 302. A glance through the small window on the door confirmed that class was in session, and the professor was in the middle of lecturing. I opened the door and stepped inside, scanning the room until my eyes landed on Rowan dutifully watching her professor.

The old man in a tweed golf cap sputtered to a stop, his stare drawing the eyes of the rest of the students. "Can I help you?" he clipped snidely.

I'd like to see him show that kind of brass when he wasn't on his throne, bolstered by the illusion of safety in the center of his little kingdom. The thought almost brought a smile to my lips.

I cut my eyes back to Rowan and gave a swift jerk of my chin toward the door. I didn't wait to see her reaction, though I caught the bright pink of her cheeks before I slipped back into the hall.

Her eyes blazed when she slipped from the classroom. "I assume since you found me here that you illegally obtained my class schedule," she hissed at me. "I guess it was too much to ask that you wait until after the lecture to arrive."

What was it about that sharp edge of hers that drove me so damn insane? It was like my emotions were hardwired to respond to her, no matter how tightly I held the reins. Anyone else could spit in my fucking face without eliciting a reaction—not an emotional one, anyway. I might fracture their jaw as a lesson, but it wouldn't be personal. Not on my end. But Rowan was different. All she had to do was breathe, and I lost all capacity to reason.

I clamped down on my need to silence her with my tongue down her throat and led us away from the door. "You asked me for help, Alexander. Take it how you can get it, or don't take it at all."

Rowan

SIX

Keir got several feet away before I worked through my shock. He'd thoroughly convinced me days before that I had no chance of enlisting his help. What had changed his mind?

Do you seriously care?

I shook free of my stupor and rushed to catch up. "Does this mean you'll look into him?"

"I've already started."

"You have? What made you change your mind?"

He stopped and stared at me but said nothing, his gaze traveling down to my lips. The lingering look heated my blood to molten lava, singeing everything in its path.

"I have my reasons." That was all he gave me. "And I don't want you over there until we sort this out."

"Having someone inside that house is the best possible source of information. And besides, Stetson is my boyfriend." Didn't he see the obvious flaws in his plan? I was in an ideal situation to gather intel. Stetson likely wouldn't notice if I made excuses to stay away, but I didn't tell that to Keir. I was the one who heard the girl cry. I felt responsible for her, and I didn't want to wipe my hands of her without ensuring something was being done.

Something about what I'd said struck a nerve. Keir's vibrant blue eyes darkened until they were as fathomless as the deepest parts of the ocean. He walked me backward, trapping me between his enormous body and the wall, his face suddenly inches from mine.

"Why do you even care about any of this? You could go about your life with no skin off your back."

I prickled at the insinuation. "I'm just a shallow sorority girl, so you'd think that's what I'd do. Maybe I'm looking for bonus points when I apply for my membership with the Colony Club. Oh, I know! Maybe I'm doing it out of a sense of obligation derived from my obvious superiority." Was that what he wanted to hear? That my station in life made me incapable of any depth or compassion?

"Don't put words in my fucking mouth," he growled.

"I didn't have to. You might as well have put them on a billboard."

I couldn't breathe. He was too much. Too disorienting.

His body blocked my escape, the same way his overwhelming presence eclipsed all thought of anything else. All I could see or feel or think of was Keir.

Then his lips were on mine, his hands gripping me tightly to him. I met his kiss with an intensity that rivaled his own. We were two magnets unable to resist one another.

The sensual press of his lips, the tug of his fingers in my hair, the delicious taste of his tongue against mine—the simple act erased my identity until I was no longer Rowan. I was whoever he wanted me to be. I was free.

His hands began to roam my body, but only for a second. Not nearly long enough. He stiffened and pulled back as though only then realizing what he'd done. A heavy veil descended behind his eyes, cutting off any chance of me understanding where his thoughts had taken him.

I didn't know what to say or do.

"Looks like staying away from the boyfriend won't be such an imposition." His well-placed jab deflated the balloon he'd only just filled in my chest.

"I suppose we can't all be perfect," I replied with a cold edge, relieved when he took a small step backward.

"No reason to be hurt. I was only speaking the truth."

I hated how right he was. "If we're back to being honest, then what is it you want from me in return for your help?" I crossed my arms over my chest. "Or was that little display your way of showing me your expectations of my role in all this?"

He'd already told me he didn't want my money, so why else would he agree to help me?

I didn't know how, but Keir's eyes went nearly black. "Don't flatter yourself." Each word was razor sharp. "The only thing you could possibly offer me that I can't get elsewhere is your father. If you owe me; *he* owes me."

I clenched my jaw so hard the muscles ached. Of course. How could I have possibly forgotten? Keir wanted my father to help him get a particular person appointed as police commissioner. *That* was what this was about. I felt like a fucking fool, so much so that an unfamiliar burn pricked behind my eyes.

"I can't make any promises," I said in a hollow voice.

Keir stared at me for a handful of endless seconds, then reached out and took a lock of my hair between his fingers. The surprising change in his demeanor stole my breath.

"You know that Rowan means redhead in Irish."

I swallowed the sudden lump in my throat. "It's also a kind of tree." The tree that had been the inspiration for my name.

"It's a particularly strong and resilient species, if I recall. Fitting."

This mercurial man was giving me whiplash. Where the hell was he going with this?

"Is this your natural color?" He finally allowed the hair to slip through his fingers.

Blood drained from my face, emotion surging to fill all the empty capillaries until I was overwhelmed with feeling.

I shook my head.

"What's your natural color?"

"Blond," I breathed.

"You always dye it?"

"Yes," I clipped, pulling away as I fought for control of myself. "What is it you want from me?" I demanded softly. The damn man turned me inside out, and I was sick of grasping for purchase on his slippery slope.

Keir's eyes finally returned to mine, an eerie calm reinstated. "I'll think of something. The more important question is, are you sure you want to go down that road?"

I studied him—absorbed every nuance of his posture and each tiny tell into his personality. I considered the way he hadn't tolerated disrespect at his club. I recalled the defacto manner in which he'd negotiated with my father, and the way I'd known innately that he wouldn't harm me. As for his kiss, never in a million years would I be able to forget how the touch of his lips had found a way to unlock a piece of my soul.

But he was still a criminal, and this was my chance to walk away. To scrub Keir Byrne from my memory banks and do my best to continue onward with the life I'd so carefully constructed.

This was a pivotal moment in my life. I could sense it as clearly as I could feel the heat radiating off his body.

One day, I'd look back at this single decision as either the beginning or the end.

If only I knew which road led where.

All I could do was go with my gut, and one word resounded in my head.

"Yes."

SEVEN

THOUGHTS OF ROWAN HAD CREPT INTO MY MIND LIKE AN invasive vine choking out all other life. No matter how hard I tried to concentrate on work that evening or clear my mind as I lay in bed that night, images of her hazel eyes haunted me.

No, that wasn't right. Calling her eyes hazel was like simplifying the vastness of the Universe by calling it space. She had entire galaxies of color in her irises—full spectrums of green and gold and brown—different hues sparking to life depending on her mood. And her moods, dear God did she try to keep control of her fiery nature with a stranglehold. She was utterly fascinating.

If I was honest with myself, that was why I went to tell her in person that I planned to help. I didn't have to. I certainly didn't have to interrupt her class, but I liked trying to rile her. She was so damn self-possessed. That was usually my role. But when she was around, I felt like I'd lost all the progress I'd made over the years and was back to being a kid—unable to string two words together and talking with my fists. I liked finding ways to shatter her control. It was only fair, considering she did the same to me.

The other reason I'd sought her out was to ensure she didn't go digging for answers and get herself into trouble. Considering she'd come to me because she was convinced something awful was happening at that house, I'd thought she wouldn't have a problem with my orders to stay away. I couldn't have been more wrong. I didn't like her involvement with the Wellington family, but I *hated* how she scoffed at the idea of staying away from her boyfriend.

How could someone so hell-bent on doing good care for a man as worthless as Stetson Wellington? I'd done the research—the kid was an asswipe. A spoiled little rich boy who had no concept of the real world. Two-dimensional. Pathetic.

She couldn't have real feelings for him. I was even more convinced of it after I felt the way she melted in my arms. So why was she with him? And why refuse to walk away?

I shook my head to myself as the man in question walked out of his apartment building. There was more than one way to skin a cat. If Rowan wouldn't stay away from trouble, I'd make sure trouble stayed away from *her*, sooner rather than later.

The day after pulling her from class, I was back near the NYU campus for a visit of a different kind.

The douche had on a polo shirt with little golfers all over it, for Christ's sake. He was making it hard to take him seriously. He'd probably piss himself if confronted by someone like me.

One could only hope.

He eyed me warily as he approached. I stood leaning against my motorcycle, which I'd conveniently parked only inches from the front of his car. He paid for a prime parking spot right out front. Handy when someone needed to track down his car.

"Hey, man, think you can move for a second so I can pull out?" He tried to be polite, but I could hear the irritation in his voice.

I simply looked him up and down and smiled as I lifted my phone to my ear. "Hey, babe. How was class?" Rowan stuttered on the other end, giving me the perfect opportunity for a genuine smile. "Good to hear. Listen, I have someone here who'd like to talk to you." I tapped the speakerphone icon and leveled Stetson Wellington with a malicious stare. "Can you hear me?" I asked Rowan with a touch more volume.

"What? Yes, I can hear you."

"Ro?" Stetson barked, his eyes rounding.

That's right, pretty boy. I have your girlfriend on speed dial.

"Stetson? *Keir*, what the hell?" Her suddenly shrill voice shot from the phone.

Wellington's face contorted with disgust. "You know this asshole?" he barked at her.

"Watch your tone, Wellington," I said with lethal calm. I didn't care how upset he was; he didn't get to talk to her like that. "Rowan wants you to know it's over between you. My relationship with her is irrelevant."

"*What?*" Rowan's voice rose yet another octave.

I clicked off speakerphone. "We'll talk later," I told her, then ended the call. Her seething anger across the line was so tangible, I'd have sworn the damn phone was on fire.

She'd get over it.

I swung my leg over my bike and met Stetson's furious glare. "Suppose it's time you looked elsewhere for your Stepford wife."

"Right, like Rowan is all of a sudden yours? She'd never be interested in a thug like you."

That stung more than I would have expected.

I flashed a menacing grin. "If that's the case, no reason to worry." I turned on my bike. When he tried to call out at me over the sound, I revved the engine. Placing my hand behind my ear, I indicated that I couldn't hear him, then flashed my teeth in a vicious grin and pulled into traffic.

Fuck, that felt good.

It was too early to go to work, but I wanted to check on a few things, so I drove to my office. We owned the entire building that housed the Moxy. Typically, I wasn't in the club all that often. It was a coincidence that I happened to be there auditioning when Rowan had come by. I spent most of my working hours in the offices upstairs, which I had expected to find empty. Instead, the main door was unlocked, and the lights were on.

"Hello?" I called out, my hand easing toward the gun holstered beneath my jacket.

Oran stepped from his office into the hall where I could see him. "Hey, man. Just me."

What the fuck was he doing here?

I lifted my chin in greeting. "Can I help you with something?"

"Doubtful," he grumbled. "I was working on getting another shipment of guns sent our way, but the supplier is skittish now."

"Suppose he has good reason." I leaned a shoulder against the wall. I'd already voiced my opposition to staying in the guns and drug business, but Oran seemed hell-bent on using the money to grow quickly. I preferred to fly under the radar. Why pursue income streams targeted by the feds when we already made bank in other, more discreet markets? Gambling, money lending, fights, and other pursuits were plenty profitable.

Oran had argued at recent family meetings that we'd never survive without acquiring more power. He specifically mentioned the dramatic decline of his wife's family as a reason for his beliefs, claiming that they would still be alive today if they'd had more of a presence. As far as I was concerned, Flynn and Caitlin were without parents precisely because of their greed for power. They grew too big, too quickly, and made too many enemies, our family among them.

"Yeah, well, it won't happen again," Oran said with conviction before disappearing back into his office.

How could he guarantee that? If we had a rat who outed the location of the guns, who was to say it wouldn't happen again? Unless ... the guns were never stolen. If they'd been sold to someone on the sly, someone he didn't want to tell us he'd made a deal with, then he could speak with authority. Had they been stolen, it was awfully ballsy of the thief to sell the shit right in our backyard. If they'd been cunning enough to get the drop on us right after the shipment arrived, why not move the guns so we couldn't trace them?

The whole thing looked more and more sketchy by the day. I hated to think we could have a traitor in our family, but I didn't want to ignore the facts either. I'd be watching Oran.

EIGHT

I WASN'T SURE MY HANDS WERE STRONG ENOUGH TO strangle a man. I needed some rope because I was going to kill Keir Byrne. He had no right to confront Stetson. No right. I'd asked for help investigating, not an intervention into my relationship.

I called Stetson three times after Keir hung up, relieved when he finally answered. "I don't know what that man said, but he was lying."

"What the hell, Rowan? How do you even know him?" Stetson's voice was curt with wariness.

"He's some mobster trying to get a favor from my

dad. He was at their house the other night when I went over, and now he somehow has my number."

My boyfriend was quiet for a beat. "Shit, Ro. Why didn't you say something?" His words lost their edge, allowing me to breathe again.

"I had no idea he'd do something like this."

"You wouldn't...? I mean ... you sounded like you knew the guy."

"I talked to him briefly while Dad was busy, but that's it. Please, Stetson, you have to believe me. You really think I'd be into that?"

"No, of course not." He sighed deeply. "He just caught me off guard. I should have known. Assholes like that love to stir up trouble for no reason."

"Exactly. I'm so sorry he upset you."

"Nah, I'm fine. Like I said, it was just unexpected." I wasn't sure if he was trying to convince himself or if he was embarrassed about the whole thing, but I could hear the uncertainty in his voice.

"Good. He had me worried," I said softly, hoping to smooth over any remaining wrinkles of doubt. "I haven't seen you in a few days. Can we hang out tonight?"

"Well, I was going to my dad's."

My heart thudded. "I can go up there," I quickly blurted. "No problem at all."

"Um ... yeah. Okay. I have practice until six, though."

"I'll meet you at the field. We can ride up there together, do dinner, then I'll head home. That work?" I asked hopefully. Any chance I had at getting inside that house was vital. It might be the only chance I'd have to figure out what the hell was going on.

"Yeah," he agreed. "Sounds good."

◊

STETSON WAS distant the entire ride up to his dad's house. I gave him space. I didn't feel like pushing the issue, but when he started up the stairs to his room without so much as a word, I had to say something.

"You don't actually believe him, do you?"

With a duffel bag full of field hockey gear over his shoulder, he paused on the stairs and slowly looked down at me a few steps below. "I just keep thinking how it's awfully convenient that he decided out of nowhere to target you. As if a guy like that gets off on breaking up relationships in his spare time."

"It has nothing to do with me. I told you that. He's using me to get at my father."

"You didn't give him any reason to come after you? What were you wearing the night he was at the house?"

Outrage set my blood boiling. How damn chauvinistic to insinuate the situation could be my fault for my choice of clothes.

You want answers about the crying woman, right?

I gritted my teeth before answering, biting back the scathing response perched on the tip of my tongue. "I was wearing the same sort of thing I always wear, Stetson," I said with forced calm. "I don't think jeans and a sweater are overly provocative." Not that wearing something sexy was an invitation to be harassed … or worse. And I would have argued that point if I wasn't already trying to smooth things over.

Stetson sighed. "Yeah, I know. I guess I'm just tired. I'm gonna jump in the shower. You want to watch some TV while you wait? I may be a minute. Practice was brutal."

"Yeah, sure. Take your time." I gave him what I hoped was a warm smile and followed him up the stairs. He turned into his bedroom while I continued to the TV room at the end of the hall, my eyes catching on the closed door to the guest room.

Things with Stetson were strained, and Keir's antics weren't the only cause. I'd thought Stetson and I made sense from the day he asked me out. Or more precisely, from the second I'd told my parents, and their faces had lit like Times Square on New Year's Eve. I didn't like the uncertainty of not knowing where things were going. I was also uncomfortable with how unbothered I was by the thought of a breakup. Was that what I wanted?

The only thing I'd ever truly wanted was to make my parents happy. My feelings had never factored into the equation, so I didn't know how to answer the question. I needed to think, and I needed more information. Whatever was or wasn't happening on the third floor could be an essential piece of my decision. What if it had all been a figment of my imagination? One quick trip upstairs could clear up everything and help reinstate the status quo. I could put all this insanity behind me and pretend it never happened. I was good at that, after all. Box it up, pack it away, and move on.

It seemed absurd not to at least try to have a look around.

I turned on the television, then snuck into the guest bedroom. Stetson had said his father was out of town, but I still felt the need to be careful. Once inside the bathroom where I'd first heard the cries, I stood motionless, straining my ears for any possible sound. Nothing.

That was what all of this could be. A whole lot of worry over nothing.

I needed to get my ass up there and see for myself.

I returned to the hallway just outside Stetson's room and listened for the shower. Bingo. This was the perfect opportunity. No one else was at the house. All it would take was five minutes to run upstairs, check things out, and be done with it—my worries, Keir, the disruption of my entire life plan.

Determination urged my feet across the main landing and into the opposite wing, but before I started up the interior stairwell to the third floor, I took out my phone and typed a quick text to Keir.

Me: Going upstairs to check it out. If I don't text back in five, call the cops.

I might have been a smidge brash, but I wasn't stupid. Should something go wrong, I wanted at least one person to know where I'd disappeared.

Shoving the phone into my back pocket, I bolted up the stairs. The two main floors of the historical home were outfitted with spacious rooms and tall ceilings, whereas the third floor had originally been built to house the nursery and staff. The wooden stairs were a simple passage up to a plain hallway that looked more like an old hotel than a mansion, if the hotel had lost power and been used to film *The Shining*. Little had been done to update the space. As far as I knew, the Wellingtons never even used it. The doors were all closed, limiting the light to one small window at either end of the hall. Every inch of my skin crawled with the need to run.

Ro, do not let your imagination run away with you. It's just an old house. Get your shit together.

And if it's not just an old house?

Then it's even more crucial that you get your ass over there and find her.

I inhaled a long breath of stale attic air. Walking swiftly but carefully, I hurried down the hall to the approximate area where the guest room would have been below. I found four doors clustered together, but two were on the wrong side of the hall. Of the two remaining, one had a deadbolt on the door with a key hanging on a hook beside it.

No. Fucking. Way.

Sure, I'd sworn I heard someone crying up here, but a part of me hadn't believed it was possible. A part of me was convinced I had missed an alternative explanation.

This was the Wellington's, after all. We'd known them forever. Could Stetson's father actually have a woman locked in his attic?

I took the key from the wall. It was time to find out.

Keir

NINE

I TEXTED ROWAN BACK TEN GODDAMN TIMES AND CALLED twice without a response. This was exactly what I'd been afraid of. The crazy woman had gone off half-cocked and would end up dead.

Fucking *fuck*.

What the hell was I supposed to do now? The Wellington house was only ten minutes from my place if traffic cooperated, but then what? If I showed up and there wasn't a problem, I might create one. The asshole knew me now and would no doubt tell his father about the incident. Bringing any more attention to myself wouldn't help me learn more about a possible abduction or the guns. So where did that leave me?

As far as I could tell, it was time to call in a favor.

TEN

I WASN'T PREPARED. NO MATTER THE TWISTED SCENARIOS I'd envisioned in my head, none of it compared to the reality of opening that door and seeing a young woman huddled in a corner of the room with a chain shackled to one wrist.

I had to close my eyes and cover my mouth to keep from vomiting all over the floor.

Get it together, Ro. This girl needs you, and you don't have time to fall apart.

I nodded and swallowed back the pooling saliva, then opened my eyes to confront the truth.

The old bedroom contained a metal bed with a stained mattress and a single wooden chair. Yellowing ancient wallpaper warped off the wall along the seams, and cool air drifted in from a poorly insulated dormer window. The girl was young, maybe nineteen. She'd fallen asleep with her head resting on one wall, knees pulled to her chest and arms curled around herself protectively.

I hoped she was just asleep. I couldn't fathom the alternative.

You'd know if she was dead. She's in rough shape, but she's not dead.

Her long blond hair was tangled, and her pale skin was mottled with bruises. She wore a floral sundress that seemed at odds with the time of year and the situation.

The sight of her sent a jagged metal spike straight through my heart.

I took a step forward to approach, making a floorboard creak. The girl's eyes shot open. My hands flew up in a rush to assure her I meant no harm and to hopefully keep her quiet.

She scurried to her feet and surged forward as far as the short chain would allow while a steady flow of indiscernible words fell from her chapped lips. I didn't have to speak her language to know her meaning. She was begging for help.

God, did I want to give it, but how?

I nodded and continued to shush her, trying to

convey that I understood without wasting time. The chain led into a tiny bathroom where it hooked around the porcelain toilet. I didn't have a key to her wrist cuff, and I'd practically have to destroy the toilet to get the other end released.

Shit. *Shit*. What should I do? Did I go get Stetson to help me free her? Was there any chance he already knew what his father was doing?

My stomach churned all over again.

Please God, no. I didn't want to believe him capable of allowing this sort of atrocity, but what if I was wrong? This poor girl would still be stuck, and I had no clue what that would mean for me.

Ro, you did not think this through properly.

You're not helping!

I couldn't risk it. What about calling the police? I could tell them anonymously that a girl was being held captive. Would that give them enough cause to search? Would they show up right away? If so, wouldn't Stetson know that I was the one who called them? What if they only did a cursory look when Stetson told them it must have been a prank, which he undoubtedly would do whether he knew the truth or not?

I wasn't sure what was best, and I didn't have the time to think it through.

This is some dangerous shit, Rowan. You need to be careful.

I know, but I hate to leave her.

Just go tell Keir, then he can help you get her out safely.

Getting yourself stuck along with the girl won't do her any good.

I hated this so fucking much.

"I can't get the chain, but I'm not leaving you, okay? I'll come back with help. I promise."

Two fat tears plunged down her cheeks as her entire body shook. She stared at me helplessly through wide blue eyes and whispered what sounded like a mix of pleas and prayer.

In the midst of heartbreak, inspiration struck. I took out my phone, noting a slew of missed messages and calls from Keir. I didn't have time to text him yet. Instead, I opened the memo app and began to record, showing her what I was doing. I wasn't entirely sure what I hoped to get—an explanation, or maybe a name? Whatever she was saying, I'd translate later.

Then it was time for the hardest part.

I started to back away, but she clamped down on my wrists.

"No, honey. Please, if I'm going to help you, I have to leave."

Her head whipped back and forth in frantic denial. A trickle of panic swelled into a flash flood, soaking my blood in a new wave of adrenaline.

I pulled at her fingers, shaking my head just as adamantly. "You have to let me go," I hissed with tears welling in my eyes. But she couldn't hear me. Not through her desperation. She was a woman drowning and would use anything or anyone to keep herself afloat.

If I had any chance of saving the situation, I had to act fast.

Whipping my arms around in sharp circles, I twisted her wrists enough to loosen her grip, then thrust my hands down against her hold. The second I broke free, I scurried backward. My eyes begged for her forgiveness.

"I'm so sorry, but I'll come back for you, I promise. I promise," I whispered hoarsely, emotion clogging my throat.

Legs giving way, she crumpled to the floor, sobbing, taking a piece of my heart with her.

"I'm so sorry," I breathed one last time before closing the door behind me.

Each step I took away from that room was physically painful. I hated leaving her—hated it more than she could ever know—but I had to do it. Saving her was the only thing that mattered, and the only way I could be sure to accomplish that was by getting the fuck out of that house.

I placed a foot on the first step on my way back downstairs when I heard my name. Stetson was calling for me.

Goddammit, couldn't I catch just one break?

He probably has no idea she's up here.

What happens if he tells his dad I was wandering around, though? What then? I can't let him see me.

Yeah, but you have to get your ass downstairs.

I know! You're not helping.

Using every ounce of stealth I possessed, I crept

down to the bottom of the stairs. Before I could take that last leap of faith and step into the hallway, sirens grew loud, stopping at the front of the house. Not two seconds later, a fist pounded on the front door down below.

"What the hell?" Stetson's voice carried to me from the top of the main stairwell winding down to the entry.

A breath I hadn't realized I'd been holding whooshed past my lips. He was going down to answer the door, and I was free to escape. I hurried into the hall and ran to grab my things from the TV room before heading downstairs.

"Look, maybe someone got the address wrong. There's no emergency here," Stetson said, arms wide.

"What's going on?" I asked as I hurried down the last few stairs. "I heard sirens, so I grabbed my things."

A pair of firemen stood fully decked out in gear across from Stetson.

"There you are. I was just about to come look for you. These guys say a call was put in for the house, but it must have been a mistake. These things happen, you know?"

One of the firemen shrugged. "Mind if we take a quick peek around, though, just to be safe?"

"Of course not. Take your time." Stetson smiled, totally unbothered. The sight of him so unruffled helped ease some of my worry. If he knew what was stashed on the third floor, he would have at least attempted to dissuade them.

. Would they check the house that thoroughly? I had thought it was too dangerous to call the police, but now that the authorities were already here, it seemed like the perfect opportunity. But not in front of Stetson. I needed to get outside and find someone I could tell in private.

The men wandered off on their walk-through, and Stetson stepped closer.

"Where were you? I got out of the shower and couldn't find you."

I clutched my stomach and grimaced. "Not sure what happened, but my stomach started to cramp. I wasn't sure if the den bathroom had been fixed, so I was using the one in the spare bedroom. Guess with the doors closed I didn't hear you."

His brow furrowed. "You okay?"

"I think so, but between that and our guests, I think I'm going to head home."

"I'd offer to take you, but I need to stay here."

"Yeah, of course," I assured him.

He leaned down and placed a kiss on my lips. It was just like the hundreds before it, yet somehow different. I had to force myself not to flinch away from him.

What did it mean? If he was innocent of any wrongdoing, would it still change the way I viewed him? Or was this how I'd felt the whole time and never realized?

Ugh, too much uncertainty and confusion. I'd figure it out later. Right now, I needed to get to one of the firemen outside and tell them what was going on.

"I'll see you tomorrow." I flashed a thin smile and slipped out the front door.

The giant red truck still had its lights flashing out front, though the siren no longer wailed. I forced myself to walk calmly to the sidewalk then around to the back of the truck where I couldn't be seen from inside the house.

"Excuse me!" I called to the back of a fireman. He was in the middle of talking to someone, but I didn't care. I need help. "There's a woman—"

I froze midsentence. When the man turned, it was Keir standing opposite him.

He surged forward and grabbed me by the wrist, hauling me away.

"What? Wait. What are you doing?" I cried, confused.

"Getting you the fuck out of here, like you should have been from the beginning. I fucking told you to stay away from that place."

I didn't know the man well, but I could tell Keir was furious. It was the first real sign of emotion I'd seen from him. I had a feeling displays like this were a rare occurrence.

Stumbling, I did my best to keep up with his long strides until we reached his car. He opened the door and tried to shove me inside.

I yanked from his grasp. "Wait! Listen for just a second." I locked my legs straight and refused to be shoved in the car. "I found her," I hissed, swatting his hands away. "Lawrence Wellington *does* have a woman captive in his house. She's chained to the fucking toilet, Keir. We have to get her out of there."

His eyes blazed. "*We* don't have to do a goddamn thing. What the fuck were you thinking?"

"I was thinking about saving a woman's life."

"And risking yours while you were at it."

Then it hit me. I peered over my shoulder at the fire truck. "You did this? You called them here to get me out?" I'd been so caught up in thoughts of the poor girl upstairs, I hadn't even pondered the coincidence of a surprise visit by the fire department.

"You think I was just going to wait and see if you texted?" Each word was a savage growl. "Fuck no. Better … better to …" He closed his eyes and took a long even breath. "Better to get you out and ask questions later," he finally said in a slow, even tone as though every ounce of emotion had dried up with his long breath. "And we are *not* going to tell those men shit. You do not rat on a man as powerful as Lawrence Wellington. Not without a plan."

He raised his hand as if to cup my cheek, but instead, his thumb tugged on my bottom lip before drifting down until his large hand cuffed my throat. "If we do this, we do it my way." His grated words were as abrasive as the asphalt under our feet.

I couldn't breathe, and it had nothing to do with the pressure his hand inflicted. Keir was simply that consuming. Being near him was like dancing on the edge of a black hole—dizzying and mystifying and potentially world-ending.

"Show me you understand, Rowan."

It was the first time I'd heard my name on his lips,

and I was instantly addicted. I was ashamed to think what I would give to hear him say it again. My promise to him felt like a simple price.

Eyes locked with his, I nodded.

He gave a rumble of masculine approval. "Good, now get in. I'm taking you home."

ELEVEN

HER PLACE WAS SMALLER THAN I EXPECTED. THE GIRL HAD grown up with money, so I had no doubt Daddy could have afforded something nicer. The living room was a good size, but the place needed updating and only had one bedroom.

I shouldn't have been surprised, though. Nothing about Rowan aligned with the stereotypes someone might expect of a woman in her shoes. She fought against her nature, but it was pointless. She couldn't be a vapid socialite if her life depended upon it. The question was why. Had the Alexanders been such attentive parents that she'd avoided the standard pretty-little-rich-girl pitfalls? Considering how much time and energy her father's career demanded, that didn't seem likely.

I'd never been so damn curious about a woman.

She'd nearly given me a stroke when I'd learned what she'd done. Considering the headache I'd gotten, my blood pressure must have been teetering on catastrophic as I raced over to the Wellington house. Even now in the quiet of her apartment, a remnant of my fear kept me tense and unsettled.

The only sense of relief I'd been given was when Rowan finally showed signs of surrender like a porcupine retracting her quills. No matter how brief, I felt that shit down to my soul, and it awakened a hunger for more. I wanted to know the feeling of Rowan standing before me, every goddamn shield at her feet, offering herself to me and only me.

The craving was so insatiable, I followed her inside her apartment when I knew I shouldn't. My father might have thought a relationship between me and the governor's daughter was a good thing, but I knew differently. This woman would complicate my life in ways I couldn't imagine. That was a problem, especially since I wasn't a fan of relationships. Commitment meant vulnerability and emotion. Those were two things I'd already seen plenty of in my life and had no desire for more.

Yet there I stood, checking out Rowan's apartment because I couldn't force myself to leave.

I was in so much damn trouble.

"It's nothing special, but it works for me," Rowan said, seemingly conscientious.

"Your father could have afforded something bigger," I observed.

She shrugged. "Yeah, but there wasn't a need. It's just me here."

My eyes cut to my right, where I could see across a small hallway into the bathroom where a large canvas painting hung over the vanity rather than a mirror. "That some new design trend I'm unaware of?"

Her gaze followed mine, then cut back to me with a touch of challenge. "Not a fan of mirrors."

Of course, she wasn't. She probably didn't like selfies either.

Who the fuck was Rowan Alexander, and why was she so goddamn addicting?

As though squirming away from my scrutiny, she bowed her head and began to dig in her backpack. "I almost forgot. I recorded the girl. She didn't speak English, so I have no idea what she said, but I figured we could translate. It's Russian, I think."

Russian. Hell. That could be totally meaningless or have enormous implications. Why the fuck did Wellington have a Russian captive in his house?

Rowan played back the recording. It was less than a minute long. We used my phone to translate the recording one section at a time. The girl rambled, begging for help, but did give a few tidbits of information. They took her, and then she was with other women in the dark for many days. Had she been trafficked on one of Wellington's ships? Was he embedded in the skin trade?

Every day that went by, the situation seemed to get worse and worse.

"You're not going over there again," I informed her. "In fact, while you've got your phone out, text the kid and tell him it's over. He needs to hear it from you."

Rowan shot to her feet. "Excuse me?"

The fight in her tone sent my temper soaring. Why would she possibly be defensive about breaking things off with him? "If you think you're about to argue with me, then save it. There is nothing to discuss."

"Pardon my impertinence, my liege." She swept her arms wide with a condescending bow. "I didn't realize you had rule over my life."

I prowled forward, just barely keeping my anger in check. "It would seem someone has to since your judgment is questionable." Each word was clipped and menacing.

Rowan wasn't the slightest bit affected. I'd seen career criminals piss themselves when I confronted them, but not Rowan. This maddening woman only seemed to dig her heels in deeper.

"If anyone's judgment is questionable, it's *yours*. How else are we supposed to get that woman out of there if I'm no longer welcome inside? She was fucking terrified, Keir—chained and bruised and who knows what else she's suffered. Things I don't even want to imagine. I'm not leaving her there alone."

Every impassioned word of her speech was another

wave on the shore, washing away my resolve. By the time she was done, nothing remained but raw desire. I'd told myself after kissing her the last time that I couldn't do it again. I was already dangerously close to addiction. One more sip from her lips, and I'd want to devour her whole. I'd want to own every goddamn inch of her body and soul.

I knew the danger, but she had me wound too tight. Lust coiled from my belly down to my straining cock. My balls were practically burrowing their way back into my body in search of release. The thought of branding her with my cum launched me over the edge.

My lips crashed down on hers.

I didn't just kiss her. I fucked her mouth with my tongue, hands branding her body, and lungs hoping to steal her soul from deep within.

Like the last time, she didn't taste like strawberry lip gloss or mint gum. That would be too typical for her. Rowan Alexander tasted like summer rain and heartbreak. Mine or hers, I couldn't be sure. Either way, I was addicted. It took every last shred of my control to finally pull away from her.

"Fuck, you drive me crazy," I said with a ragged breath.

"Is that why you kissed me?"

"I was just shutting you up." I wished it were that simple.

The corners of her lips twitched before she sobered again. "I'm not breaking it off with him."

I locked eyes with her and dropped every barrier so

she'd hear the truth in what I was about to say. "If I see him near you again, I'll kill him."

Her lips parted twice before she found her words. "Keir, he has nothing to do with this."

"You don't know that."

She frowned. "I don't think he's involved, but I'll stay away from him for now."

"For now?" I stepped away, turning my back to help calm myself. "Why the fuck are you fighting for him?"

"It's not just him. Don't you understand?"

"No, I don't." My voice raised dangerously close to a shout. "*Enlighten* me."

Rowan's shoulders relaxed, and a veil of callous determination settled over her features. "Stetson is the man I'm supposed to marry. If that falls apart, and his father is arrested, my father will be devastated. It may even end his career because of the family ties. I will *not* let that happen if it's remotely in my power."

"You'd rather let your father live in some fairy tale while you're miserable than make him face reality?"

"*Yes*," she hissed, emotion seeping past her walls.

Fury and revulsion carved my voice into a steel blade. "That, Miss Alexander, is fucked up." With nothing left to say, I walked past her and let myself out.

TWELVE

THE SCREAM I SO DESPERATELY WANTED TO UNLEASH reverberated in my head. It filled every crook and crevice of my mind until I couldn't breathe. Frustration filled my lungs instead of air, and I so desperately wanted to let it out, but I'd spent my entire life learning to keep it in.

More than that, I'd taught myself to keep emotions so buried that they couldn't find the surface. If they didn't even exist, I didn't have to rein them in. Life was a series of check marks. I knew what was expected of me and accomplished tasks to further those goals. Everything was so much easier that way.

And then I met Keir.

He was an earthquake that split my surface wide open. He'd created a crevasse down to the deepest parts of me, allowing everything I'd buried to leak free. The damage to my defenses was too catastrophic to duct tape over. I'd tried, but it wasn't working. A hurricane of emotion was brewing, and I had no idea how I'd survive it.

Keir's parting words were the distant rumbles of thunder, teasing devastation. I'd never hated my last name so damn much.

That, Miss Alexander, is fucked up.

"Fuck you, *Mr. Byrne*. You don't even know the half of it."

I bent and shoved my sofa as far as it would go into the kitchen area, then put in my AirPods. Normally, I would change clothes before dancing, but I didn't usually have an overbearing Irishman challenging the very core of my identity.

I kicked off my shoes and put on my most angsty, emotional playlist. Lana Del Rey's "Happiness is a Butterfly" filled my ears, the perfect balm to my aching soul. It was times like this my ten years of ballet training seeped into my dancing. If I was working out frustration or expressing joy, I tended to go with much more contemporary choreography, but tonight, no matter how angry I thought I was, the music and my moves were born out of elegant anguish only ballet could capture.

I pushed myself until my calves ached and my

stomach growled with hunger. Until I'd relived our kiss a thousand times over and could no longer remember why I hadn't begged him to come back.

I felt more alive around Keir than I'd felt in years, more like myself, and that terrified me. I'd thought there was only one thing I feared, but I'd been wrong. Being me—giving a voice to my desires and emotions—truly scared me because that path led to nothing but heartbreak and shame.

My choices weren't my own. My choices impacted other people, and I couldn't forget that. If I allowed myself to want what I couldn't have, I'd be more miserable than Keir thought I already was.

I'd already put Dad's career at risk because I couldn't set aside my curiosity. I didn't regret finding the girl, but I worried about the fallout. If Wellington's activities became public knowledge, what would that do to my father? He already had that hanging over his head, how could I even entertain a relationship with a known criminal? My parents would be devastated. Not that I could avoid that fate. They'd be crushed no matter what when I broke up with Stetson. I knew it was over with him, but I'd been unable to admit it to Keir. He'd already turned my life upside down and conceding the timing and manner of my breakup to him was one step too far. I needed to maintain some illusion of control.

That need for control was the same reason it had made sense to ration my hopes and desires. If I didn't allow myself to want something other than what I could have, there would never be any disappointments. The only thing that was important was protecting the people I cared about. And while I didn't truly know the Russian girl, I felt responsible for her as well. If I could get her to safety without damaging my father's reputation in the process, all of this turmoil would have been worth it.

The wisp of a quiet voice in my head tried to gain purchase. I knew what she'd have to say. She'd try to convince me emotions weren't the problem like she'd done so many times before, but I didn't have the capacity to listen. I turned up my music instead and relished the absence of thought.

♦

STETSON CALLED THE FOLLOWING MORNING. I was ashamed of my disappointment when it wasn't Keir. My irritation at my reaction was part of the reason I answered the call. The other reason was the fact that technically taking a call from Stetson wasn't breaking Keir's rule of staying away. I still saw merit in keeping our relationship alive for the sake of the girl.

"Hey, I thought I'd swing by and walk to class with you," Stetson said in a warm voice. "I had a meeting with our finance guy, and your place is on the way back to campus."

I'd already been debating what to do because that morning's economics class was the one class we had together. "I was about to call you. My stomach is still acting up. Think I need to stay in today. You good with taking notes?"

"Yeah, no problem." He paused. "You don't think …
you could be … I mean…"

"What? No! Not at all. This is just a bug, promise."

A whooshing exhale filled my ear.

"Not that we couldn't figure that out, but we've both
got plans. You understand, right?" He tried to smooth
things over.

"Yeah, Stetson. I get it. Babies are not on the
agenda."

"That's my girl," he said with a smile I could hear. "I'd
ask if you need anything, but I'd hate to catch whatever
you have. Guess I could drop Gatorade or food at your
door if you really needed something."

Our highly independent relationship had always
suited me just fine, but it suddenly seemed so vacuous
and insincere. I wasn't actually sick, but would it have
been so terrible for him to want to take care of me if I
was? Mom and Dad would never have stayed away from
one another in that instance just to keep themselves
healthy. That defeated the purpose of being partners—of
being that one person you could count on no matter
what.

I shook my head, disappointed in myself for having
been so blind. "That's okay, Stetson. I wouldn't want to
get you sick."

"Let me know if it gets worse. Dad has a family doc
who does house calls. I could send him your way."

"Thanks, I appreciate that." It was strange talking to
him, knowing I'd be breaking things off while he was in
the dark. I had to pretend nothing had changed and

there wasn't an abused young woman chained in the attic of his house. I shuddered at the memory of her.

"Yeah, we need to get you better. I have a game tomorrow night over in Jersey. You know I like having my girl in the stands." His words planted the seed of an idea.

"Well, if I can't, hopefully your dad can make it." I held my breath in anticipation of his answer.

"Nah, he's got some meeting here in the city. Man was he pissed when I told him about the fire department showing up yesterday—well, about the fact that they insisted on a walk-through. I bet he reamed the chief today."

"They were just making sure everything was okay." I hoped no one got in trouble because of me.

"That's what I told him. No harm, no foul. I had it all under control."

"What time is the game tomorrow?" I asked nonchalantly.

"Five. I'll drop a pin and text you. Let me know if you think you can make it."

"I will."

"Get some rest, Ro."

"'Kay, talk to you later." I hung up, my mind racing.

If Stetson and his father would both be out of the house, I could get a message to the girl. Hannah would still be on duty until five. She could let me in, and I could run a message upstairs and be back out in five minutes flat—something translated into Russian to let her know we were going to get her out of there. Keir didn't want me around the Wellingtons, but I never promised to stay away from the girl. One quick trip inside. After that, I would feel I'd done what I could to reassure her, and everything else could be done from a distance.

THIRTEEN

"OH HELLO, ROWAN," HANNAH GREETED ME AT THE DOOR. "I'm afraid Stetson isn't here right now."

"I know. I wasn't able to make his game this evening, and he mentioned staying here tonight, so I thought I'd drop a little surprise off for him. Hopefully make up for missing his game." I gave her a bashful smile.

Hannah had to be closing in on sixty. She wore her hair in a tidy bob cut and kept the house running seamlessly in her white button-down and navy slacks starched to the point of standing on their own. She saw it as her personal mission to mother hen the Wellington men, so I was counting on her being sympathetic to the plight of an errant girlfriend who had fallen behind on her duty to support her boyfriend.

"Of course, sweetie. Though, I can't say what condition his rooms are in."

"No worries. I heard you weren't cleaning that part of the house. I say it's good for Stetson. Some things are life skills everyone should have," I said conspiratorially.

Hannah winked. "You said it, not me." She closed the door behind me once I was inside.

"I'll just drop this in his room and let myself out."

"All right, dear. Holler if you need me."

"Thanks, Hannah."

She smiled warmly and headed back toward the kitchen. I bolted up the stairs. Instead of turning right toward Stetson's room, I hooked to my left and hurried up the small second floor stairwell to the third floor.

Hands trembling, I used the key to unlock the deadbolt and opened the door. My lungs seized at the sight of the girl huddled in her corner with a small blanket around her. From what I could tell, the floral dress was gone.

Outrage burned the back of my throat. The injustice of it all threatened to take my legs out from under me— that she was being forced to endure such inhumanities, and that I was forced to let it happen. I'd never felt such crippling anger in my entire life.

The helplessness, however, was familiar, and I hated it.

The girl jumped to her feet at the sight of me. Her face lifted with desperate hope that this was the escape she'd been praying for. That this time, I was here to save her.

I suddenly questioned whether my return would do more harm than good because now I had to crush her hope all over again. "I'm so sorry," I pleaded, extending the small piece of paper I'd prepared for her.

I'd translated a message into Russian explaining that the man holding her is very powerful and that we were working on freeing her soon. As her eyes scanned the words, her trembling intensified until I didn't know how she could possibly see the words.

"I'm ... I'm so sorry." My voice failed me. All I had was a wisp of breath that managed to squeeze past my heart lodged in my throat.

The paper drifted to the floor, two heavy tears from her cheeks following after it.

"So, so sorry," I continued to murmur as I picked up the paper and stuffed it in my pocket.

Regret engulfed me with enough fiery shame that I felt as though my skin was burning from the inside. How dare I let this girl's suffering go on when I could free her? Had I been brave enough, I could have brought bolt cutters and gotten her out of the damn house. I could have gone into hiding—better that than know I was the reason she was still trapped in hell.

Ro, please don't do this. It's not your fault.

Maybe not initially, but the fact she's still here is on my shoulders.

Was there still time? Maybe I could find something

that would cut the chain in the garage. I had to save her. I had to at least try.

I clasped her hands in mine and explained I'd be right back. She seemed to understand my sudden urgency, her face lifting warily to study mine. I gave her hands one last squeeze and rushed out the door, not wasting time to lock it behind me.

I hurried down to the second floor and had one foot on the main stairs before I realized I wasn't alone. My entire body froze—heart and lungs and internal organs all suspended in time—as I registered that Lawrence Wellington was walking up the stairs with another man. A man with a gnarled scar stretching from his left temple to the corner of his mouth and frigid eyes so light blue, they looked bionic.

A hailstorm of questions rained down in my mind. Why was he here? Who was the scarred man? Were they going for the girl? Had they seen that I'd come from the wrong direction? Even if they hadn't, if they went to her room, they'd surely notice that the door had been left unlocked.

Shit! Shit, shit, shit, Ro. You need to get your ass out of here now.

I smiled broadly. "Hey, Mr. Wellington!"

"Rowan, I didn't realize you were here."

"Yeah, sorry about that. I just stopped in to leave a note for Stetson since I couldn't make it to his game." I took a couple of casual steps downward, desperately trying to control my breathing so I didn't sound winded.

"That's very thoughtful of you," he said without any real feeling.

"I was in the area helping Mom anyway, so it wasn't a big deal. Hope you don't mind." I flashed him another grin, this one dripping with beguiling innocence, though the mask almost cracked when my eyes cut briefly to the scarred man. His eviscerating stare cut straight through me.

"Not at all," Wellington said.

"I'll just get out of your way and head back to my parents." I seized the courage to rush past them. "Sorry again to interrupt."

"Tell your father hello from me," he said in an even, chilling tone.

"Sure thing," I called out without turning around. I couldn't because fear had drained the blood from my face. Had that been a threat? Would Lawrence Wellington hurt my father to keep me silent? Was I just being paranoid?

I pictured the poor girl shackled upstairs and knew that every fear where he was concerned was reasonable. The man was an evil monster, and I'd just put myself square in his sights.

◊

I NEVER MADE a conscious decision to go in search of Keir, but that was where my feet took me. I texted him and called but got no answer. Giving up wasn't an option. I had to find him.

The afternoon sun had descended enough to streak the sky with hints of tangerine by the time I walked up to the entrance at Moxy. This time, I didn't pause before pulling open the door and marching inside. I came face-to-face with a behemoth of a man working the entrance.

"I'm looking for Keir." Please, please don't be difficult.

"Boss ain't here," he said without hesitation. He was telling the truth.

I swallowed back the bitter taste of disappointment. "Can you tell me where he is? I tried to call him, but he isn't answering."

The man smirked. "Maybe that means you should take a hint?"

"I'll just wait, then," I bit out, folding my arms over my chest to indicate I wasn't going anywhere.

He glanced back into the club. "That's not a bad idea, now that you mention it. You were pretty fuckin' hot up there. Maybe while you wait, you can show us what else you can do." He rolled a piece of gum from one side of his mouth to the other with a lascivious grin.

I refused to react to his goading.

"Look, princess. You can't stand there all fuckin' night."

"I'm happy to leave. Just tell me where I can find your boss, and I'll be out of here."

He took two intimidating steps forward. "Or, I can just pick that skinny ass up and toss you out onto the street." He'd donned his professional bouncer demeanor, which was admittedly unsettling.

"Listen, I really, *really* need to talk to Keir. This is urgent. And I told you—"

"There a problem here?" The scowling man who'd been working at the front the last time I was at the club joined us by the door. I tried to recall his name—Thor or Tor—that was it, Torin.

"Chick wants to see the boss, but he ain't here," the bouncer eloquently explained.

"Keir and I are working on something, and there's been an urgent development. I need to talk to him. My name's Rowan."

"I know who you are, Rowan."

Relief collided with worry because I couldn't tell if knowing me was a good thing or not. "Can you help me? It's incredibly important."

He studied me like a wolf might warily assess food suspiciously left in the open. "Yeah," he eventually muttered. "Asshole left his phone in his office. Need to take it to him anyway. Come on."

He pushed through the entrance without looking back, expecting me to follow, and walked up to a green and red motorcycle parked on the sidewalk. He threw a leg over. The machine roared to life. It was sleek with smooth jet-black tires and a low profile that denoted this beast of a machine was made for racing. It looked like it had rolled right out of a video game.

"You gonna get on or stare at it all night?"

"Uh, yeah." I'd never been on a motorcycle, and certainly not something like this. I had no idea what I was doing.

"Step on this peg, grab my shoulders, and throw your other leg over," he instructed. "Careful not to touch the shit below. It's gonna be a tight fit. She's not made for passengers." Nor helmets, apparently.

I sucked in a deep breath and took the leap. It felt awkward to cling to a stranger's back, but I planned to hold on for dear life.

"You part monkey?" he called back to me, peering down at my death grip around his middle.

"Shut up and drive," I hollered back, my cheek on his shoulder. I was pretty sure he chuckled, which I only felt because I'd molded myself onto him like a second skin.

Five minutes and ten Hail Marys later, he parked the bike at a building in Midtown East. He helped me off the bike and led us to the front entrance without ever saying a word. That worked for me. I wasn't feeling overly talkative. We went to the twenty-second floor, where he pounded on one of three doors on the landing.

It took almost a solid minute before the lock clicked open. Keir opened the door, shirtless with his hair dripping wet. He stilled, eyeing his unexpected arrivals.

"You left this shit at the club." Torin handed Keir his phone.

"Thanks, man. I was just about to come looking for that."

"No problem." He began to turn for the elevator.

"Wait," Keir called. "You bring her here on the bike?" His voice took on a menacing tone.

"It's what I had with me."

"You don't have any goddamn helmets. Next time,

take a fucking Uber if you have to. *Jesus.*" Keir grabbed my wrist and hauled me inside, slamming the door behind us.

Between my shock at his outburst and the intoxicating cloud of body-wash-scented air teasing my senses, my mind grew hazy and vacuous.

"You were showering." I spoke the first words that popped into my head.

Keir turned to face me, giving me an unobstructed view of his smooth inked skin taut over toned muscle. I'd known he was tattooed. The designs bled up his neck and covered his arms, some even dipping down onto his fingers. Odds were good that the rest of him was covered too, but the reality of his inked perfection was so much more overwhelming than I'd anticipated. I wanted to trace every crease and crevice—memorize each brightly colored design as he told me their meanings.

By some miracle of God, I realized how unabashedly I was staring and shook free of my trance. "Um, I called. You didn't answer."

Keir stared at me with an intensity that stole my breath. It was no wonder he wasn't overly talkative. His eyes spoke a thousand words in a single look, and right now, they were telling me if I didn't stop staring at him, I would end up bent over his couch and fucked within an inch of my life.

I swallowed, hard, and kept my eyes on his.

"What was so important?" he finally asked.

Now came the hard part. He wasn't going to be

happy about what I'd done, but that was tough. Having a clear conscience was imperative to me. The girl was important to me, and I'd needed to see her one last time.

I squared my shoulders and relayed all that had happened as factually and unemotionally as possible.

Keir could have passed for carved granite, he stood so inhumanly still. When I was done, an abyss of silence stood between us until he shattered the air with a roar.

"*Fuck!*"

He turned his back to me and lowered his head. Meanwhile, contrition and conviction started a raging battle in my head. I felt bad for complicating things, yet unapologetic for following my heart.

"This doesn't have to involve you," I murmured. "I can go."

"Don't. Fucking. Move." He growled each word but still didn't face me.

From behind, I watched his rib cage expand and contract with practiced intent.

Once. Twice. Three times.

Eventually, he turned, his stare sharp as a lashing. "The man with the scar is spoken about as though he were the devil incarnate. His name is Damyon, but most call him the Shadow because no one knows anything about him except that he's Russian. And in case you couldn't guess, this situation is fucking *lightyears* beyond bad."

FOURTEEN

I STARED AT THE GROUND, COMMANDING MY HEART TO calm, my breaths to slow, and my fear to release its stranglehold on my thoughts. The situation was so much worse than I imagined—both for Rowan and myself.

Had the men I'd seen outside Wellington's place worked for Damyon? Surely, Oran hadn't been stupid enough to do a deal with such a psychopath. Although, that would explain why he might lie about the guns being stolen. He would have known we'd never approve of a deal with the Russian.

I hated that we might be linked to the man, but the

fact that he now had Rowan on his radar terrified me. Wellington was bad enough; Damyon amplified the threat ten times over.

"I can't believe you went back there when I *told* you to stay away from him." My fear was so consuming, I knew of no other way to express it besides blistering anger. The emotion strained against the thin membrane of my control, threatening annihilation.

"Stetson and his dad were supposed to be out of the house," Rowan said softly. "None of this was supposed to happen."

"No, you weren't *supposed* to step foot back in that house." My elevated voice echoed the emotions brewing inside me, and I didn't fully understand them. Rowan was most at risk, not me or my family. I had no obligation to help her. Nothing forced me to continue associating with her. I could cut all ties and hope the angry black cloud over her head didn't follow me.

The reason I was so upset wasn't about Damyon or her going back to that house. I was furious because I knew I wouldn't walk away from her. I couldn't. Something intangible bound me to her. Something I couldn't name. She had come to me, of all people, for help. Twice. Some unevolved, half savage part of me had decided she was now mine to protect. Logic had no say in the matter, which was the true source of my anger.

Rowan didn't yell back at me.

Had she done that, it would have been far more satisfying than the eerily detached way she responded.

"I couldn't leave her there without knowing help was coming."

"Couldn't or didn't want to?"

Her eyes cut to mine with a spark of fight. "Same damn thing."

"No. Not unless you have some sort of savior complex." I moved closer until only a matter of inches separated us. "So what is it, Miss Alexander?" I asked with lethal precision. "Were you thinking of the girl, or just satisfying your own need to play the hero?" It was hypocritical, considering my recent revelation, but my frustration had taken aim at her emotional barriers with the intent of watching them crumble.

Rowan slammed her hands against my chest. "Don't fucking call me that!"

There we go. I want to see the real Rowan come out to play.

Any other woman would have been coming apart at the seams by now—hell, man *or* woman. But not Rowan. She'd mastered the ability to suppress her natural responses. This display of anger was the perfect thread to pull for more. I wanted to unravel each impenetrable layer of armor until I'd exposed every captivating inch of her.

I reached around her and wrapped my fist in her long hair, pulling her body flush with mine. "Is it the name you don't like, or my implication that you're acting like a child?"

"*Neither*," she snarled.

My eyes narrowed, and I tugged her head back a

fraction farther. "It's the intimacy," I mused. An unexpected sense of satisfaction swelled in my chest, but I didn't let it show. "You want there to be some sort of connection between us."

Be careful what you wish for.

"I never said that." She tried to backpedal.

"You didn't have to. It's written all over your face."

She tried to school her features, but it was too late. I had her in my web. "Just because I want to fuck you doesn't mean I want to keep you, Miss Alexander."

Point. Set. Match.

An aggravated scream bellowed up from deep inside her as she twisted and fought her way out of my grasp. She lunged for a glass bowl on the entry credenza and flung it at me with all her might. I ducked just in time, and it shattered against the door behind me. Before I could react, she already had a small ceramic lamp in her hands.

"You think you can just break into my house, turn my life upside down, then waltz away?" she yelled. Her face was mottled an angry red, eyes growing glassy.

"You turned your life upside down, not me. I told you to stay away from him."

Show me all your fury, beautiful. Unleash it all.

"Ugh! This has *nothing* to do with him or that fucking house!"

She launched the lamp. This time, I ducked then flowed straight into a lunge, rushing at her before she could grab anything else. I forced her back against the wall, her hands shackled in mine and pinned on either side of her head. Our heavy breaths mingled in a cloud of frustrated desire.

"Then tell me what it does have to do with," I demanded.

Her lips pursed in refusal, a fiery gold dominating her hazel eyes. "Fucking *tell me!*" I roared in her face.

"*You,* you fucking asshole!" she screamed back. "It has to do with *you* and the way I feel alive every time I'm around you. Like I can fucking *breathe* for the first time in my life." She paused, her body shuddering on a shaky breath. I wanted to inhale every last morsel and saturate my lungs with her.

I wrenched her hands above her head, securing her wrists in one of my fists, then slammed my mouth down on hers. Her body gave way to mine like clay molded to stone.

The taste of passionate defiance on her lips sent a jolt of electric need straight to my cock. I was so damn hard I could have come in my fucking pants. I wanted to punish her for making me lose control. Judging from the way she bit my lower lip, then sucked it between hers, she struggled with the same sense of conflict. We were two trains on the same track with no way to avoid the collision.

I hooked my fingers into her leggings, making sure to include her panties, then dragged them both down enough that I could use my foot to stomp the fabric to the ground.

"I'm going to fuck you against this wall," I informed her, sounding half savage even to my own ears. "I do something you don't like, I expect you to fucking tell me."

She nodded quickly.

Greedy lust coiled at the base of my spine as I tugged down my joggers and freed my cock. When I released her arms, she draped them around my shoulders. I lifted her, securing her legs around my waist and her back against the wall. My cock throbbed insatiably when it made contact with her warm folds.

"Already so goddamn wet for me." I was about to plunge deep inside her when three loud knocks sounded on the front door.

"Go away!" Rowan called.

"You okay in there?" The man sounded uncertain. One of my neighbors must have heard us arguing.

It pissed me off that someone would think I'd ever hurt her. An angry retort died on the tip of my tongue when Rowan beat me to the punch.

"Seriously, fuck off!"

Goddamn if I didn't grin as I thrust inside her.

Jesus, this girl.

Rowan let out a guttural moan that made me want to lock her in my bedroom and spend every damn day for the rest of my life coaxing that same sound past her lips. "Oh *God*. This feels so good." She sounded incredulous.

Just wait, princess, it gets better.

I buried myself inside her, one voracious thrust after another. It was a miracle we didn't put a damn hole in the wall. I kissed and nipped down the column of her neck. She tugged at my hair and arched into every movement, welcoming my body into hers.

When I reached between us and pinched one of her nipples, her inner muscles squeezed me so hard I saw fucking stars.

"Oh *shit*! Keir, I think I'm gonna come."

"You better, baby, because I'm right behind you." I was so damn close it was a struggle to speak. Every ounce of my blood had migrated into my dick, clamoring for release.

"No, I...I haven't...*oh!*" She gasped, then cried out as her entire body began to shudder and shake, her thighs squeezing so tight they almost kept me from moving.

Fortunately, that didn't matter because feeling her come undone in my arms shoved me over the edge with unexpected force. Like a teen unable to control himself, my orgasm exploded without warning, from deep in my balls to the base of my spine and outward to every extremity.

I held her in my arms for countless seconds. She relaxed into my hold, and a piece of my soul shifted deep in my chest. Rowan was changing me. She carved out a place for herself within me until the boundaries between us blurred and overlapped.

"That's never happened before," she murmured absently, her lips close to my ear.

"You've never come before?"

"I've come, but never during sex."

Equal degrees of smugness and violence fought for dominance in my head. I liked knowing I could give her something he couldn't, but I fucking abhorred thinking of that worthless piece of shit inside her. Instead of saying something I'd regret, I carried her to the bathroom.

Reality slowly trickled back in, leaving us both silent.

I lifted her shirt over her head and unclasped her bra. When my gaze lifted to the mirror, I discovered she had a vine tattooed the length of her spine. Again, not what I expected. Would I ever begin to know this woman, or was it in her nature to keep everyone guessing?

My need to find out overwhelmed me.

"Is that ivy?" I asked, moving close enough to trail my fingers down her spine, watching the movement in the mirror.

A full-body shiver overtook her. "Yeah," she said softly. "You have so many tattoos, it would take a lifetime to identify them all." Her hand hesitantly grazed my chest, drifting along the trunk of a Celtic tree of life tattooed over my heart. A constant reminder of my roots.

"Not quite that many, but yeah. I've spent some time under the needle." I could stand there and let her touch me all damn night, but I didn't want her to freeze to death. "Let's get you showered. Then we need to talk."

FIFTEEN

I DIDN'T CORRECT HIM. BETTER HE THOUGHT I WAS COLD than know it was his attention on my tattoo that had shaken me.

Keir turned on the water, which was instantly a perfect steamy temperature. He guided me inside but didn't follow. Instead, I watched through the glass while he used a washcloth at the sink to clean himself then disappeared into the closet. The hot water was ineffective at warding off a cold uncertainty that settled deep in my bones.

I'd just had sex with Keir Byrne.

No, I'd just been fucked by Keir Byrne. There was a

difference. Hell, we hadn't even used a condom. I was on birth control, so I wouldn't get pregnant.

And what about STDs, Ro?

If I got a disease, I deserved it. I probably deserved that and more.

I scrubbed myself clean with his body wash, trying to ignore what the familiar scent did to my insides. I hadn't planned to wash my hair when I stepped in the shower but found myself stepping back into the stream of water and letting the liquid heat soak my head. Heavy rivulets poured down my face. It was too bad they couldn't take my shame with them.

Maybe if I quit trying so hard to do the right thing, it might happen for once.

It's not all that bad, whispered that inner voice. *We'll figure a way out of this.*

God, I hoped so.

It would be a little easier if I had the tiniest clue what Keir was thinking. Not that it should matter. We weren't in a relationship and never would be. The best thing I could do for myself right now was accept that I had a big problem and would have to find a way out myself. My life hung in the balance. I couldn't sit back and hope Keir or anyone else would jump into the burning building to save me.

I willed all weakness and doubt to drain away with the water at my feet before getting out of the shower. Keir had placed my clothes on the vanity. I chided myself when the sight triggered a degree of disappointment.

You're allowed to be a little hurt when every sign says he's ready to send you on your way. Wham, bam, thank you ma'am is so not cool.

"No, I'm not allowed to be disappointed. That indicates I'm still counting on him to stick around, and that's a big mistake." I was suddenly unsure I'd made the right choice seeking out Keir.

"Am I interrupting?" His low rumble startled me. I whipped my head around toward the door, wincing when I pinched a nerve with the quick motion.

"No. I sort of have a habit of talking to myself." I hung my towel on a rack and prayed he hadn't heard what I'd said.

On second thought, maybe it was best. I didn't want him to think I was some simpering girl who couldn't take care of herself.

"I put some food together. Come eat."

"I'm not hungry."

"Never asked if you were. Now, come on." He walked away, giving me the chance to roll my eyes without him seeing. "Do that again, and I'll spank that ass."

"Do what?" I asked innocently. He sent a warning glare over his shoulder.

What was it about Keir Byrne that made me so damn obstinate? I'd spent my life not making waves, but with Keir, I couldn't stop from splashing water everywhere.

Once in the kitchen, he slid a plate with half a sandwich across the island to me and stared at me until I reluctantly took a small bite.

"You're staying here tonight."

I stilled, meeting his stoic gaze. I'd gotten the feeling he was working on cutting me loose. Hiding me away at his place was unexpected.

"I'll take you to your parents' place tomorrow. You'll need to stay there for a while, and I'll need you to stay inside—no outings at all while I sort this out."

I forced the food down my suddenly dry throat. "You don't have to do this, you know. None of this is your problem to solve."

He took a huge bite of his sandwich and stared at me while he chewed, not responding until he'd swallowed and taken several long swigs from a bottle of beer. "I'll keep that in mind."

My eyes drifted down and over toward the entry. "I'm sorry about the bowl and the lamp."

"Don't be. I'm glad you did it."

"Glad I broke your stuff?" I gawked at him.

"Glad you finally lost control and let it out."

I'd never felt more damn exposed than I did at that moment. Not up against the wall while he fucked me. Not naked in the shower with every inch of my body on display. This was different.

I felt like he had opened a window into the darkest parts of my soul.

I broke eye contact, the weight of his stare unbearable. "I'll get it all cleaned up," I muttered.

We swept up the broken shards of glass and pottery in silence, working together but separated by an ocean of unspoken words. I hadn't expected him to help. I almost wished he hadn't. Seeing the aftermath of my tantrum brought on a new wave of embarrassment only intensified by knowing he was there to witness the destruction I'd caused.

Then again, if he was going to hang around me for long, he needed to get used to it because that was what I did. I brought devastation to the world around me. It was only a matter of time before my dark influence touched him as well.

SIXTEEN

ROWAN INSISTED ON STAYING IN THE GUEST ROOM. I figured she'd been through enough for one day to argue, but I wasn't happy about it. My entire being vibrated with annoyance knowing her soft body was right there in my house, yet still out of my reach. Between my irritation and racing thoughts about how to handle our situation, I hardly slept.

As though manifested by my mood, the next day began under heavy skies and sheets of pouring rain. Bad weather meant traffic, which meant it took us an extra half hour to drive to her parents' place on the Upper

East Side. More time to think, for better or worse. Specifically, I thought about the conversation I was about to have with her father and how if I didn't make this happen, Rowan would disappear in a heartbeat.

The suffocating emotions that thought had brought about while I lay in bed last night had become the foundation of a plan. I had to find a way to protect Rowan. Her father was influential but not powerful enough in the right circles to keep her safe—not with his steadfast determination to remain lawful. Not like my family. While we weren't the biggest, baddest fish in the pond, we had a reputation and plenty of allies. If Rowan were connected to the Byrnes, it would shed a whole new light on the situation.

It looked like my father was getting his wish after all. Assuming I could orchestrate it all. I needed Evan Alexander's cooperation, but if he knew the full extent of my plan, he'd never agree. I'd have to give him just enough information to accomplish my goals but not so much that he called the feds on me. It would be a delicate balance.

"You don't have to walk me to the door," Rowan tried to assure me after I parked out front of her parents' house. "I'm pretty sure it's safe enough."

"I'm coming in to talk to your father."

She stilled. "Are we going to tell him everything?"

"*We* aren't doing anything. *I* am going to discuss matters with him while *you* go upstairs and make yourself scarce."

Her jaw dropped in preparation of an argument. I

held up my hand to stop her. "I don't want to hear it. What I have to tell him won't be easy. I don't need you there adding fuel to his emotions. I need him to listen and understand how serious this is."

Her lips came together in a thin line. "Fine, but I want a full report," she grumbled as she opened the car door.

I'd reached out to Evan Alexander the night before to request a meeting. He flat-out refused until I told him Rowan was in danger. I left out the part about her staying at my place so that I didn't end up with half the police force banging down my door. However, the way he eyed me when we entered the house told me he suspected as much and was pissed about it.

Adding an entirely separate layer of tension to the scene, Rowan didn't greet her father with the same warmth she'd done the first time I saw them together. She bit her lip, peering up at him apologetically, then walked past to the stairs.

"Have a seat." Alexander motioned to the living area. "I'd take this to my office, but it's right across the hall from Rowan's bedroom, and I get the sense this is a private conversation."

"It is. A situation has developed."

"That somehow involves you *and* my daughter? You get my girl into trouble?" He was already geared up to blame this on me. I'd come prepared for that and didn't let it bother me. Soon enough, he'd know this was his own damn fault.

"About a week ago, Rowan heard a woman crying over at the Wellington house."

Alexander stilled, his arms slowly uncrossing. "She mentioned it. I told her to let it go."

"Well, she didn't." The gravity of my words was a physical force that caused him to clamp his eyes shut.

"A few days later," I continued, "she went looking for answers and found a woman chained in a bedroom on the third floor."

His eyes shot open. "Jesus *Christ*." He turned around, jabbing his fingers through his hair.

I gave him a moment to process.

"Lawrence wouldn't … he couldn't. I've known him so long …" Whether it was denial or sheer ignorance, I wasn't sure, but Evan Alexander was in complete shock about what his friend was into.

"None of this is going to be easy, but I need you to listen and understand. Rowan needs you."

His spine stiffened before he turned around and met my stern gaze with cold determination. He might not have been a criminal, but he was a politician, so that wasn't far off. This wouldn't be the first time he'd faced adversity. "And how do you play into this?"

"She knew she needed help but didn't want you involved. She was worried the fallout would rub off on you and your career. She came to me at the Moxy."

He gripped the edge of the marble countertop and leaned against it, hanging his head toward his arms. "Why do I get the feeling this somehow gets worse?"

"Because it does. The woman being held captive is Russian. Rowan wanted to assure her we were working on freeing her, so she translated a message and went over when the family was supposed to be gone, but Lawrence Wellington returned, and he wasn't alone."

"Shit." The exhaled curse was wrought with defeat.

"He and a man known as Damyon saw her in the house. She made it out, but they will have been able to tell she was up with the girl. They'll know that she knows. And this man, Damyon? He's utterly ruthless."

Alexander's body shook with shuddering breaths. In and out, minutes went by until he finally spoke.

"I knew he wasn't totally above board, but I never imagined … This is all my fault. I shouldn't have brushed her off." He lifted his head just enough to meet my eyes, his glinting with fear. "I'll hide her away."

I cut my head to the side. "You're a public figure. Everything about you is searchable—they'll find her."

He pushed away from the counter and stood tall, determination mingling with desperation. "I have security."

"You think that means anything to them?" I pushed.

"Then we'll get her into Witness Protection!" he shot back.

I took a menacing step forward, sensing my moment had come. "You prepared to lose your daughter forever?" I snarled. "Because that's what happens if she goes in the system, and you know it. You'll never see her again."

"Then what?" he hissed, desperation bulging his eyes wide. "What the hell am I supposed to do?"

I let the question linger and took a slow even breath before tossing the drowning man a life raft. "I have a solution, but you won't like it."

SEVENTEEN

I TOOK THE TIME ALONE TO FINALLY WASH MY MAKEUP OFF and reapply a fresh face. I'd been in desperate need of a cleanse, and it gave me a distraction from obsessing over what was being said downstairs. No matter Keir's reasons, I still thought I had a right to be present for the conversation. It was my damn life in the balance.

The instant a knock sounded on my bedroom door, I was on my feet. "Come in!"

Dad looked like he'd aged ten years since I'd seen him an hour earlier. I rushed over and wrapped my arms around his middle.

"I'm so sorry, Daddy. I'm so sorry."

"Shhh, there's nothing to be sorry about. If there's anyone who should apologize, it's me. I never imagined ..." Pain carved away the usual confidence from his voice.

"None of us did." I pulled back and peered up at him. "No one wants to think someone close to them could be capable of something so ... horrendous."

"I'm just glad you're here." His eyes danced across my face as though reassuring himself I was unharmed. "I only ever wanted the best for you. Sometimes it's so hard to know what that is." His brow furrowed and lips parted like he wanted to say more, but then his mouth clamped shut.

"I know, Daddy," I whispered.

I could only imagine the guilt he felt. He'd introduced me to the Wellington family and encouraged me to date Stetson. Dad wasn't afraid to take responsibility for his actions—that's what made him so popular among the people—but I hoped he didn't try to shoulder too much of the blame.

He forced a withering smile. "Keir seems to have a plan, though he hasn't shared all the details with me."

"What did he tell you?"

His brow furrowed as his gaze dropped. "He said he wanted to tell you himself. That it would be better coming from him."

"Should I be worried?" My attempt at levity fell short.

Dad tucked my hair behind my ear. "You tell me, kiddo. How do you feel about Keir Byrne?"

The question felt odd. "What do you mean?" Why was he asking about Keir?

"Do you think he's a decent enough man? I assume you went to him for help because you trusted him on some level."

"Well, yeah. It's hard to explain, but we had this strange sort of connection from the moment we met. I didn't tell you at the time, but Keir was already in the house that day when you came home. He'd broken in."

Dad gaped at me. "And you didn't say anything?"

"I know, and that's exactly my point. I can't explain it, but I didn't want him to get in trouble, and I know he'll do what he can to protect me." I looked at him pleadingly. "It's not like it's forever, though. In a few months, it'll all be a distant memory." I wasn't sure I believed myself, but I hoped my reassurance eased Dad's conscience.

"You're right." He nodded, then stilled. "Have you talked to Stetson about any of this?"

"No. I can't imagine he has any idea what his dad is doing, and I'm not sure it's my place to tell him."

"Then you two haven't broken up?"

Was that hope in his voice? A wave of weariness made my entire body feel as though it had been cast in lead.

"No, we haven't."

Dad's brows met in a hopeful peak on his forehead. "Well, then. He's sure to understand when the truth comes out. You've already faced so much, sweet girl; I'd hate for you to lose him, too."

My answering smile was sickly at best. "I'm sure everything will work out for the best." My voice betrayed me, growing weak and wobbly.

He hugged me close again, then pulled back. "I'd say we could both use a distraction. How does a movie sound?"

"What about work?" Dad was practically a workaholic and had been almost as long as I could remember.

"Work will be there tomorrow, trust me." He winked just like he used to do when I was little. I clung to the tiny reminder of happier times.

"Sounds like a plan." I wasn't sure how we'd handle explaining all this to Mom, but I'd let him worry about that. I could only take on so much, and I was barreling toward that limit at lightning speed.

◆

I KNEW Dad had told Mom the next day when she could hardly make eye contact. She wasn't the best at handling adversity. Mom was generous and loving and wonderful in so many ways, but when things got rough, she didn't cope well.

I tried extra hard over the next two days to smile and be reassuring. She tried extra hard not to be around. In some ways, her escapism was a blessing. I didn't have the mental energy to be strong for both of us.

Keir brought over a ton of my clothes and other

necessities from my apartment on the morning of the third day. The thought of how much school I was missing made me nauseous. I'd contacted my professors and told them I was sick, but that excuse would only get me so far. I had no idea how long Keir planned to keep me sequestered. I prayed his packing wasn't an indication of the length of my sojourn at my parents' house because that would mean I might be there for months. Three large suitcases. Denial kept me from fully unpacking any of them.

When I finally decided to at least glance through them and see what all he'd brought, things only got more awkward. Laying on the very top of the first bag I opened were all three of my vibrators. I stared, eyes round and stomach bottoming out.

Keir Byrne had seen my vibrators and wanted me to know it. What did it mean? What had he thought when he first saw them?

For the hundredth time, memories of him fucking me senseless flooded my mind. I couldn't believe I'd let that happen or how desperately I craved more.

I clutched my favorite butterfly toy in my hand as a tingling anticipation rippled beneath my skin. Sex was the very last thing I should have been thinking about. My freaking life was in danger!

It's not so unreasonable. And besides, what else do you have to do? You're trapped here.

That's when I noticed what was packed beneath the toys. My dance clothes. He'd packed every single piece of dance gear I had—sports bras, tanks, leggings, tights

—all of it. He even had both pairs of my lyrical shoes at the bottom, and there was a note inside one.

I want to see you dance again. Just for me.

My heart skittered haphazardly.

There might have been others watching the last time, but even then, I'd been dancing only for him. Not that I'd admit it aloud. He probably just thought it was hot, but he didn't realize dance meant so much more to me. Dancing was an expression of my soul. The one outlet I allowed myself. Giving him that part of me meant so much more than he could know.

I selected a tank and shorts and went to change. With my mind turned toward dance, I could think of nothing else. The one silver lining about returning home was the dance studio my parents had built for me in the basement. I had twenty-four-hour access to the perfect wood flooring, adjustable lighting, and a wall of frosted glass mirrors. Down there, I could escape the myriad of questions running circles in my head and simply feel the music.

I danced for two solid hours.

It felt incredible—so relieving that I even had the capacity to handle a text that had come through from Stetson.

Stetson: I know you said you're sick, but I'd like to come by. I'm getting worried.

I sat on the ground cross-legged and typed my response.

Me: Mom and Dad insisted I stay with them, so

there's nothing to worry about. I'm already feeling better.

I was desperately curious how much he knew. Had his father or Hannah told him I'd been by the other day? He'd never mentioned it. We'd texted some about superficial things. I hated stringing him along, but I also felt shitty about breaking up over text. Considering how unexpected it would be, even a breakup over the phone would be unnecessarily harsh. Stetson was just as much a victim in all this as I was.

Stetson: That's good to hear. You need for me to talk to professors or anything?

Me: I've emailed all of them. It shouldn't be a problem, but thanks!

Stetson: K, get some rest. I'll come see you tomorrow. 😘

Me: 🖤

I wasn't sure if Keir would be okay with Stetson coming over. I made a mental note to ask as I set my phone on the ground and lifted my gaze to the mirror. I'd never liked mirrors, so my parents hadn't questioned when I'd asked for frosted glass in my studio. The effect was perfect. I could see the flow of movement without any distracting focus on details.

Like now, I could tell my hair was probably a mess in an auburn pile on my head, but I couldn't see enough to stress over it. I used a small magnifying mirror to apply my makeup. That was it.

Who hates mirrors but wears makeup religiously? It didn't make sense to most people, which was partly why

I'd stopped trying. Other girls couldn't relate to me, which made me a loner in school. As I got older, I learned to better mask my irregularities, but I was still that messed up girl underneath it all.

Stop, Ro. Stop right now. Negative self-talk is beneath you.

I huffed, not sure anything was beneath me.

My phone dinged. I turned it over, surprised when it wasn't Stetson.

Keir: I'm taking you out tonight. Wear something nice.

Going out was the last thing I'd expected. Wouldn't it be dangerous? What if someone I knew saw us?

Me: Would this look like a date??

Keir: Yes.

Me: What about Stetson? I can't be seen going on a date with someone else.

My phone rang.

"Hello?" I answered with a question because even though I knew it was Keir, I wasn't sure why he needed to call.

"Tell me you're not serious."

"It's not a joke. I technically have a boyfriend."

"Not anymore, you don't." His voice was a silken tongue lapping at my core.

I closed my eyes briefly and demanded focus. "But he doesn't know that. I haven't officially broken up with him. Finding out from someone else would be cruel."

"That piece of shit doesn't deserve your kindness.

And besides, my cock's been inside you. That means he no longer exists."

I was stunned. That wasn't the impression I'd gotten when he'd been so distant after we had sex. Hell, I hadn't even stayed in his bed that night. Granted, I'd offered to sleep in the guest room, but he hadn't argued. This man was so damn confusing.

"I ... don't know what to say." My voice trailed off, unsure how to continue. "I didn't realize..."

"Now that you do, try not to forget. I'm not at my most reasonable where you're concerned. Dinner will be nice, cocktail appropriate. I'll pick you up at seven." The phone clicked dead.

EIGHTEEN

Had my eyelids turned to sandpaper? And oh my God why did my head hurt so bad?

This was the second time I'd tried to wake up. The first time, I'd decided it wasn't worth the pain and passed back out. While the throbbing in my head was only mildly better, I felt enough confusion and alarm to push past the pain. I had to figure out what the hell was going on.

I cracked open my eyes one sliver at a time. The room around me was garishly bright, like I'd fallen inside of a giant light bulb. Okay, maybe not garish, but it looked to be midday, and the gossamer drapes over the enormous windows did nothing to block the sun.

I was in a bed. The room was luxurious though unfamiliar.

I racked my brain trying to figure out how I'd gotten there but came up empty. I remembered getting ready to go out, and Keir coming to pick me up at my parents' house. He'd looked so incredibly sexy, I'd been speechless, and when he'd whispered close to my ear that I was the most breathtaking woman he'd ever laid eyes on, I thought my cheeks might be permanently tinged pink.

I could see it all so clearly. The expensive steakhouse he'd taken me to. The chardonnay we'd shared. I could recall some of our conversation, but that was when things got fuzzy, as though paint thinner had been spilled on my canvas and erased the rest of the image. What the hell had happened?

I took a slow, even breath, then pushed myself upright. My head pulsed so angrily I had to close my eyes momentarily. When they re-opened, I saw that I wasn't alone. Keir lay in the bed beside me, watching me with interest.

"Where are we?" I rasped. My throat felt like I'd been gargling with gasoline. "Why can't I remember anything?" I was wearing one of Keir's shirts. His torso was bare, but I didn't know what lay beneath the sheets. Did we have sex again? Wouldn't I remember if we had?

Panic trickled from my scalp down to my fingertips. I was instantly covered in a thin layer of sweat, and my pulse began to throb in my neck as my stomach lurched upward to join it. I clamped my hand over my mouth and tried to drag myself from the bed, but before I could, Keir was there with a small trash can. As though the mere sight of the can signaled permission to my body, I vomited into the container repeatedly.

"That's it. Let it all out," he said softly while holding my hair back.

Nothing, absolutely *nothing*, was more embarrassing than getting sick in front of someone else, let alone the sexiest man you'd ever known. If I hadn't wanted to die five minutes before from the ice pick in my skull, I sure as hell did now.

Despite how I might have felt, however, the Grim Reaper hadn't come for me yet. After a round of dry heaving, my body finally stopped convulsing. Keir handed me a washcloth from the nightstand, then a glass of water. I dabbed my mouth as he collected the soiled plastic liner from the trash can, tied it off and took it out of the room.

The trash had been double or even triple lined, leaving the can ready for a possible reoccurrence. Even in my disoriented state, I noted that the trash can, washcloth, water, and even a bottle of painkillers had been set out as though in preparation. As though Keir had known I was going to be sick. I wasn't the type to get blackout drunk, especially at an expensive steakhouse. If this wasn't alcohol induced, then what? Drugs? That was even more absurd. But as I peered at my unfamiliar surroundings, no other explanation came to mind.

"Keir, what the hell is going on?" I asked as soon as he returned.

"How much do you remember?" He was wearing boxer briefs. Not naked, but that didn't necessarily mean anything.

"Not much. I remember going to dinner, but I'm not sure I even remember leaving."

He stood in front of me, hands on his hips, eyes guarded. "I'm going to tell you what happened, but I need you not to overreact."

I huffed out a sarcastic laugh. "You might as well tell me to do the opposite. I'm already halfway to freaked-the-fuck-out. What the hell happened? Was I drugged?"

The muscles in his jaw flexed with strain. "You were, and more importantly, we got married."

Keir

NINETEEN

I'D BEEN DREADING THIS FOR DAYS. IF I HADN'T BEEN SO certain she'd reject a marriage, I would have told her my plan beforehand like I'd assured her father I'd do. I knew that never would have worked. She would have refused, and that wasn't an option. But as thoroughly as I'd known this moment would be a challenge, I hadn't expected the horror on her face or the painful sting it would elicit.

Rowan looked down at her trembling hands, gaping at the Celtic ring tattooed on her finger. That would be a little harder to explain.

"What have you done?" She breathed then shot me a

look rife with betrayal.

Every muscle in my body coiled to lash out. "I did what I had to do to keep you safe."

She looked back at the ring, her head shaking in disbelief. "No. You're lying. I would never have married you. It never happened." Her words were a blade slicing through all but the very last thread of my control.

"Oh yeah? Then tell me how I got these?" I pulled up the camera roll on my phone and displayed an image of me with Rowan, her grinning ecstatically while holding a small bouquet of fresh flowers and displaying her new tattoo for the camera.

She jumped to her feet and snatched the phone from my hand. One by one, she scrolled through my record of the past twenty-four hours. Our arrival at the small chapel. Our kiss. Her grinning through the pain of her tattoo. Us dancing at a nightclub decked out in celebratory decorations. It had taken me a couple of days to put it all together, but the night had gone off without a hitch. Granted, she'd been high as a kite, and the paperwork was all forged, but none of that mattered. My objective had been to make sure the world knew Rowan and I were married, and now they did.

"How? How could you do this without telling me first?" She looked up, eyes glassy. *"How could you?"* she screamed, then threw my phone at me.

I ducked on instinct and grimaced when I heard the thing crash against the wall behind me. "I did it for exactly this reason," I roared back at her. "I knew ... you

... this wouldn't ... Jesus *Christ!*" I roared, turning around to try to regain my composure.

It pissed me off even more that I was upset because the words seemed to get lost on their way from my head to my mouth. It had always been that way. I'd learned to manage it by keeping calm, but fuck if Rowan didn't make me feel like a stuttering kid again.

"If you knew I wouldn't agree, that should have been a sign not to do it."

I turned back around and forced my words to come slow and steady. "So I'm allowed to fuck you, but I'm not good enough to stand beside you? Is that how this works?"

She flinched. "No, I...I had plans."

"Yeah, I know your plans. Marry some panty-waste socialite who probably has a secret fetish for little boys and work for Daddy's campaign while doing charity work on the side. Maybe have two-point-five kids and drink away your misery every night. That's one hell of a plan."

"You presumptive, condescending *asshole*. You don't know anything."

"Well, I know that your father agreed with me that a marriage was the best way to protect you." That's right, princess. Your daddy knew.

Her face went so white, I was surprised she didn't pass out. "He knows?"

All the oxygen seemed to leak from the room.

"I told him that day I took you home when he and I

talked privately. I didn't exactly spell out how it would all go down, but he knew the goal."

Her eyes cut to the side a split second before she bolted for the bathroom, slamming the door behind her and locking it. Had it been anyone else, I would have written off the outburst as normal. People got upset and lashed out. I would have given her some time to cool off and hoped we could discuss things rationally later.

But this was Rowan.

She didn't do emotions like other people. My instincts were screaming at me that something was horribly wrong, but I had no idea what.

I lifted my gaze to the vaulted ceiling, breathing deeply before sitting down on the edge of the bed. I didn't feel right leaving her, so I resigned myself to wait. I didn't have to wait long. Minutes later, her scream and the crash of shattering glass had me shooting to my feet.

TWENTY

I LEANED MY BACK AGAINST THE BATHROOM DOOR, MY breaths coming in such rapid bursts I was growing lightheaded. But the universe had no plans to let me escape from reality. Escape from myself.

Directly across from me was a large circular mirror in a gold frame, and within it was a set of eyes staring back at me with such innocence and heartbreak, I felt my own heart incinerate into a pile of ash at my feet. Tears ran like rivers down my cheeks.

"I didn't mean for it to happen," I whispered to the girl in the mirror, inching closer. "I'm so ..." A sob hitched in my throat. "I'm so sorry."

Her arms reached out for me, and for the cruelest second, I almost believed she was with me. That I could reach through the glass and finally hold the other half of my heart.

She wept for me just as helplessly as I cried for her.

Same heartbreak, different reasons. She hated to see me in pain, and my heart shattered to know I'd never get her back.

The desire was so intense that I kept moving forward, desperate to reach her. Except, when my fingertips finally made contact, I was met with cold, hard reality. She was gone, and the only person left was a sad, pathetic replica who couldn't do anything right.

"*No,*" I cried. "Please, come back. *Please.*" I pressed my palm flat against the mirror as wave after wave of crushing sorrow battered me from the inside. "I don't want to be here without you. Please."

The unfairness was so cruel. So pointless and arbitrary. I couldn't take it any longer. I didn't want to.

My face crumpled with the weight of the crushing expectations and my monumental failures. My chest heaved with a quaking breath as I pulled back my fist and let it slam into the sadistic mirage of a life I'd never get back, letting loose a scream filled with every suffocating, heart-wrenching emotion festering deep inside me.

Keir

TWENTY-ONE

I BARRELED INTO THE DOOR WITH ENOUGH FORCE TO TAKE it clean off the hinges. I wasn't wasting time convincing Rowan to let me in. Not after hearing such soul-crushing agony in her cry.

I wasn't affected by much—I'd seen some pretty fucked up shit in my thirty-two years—but the sight of Rowan rocking herself in a sea of broken glass and blood flayed me wide open.

The girl I'd come to know was a pillar of strength. I'd started to wonder if she was fueled by an endless supply of courage and resolve, but seeing her now curled in on herself and sobbing uncontrollably, I knew I'd finally been shown a glimpse of the real Rowan. I hated that being married to me had been the trigger but not enough to begrudge her my help. At that moment, I would have carved out my own heart and handed it over if it would give her comfort.

"Ro, baby. I'm coming. I've got you." I hurried to her side, ignoring the shards of mirror under my bare feet. I slid one arm under her knees and the other wrapped around her back to lift her, cradled like a child.

She reached her arms around my neck and clung to me as though I were God himself come to take her home. That sort of open vulnerability was a balm that healed all wounds. Any lingering hurt I'd felt at her outburst flickered and died beneath her suffocating hold.

Whatever had upset her wasn't truly about me or what I'd done. This was something deeper—a jagged emotional wound that had reshaped her from the inside out. All I'd done was bring it out into the light.

I set her on the vanity but kept my arms banded securely around her. "Let it out, Rowan. You need to get it out," I said softly.

My encouragement was admittedly hypocritical, considering I rarely displayed emotion outside of my home gym, but she wasn't me. I found ways to open the pressure valve and relieve the pressure. Something told me Rowan had no outlets. She'd been a ticking time bomb, and something about our marriage had lit that fuse.

I absorbed each of her shuddered sobs, her tears

marking me far beyond the salt left on my skin. Eventually, she regained control of her breathing and relaxed into my hold. Long minutes passed in silence before she finally spoke.

"Her name was Ivy." Rowan's whispered voice was as fragile as a single snowflake fallen from the sky. "We were identical in every way. She was my other half. Not just my sister, she was me, and I was her. We were two halves of a whole."

Jesus Christ. How had I missed this?

How had I not known Alexander had had two daughters? I'd looked into his connections and business history and done a cursory look into Rowan, but it had never occurred to me to look for a deceased sibling.

Everything made so much more sense now. Her heart had been shattered years ago, and she'd never healed. If I could have, I would have unmade the world and rebuilt it with her sister alive and well. I knew at that moment that I would give just about anything to take away her pain.

What I still didn't understand, though, was how any of this related to our marriage. How had marrying me ripped open that wound? I had so many questions I wanted to ask, but she wasn't ready. I would have to let her explain on her own terms, so I continued to hold her and listen.

"Ivy died when we were six. Our family was devastated. Dad consumed himself with work, Mom spent half her days on sleeping pills, and neither of them could look at me for ages without bursting into tears and rushing away. My face was a constant reminder of what we'd lost. We couldn't escape it. I couldn't escape it."

No wonder she didn't like mirrors. That and the dyed hair and heavy makeup—it all made sense now. She was hiding from herself.

Fuck, that was brutal. I couldn't even fathom what it had been like.

"I'm so goddamn sorry, Rowan."

"This life I'm living, it's not my own." She finally lifted her head, bringing bloodshot eyes to mine. "I'm living for her and for my parents because I'm all they have left. They suffered so much, and I've only ever wanted to bring them joy. To give them the things out of life that they wanted for me and for Ivy. You should have seen Dad when I told him Stetson asked me out." The tiniest hint of a smile teased the corners of her lips. "He was so damn excited. I've done everything —*everything*—for them. And now it all feels like it was for nothing. If my involvement with your family tarnishes my father's career, I'll have been yet another source of loss and disappointment. My feelings for you and the reasons behind it all are irrelevant." She shook her head helplessly.

"That's not true." I stopped her. "Remember, I spoke with your dad, and the only thing he was worried about was your safety. Those reasons were *very* important to him. He understood this was the best way forward." Relief coursed through me when her gaze returned to mine, and she slowly nodded.

"I've made a mess again," she whispered, eyes drifting over my shoulder. "And I'm bleeding everywhere." She released a breath that was half laugh and half sob. "I swear I'm not always such a lunatic."

I had to bite my cheek to keep from laughing. "We all have our moments." I pulled away enough to take her hand in mine and examine the damage. "You've split your knuckles, but I think we can clean you up without a trip to the ER."

"Good because I'm not a fan," she grumbled.

"I'll remember that. Any other tidbits I should know?"

She set her feet into the sink and shook her head, her bottom lip pulled between her teeth. Fuck if she wasn't the hottest, most mesmerizing mess I'd ever seen. And now she was mine, whether she wanted to be or not. As for me, I was more convinced than ever that we'd been sent down this path for a reason. Rowan was meant for me, and one way or another, I'd find a way to prove it to her.

TWENTY-TWO

I UNFOLDED MYSELF TO DANGLE MY LEGS OVER THE counter's edge, making sure to keep my bloody hand over the sink. Keir dug through the cabinets until he located some first-aid supplies, then washed my hand. I watched as he poured peroxide over my knuckles and gingerly patted my hand dry.

I felt like an empty eggshell, my insides drained clean until I was perfectly hollow.

Until Keir lifted my hand and gently blew on my knuckles. He only meant to dry my skin, but I swore I felt his breath swell in my lungs, filling me with warmth.

"Where are we?" I asked as he wrapped gauze around my hand.

"A friend's place down at Virginia Beach."

"Virginia! We're at the beach? How did we get here?" I strained my ears to listen for the water but heard nothing.

"Yes, the beach is right outside," he confirmed with a hint of amusement. "We flew down earlier today. You were out cold, so you definitely wouldn't remember."

"Please tell me you didn't stuff me in a suitcase."

"It was that or *Weekend at Bernie's* style flying with an unconscious woman in a wheelchair." He smirked. "We have a jet, Rowan. You slept comfortably on a leather sofa the whole time."

Hearing him say my name made me recall screaming at him back at his place, demanding he not call me Miss Alexander.

A new set of tears dripped from my lashes down to my shirt. His shirt.

He must have noticed because he stilled, then lifted my face to his, silently demanding an explanation.

"I'm so sorry ... for all of this. For yelling at you. For breaking things, things that don't even belong to you." I gestured to the scraps of mirror still strewn about the floor. "For getting myself into trouble. For everything." My voice had completely dried up by the time I finished my apology.

Keir swept my tears away with his thumb. "It's nothing that can't be fixed." His gaze drifted to my hair, his fingers slowly weaving their way through the messy strands. "That's why you dye your hair. And the makeup, too?"

I nodded. "You took it off."

"I thought I was supposed to. Aren't women supposed to take off their makeup before they go to bed?"

A small chuckle tickled my lungs. "Yeah, I just wasn't expecting it. I only use a tiny mirror to put on my makeup, so I never see the whole picture. If I happen across a mirror during my day, the hair and makeup keep me from seeing her. When I walked in here, it was like she was standing there waiting for me. I sort of lost it."

"I'm only going to say this once, then we're going to grab some food in the kitchen and sit on the back porch. You need to talk to someone about all that. A professional." His tone was kind but firm.

I didn't argue with him. How could I? Clearly, I wasn't coping as well as I'd thought. In fact, ever since Keir burst into my world, every single day had been further proof just how poorly I'd dealt with the loss of my sister.

"Bandage is secure, and we're clear of the shards, so you should be safe to walk."

I scooted off the counter and followed him to the bedroom. It was a beautiful space decorated in pale beige, blue, and white in honor of the magnificent landscape right outside the window. I hadn't even noticed the shoreline through the sheer drapes when I'd first woken. I'd been too upset and disoriented.

"Bundle up. It's warmer than back home but still cool." He motioned to one of the suitcases that had been brought to my parents' house. Hopefully, it wasn't the one filled with dance gear and dildos.

Glad to see your sense of humor isn't as dead as me.

My breath hitched. *Hey, you.*

No crying. You've done enough of that today. Get something warm on and go talk with that gorgeous hunk of a man.

I bit down on a smile and shook my head as I opened the bag and sorted through its contents.

"Something funny?" Keir had put on a long-sleeved Henley to go with the joggers he was already wearing.

"Uh, I feel like telling you will make you think I'm crazy, but considering you probably already think that, I suppose there's no harm." I slid a heavy hoodie over my head. "Ivy sort of lives in my head. I talk to her, and she talks to me."

"You're right. That's pretty fucked up."

I whipped my head around to gape at him, shocked he'd be so harsh, only to find him grinning the most delectable, playful smile I'd ever seen.

"Oh, that was just mean," I said in a mock pout, tossing one of my shirts at him.

"Damn, my wife does like to throw things."

All levity evaporated as our eyes locked. Wife. We were married. I wasn't sure how legal it was, but I also wasn't sure that mattered.

Keir cleared his throat. "Let's eat. You'll need some food in your system to clear out the drugs."

❧

KEIR RUMMAGED through the fridge and put together a selection of meats, cheeses, and fruits for lunch then joined me at the bar.

"You know, considering you're a big-bad gangster, you're pretty good at taking care of people—and I don't mean in the six-feet-under way, although you may be good at that, too. I'd prefer not to find out."

"I'm just a man, nothing more, nothing less."

"Mmm, I'm not so sure about that."

"No?"

I shook my head, plucking a grape into my mouth. "You have this larger-than-life quality."

He huffed. "Wait till you meet my dad. He fills a room like no one else I know."

It occurred to me that I knew nothing about his family. "Tell me about him and your mom. Do you have siblings?"

He nodded. "Three, all younger. My brother, Quinn, then the girls, Nora and Maeve. She's the baby, just turned twenty-four." Baby? She was two years older than me.

My eyes lifted to him. "So ... how old are you?"

His gaze met mine. "Thirty-two."

Wowza, ten years older. That's pretty hot, Ro. Think of all the things he can teach you.

Blood rushed to my cheeks.

"That a problem?" he asked, though his voice didn't carry any concern.

"Nope." I popped the P.

"Good. Grab those plates and let's go outside." He picked up the remaining dishes and walked to an enormous sliding glass door.

We set the plates on a double-wide chaise lounge overlooking the shoreline. A small row of grass-covered dunes lay between us and the waves, but the house sat high enough to see over them. The sky was overcast, and the churning water a soupy brown, but it was still beautiful. The steady rolling of the waves was a cathartic reminder that life was more than the sum of my current problems.

We sat together in the lounger, my crossed legs occasionally making contact with his thigh and sending a burst of tingles up to more intimate areas. We ate and watched the gulls. Some came close in hopes of scavenging our leftovers. I could hardly wrap my brain around the fact that I was sitting on a beach, eating lunch with my new husband.

Keir Byrne. Did that make me Rowan Byrne? I supposed so, but the whole thing felt so odd. How long would it last? Surely, he hadn't meant for this to be permanent.

"Keir?" I ventured, breaking our comfortable silence.

"Hm?"

"Why did you do it?" I didn't explain what I meant. I didn't have to. He knew. Once the words were out, however, a part of me wished I could gobble them back down. I wasn't sure if I wanted to hear his answer. I felt like a grade-schooler asking a playground crush if they liked me. It seemed absurd, but so was my entire situation.

"The man you saw with Alexander—the man with the scar—is incredibly dangerous. The only way to make him think twice about touching you was to claim you. That way, he has the government and the Irish to contend with if something happened to you." His answer made perfect sense, so why did it sting? What exactly had I been expecting him to do, profess his unrequited love for me?

He wanted to keep you safe. That says something, right?

"I suppose I should thank you. I can't imagine you wanted to find yourself married out of nowhere."

"It definitely wasn't how I saw things unfolding," he murmured, eyes on the horizon.

Another zing of pain confirmed my suspicion. I wanted Keir to want me. Not just to protect me or feel a duty toward me, I wanted him to see me as more.

I was a piece of work.

"So why bring me here?" Our ruse hadn't exactly required a makeshift honeymoon.

"Give you time to process and for word to get out." He slid a piece of cheese into his mouth, totally oblivious to the impact his words would have.

The food in my stomach turned rancid.

News of our wedding would be in all the papers and blasted on social media. ***Governor's Daughter Wed in Shotgun Ceremony.***

Stetson would be crushed.

I stood on shaky legs. "Um, where's my phone? I need my phone."

"In your purse next to your suitcase."

I nodded numbly. "I'll be back ... I just need to..." I wandered back inside without finishing my thought. My phone thankfully hadn't died and showed several missed texts from Stetson from yesterday asking about plans for the weekend. Nothing after that. He knew. I knew in my gut that he knew.

God, what a shit thing to do to someone. I felt absolutely wretched.

My heartache drew me back to the bathroom where I approached the vanity, this time prepared to confront the girl in the mirror. It was the first time since I was a little girl that I'd looked at that face. Really looked.

"I'm sorry, V," I whispered to her. "I hope you understand everything I've done—that I couldn't leave her there alone. I hope you understand."

I could have sworn the reflection lift her hand toward me.

I would have done the same, Ro. You did good.

"Love you, sis," I said with tears in my eyes.

Love you more.

TWENTY-THREE

"Hey, Keir?" I found him back in the kitchen cleaning up our dishes.

"Yeah?" He placed the last dish in the sink and wandered toward me.

"I'd like to clean up—I feel pretty gross—but I'm not sure what to do about the bandage." I wasn't sure why I was asking him except that he was the one who wrapped my hand. That, and the fact that my head still hurt, and decisions felt hard.

He continued forward and took my hand in his, rolling it slowly to the side as though examining the bandage. "I could help with that." The coarse rasp of his voice sucked every last thought from my brain. I was lucky to remember how to breathe as I nodded my assent.

He walked over to a drawer at the edge of the kitchen and rummaged around until he found a couple of rubber bands, then returned. "Come with me." He took my good hand and led me to another bathroom, not quite as grand as the master but still luxurious and much less hazardous to bare feet. "Let's get the hoodie off first."

I did as he instructed, then watched as he wrapped a hand towel over my bandage and secured the clubbed fist with rubber bands.

"You still can't get it in the water, but that'll keep the splatter off."

My hand was now completely dysfunctional. I peered down at the T-shirt I was still wearing, deciding I could surely get it off on my own, but before I could try, Keir's large body filled my view.

"Let me," he breathed.

Again, I nodded.

His hands brought the fabric up achingly slowly, his fingertips grazing my sides on the way. My lungs began to ache until I realized I was holding my breath. I inhaled, making my head spin. Then again, that could have been a reaction to Keir squatting before me to pull down my joggers. His face was inches from my belly.

Goose bumps danced across my skin.

Keir slid his fingers into the waistband of my pants and panties, lowering them inch by inch over my hips and letting his hands continue the slow path downward even after the fabric had fallen to the floor.

"You didn't get your fill when you changed me out of my dress last night?" A small piece of my typical snark resurfaced when I realized he must have changed me.

He met my eyes, his a liquid azure ringed by a forest of thick lashes, then rose without breaking our connection. "I changed you twice, and no, I'm not sure I'd ever get enough of your body." His reply winded me almost as much as the sight of his naked body when he whisked off his shirt and pants before stepping into the shower.

"You're getting in, too?" I blurted.

He stilled. "That a problem? It would be hard to wash you from out there." Wash me?

Yeah, slick. What did you think was happening?

I don't know! My brain is too mushy to think.

"No, I … it's just … you didn't shower with me last time." I walked to the glass door and hesitantly stepped inside.

"A lot's changed since then." He guided my bandaged hand away from the spray, but I got the sense he wasn't talking about my hand. Not at all. He switched the spray over to the wand and began to wet my hair.

I stood transfixed as Keir Byrne shampooed and conditioned my hair. When he squirted a dab of body wash in his hand, I almost hyperventilated.

Stetson and I had sex for the first time a month into our relationship. He wasn't my first, but he was the most serious boyfriend I'd ever had. Not once in almost a year of sex with him had he ever done anything so intimate with me as what Keir was doing right now. He was tattooed and scarred and could be abrasive when he wanted to be, but the way he touched me was nothing short of reverent.

He made me feel cherished. Safe. Beautiful. All without even trying.

Nothing about his actions in the shower were overtly sexual, yet his hunger for me was palpable in every single touch. Scarred knuckles grazed the bottom of my breasts. Calloused palms glided down my hips. When his soapy hands slid to the inside of my thighs, rising higher to my cleft, I thought I might black out from the intensity of my arousal.

How could I feel so turned on by someone who had kidnapped and married me after drugging me out of my mind? It shouldn't have mattered that he'd talked to my father beforehand. It was my life he had derailed. Yes, he was trying to help. Yes, I was obscenely attracted to the man, but did that negate the other stuff—the fact that our involvement could harm my father's reputation? The fact that he'd tricked me, and our entire fake relationship was an illusion only serving to keep me safe?

You're overthinking this, Ro.

Am I? Maybe for once, I should do a little more thinking, and a little less denying the truth. I'm messed up, and he's a criminal—what kind of relationship could we possibly have?

"I think I'm ready to get out," I said breathlessly, the contents of my stomach growing more unsettled.

"Thank you." I met his impenetrable gaze before stepping into the cool bathroom air. I toweled off, forcing myself not to stare while Keir finished his shower, then grabbed my clothes and fled for a minute of privacy.

After taking off the towel wrapping, I was able to get dressed and brush out my tangled hair. I even brushed my teeth and was feeling halfway human again when I went back into the living area and found Keir watching television on the sofa.

God, how was this supposed to work? It didn't feel right to just cuddle up next to him. We'd only known each other a week! But we'd also been through a lot together in that short time.

I did my best to let my instincts guide me, sitting near him but making sure to leave a foot of space between us.

We both stared at the television—a documentary about World War II. It could have been worse, though I wasn't exactly tuned in.

"I can change it, if you want," Keir offered after a minute.

"No, this is fine. I like history."

Keir grunted.

The awkwardness seemed to intensify exponentially as each second ticked by until he huffed and scooped my entire body up to plant me right next to him. He kept his arm around me, forcing me to relax into his side. Instantly, the tension settled, like a missing puzzle piece locking into place.

We sat together companionably watching television until it was time to order dinner. It was one of the most peaceful afternoons I could remember in a very long time.

♦

"Does your family know what's going on?" I asked once we were seated back at the kitchen island sorting through the takeout that had just arrived. He'd ordered enough food for a small family. Though, with his size, that might be a normal meal for him.

"No reason to keep it a secret."

Guess that was true. I wondered how they felt about it. Did they care that I wasn't Irish? I mean, I had Irish in my blood, but not in the same way as the Byrnes. They probably would have preferred he married someone fully Irish and not so ... law abiding. Of course, he was thirty-two and unmarried, so maybe they were just glad he'd settled down.

Oh shit. Had he been married before? Surely, he hadn't been dating anyone when I met him.

A stab of jealousy struck between my ribs. I didn't like the thought of him with someone else. Would he go through with all this and still plan to find an Irish girl later? It wasn't like this marriage was real.

Take it easy, tiger. You're deep diving down that rabbit hole.

Yeah, well. This whole surprise marriage to a gangster thing is new to me. I grumbled back at Ivy.

And you've always been sooo good at adapting to change. Ivy's voice dripped in sarcasm.

Easy to say from a dead girl.

Ouch!

I smirked.

"You've got that look on your face again," Keir murmured. "It's like someone's told a joke, but you're the only one who knows the punchline."

My eyes rounded. "I can't help it. She's pretty vocal."

He lifted a single brow.

"Yeah, I suppose I can be too, when I want to be."

He took a giant bite of his breadstick and stared pointedly at me.

"Well, anyone compared to you is a Chatty Cathy."

He slowly shook his head as he finished chewing. "I swear I've said more to you in the past week than I've spoken in the past year."

My cheeks warmed. "I think I'll take that as a compliment," I said softly.

He took another bite, his eyes darkening in a way that shouldn't be legal.

We didn't talk much the rest of dinner, and by the time we'd cleaned everything up, a wave of exhaustion threatened to drag me under.

"Think I'm ready to call it a night," I told Keir.

"Same, I didn't sleep much last night."

"Guess you had a lot going on." I stood and clicked off a nearby lamp.

"That, and I didn't want to sleep while you were

drugged. I finally decided in the early hours that you were in the clear."

So that was why we'd been in the same bed. It hadn't been a statement about our new marital status. Disappointment made each of my steps that much heavier.

"I can stay in one of the other rooms tonight," I offered quietly. I wouldn't blame him if he wanted a little space to process things as well.

His hand snagged my hair gently and pulled me back around to face him. The intensity in his eyes caught me off guard, sucking the air from my lungs.

"My bed is your bed. I wake alone, and I will *not* be happy. Understood?"

Holy hell, why did I feel like saying yes, sir? It was there on the tip of my tongue, but I kept it at bay, nodding instead.

He made a masculine rumble deep in his chest, then swatted my ass. "Good, now keep moving."

Suddenly, I wasn't so tired.

TWENTY-FOUR

I'd watched Rowan sleep the night before long enough that I should have had my fill. But every time I learned more about her, it changed the way I saw her. Yesterday, she'd unloaded a mountain of information. We'd both been exhausted after an eventful twenty-four hours and passed out early. I woke the following morning just as the sun warmed the horizon, providing me with the opportunity to watch my new wife sleep yet again.

Without makeup, she had an innocence about her. A smattering of freckles and a softness. Knowing what she'd gone through, however, made me see her in a different light. That little girl had to grow up so much faster than she should have. It was no wonder she wasn't like other women her age. She'd had to mold herself early on for survival, stealing away her childhood.

I'd seen and done some heavy shit in my life, but my childhood had been happy. I'd never had to face personal loss until well into adulthood. I couldn't even imagine what it had been like for her.

Alexander was a decent man, and he probably coped the best way he could at the time, but it still pissed me off that Rowan's pain hadn't been addressed. I got the sense she was the glue that held them together—that was why her father's career and being Little Miss Perfect had been so damn important to her.

Her father never should have allowed her to fill that role. And letting her date Wellington like he was some sort of catch? When it came to his daughter, Alexander had his head up his ass.

My sudden irritation coaxed me up out of bed. I needed to move, to get things done. My dad would be up already. He'd always been an early riser, so it was time to check in with the family.

I threw on some clothes and went across the house to the breakfast nook, hoping my voice didn't carry. Rowan needed all the sleep she could get.

"Hey, boyo. I've been anxious to hear from you," Dad greeted heartily.

"Hey, Pops. Sorry about the wait. We've had a lot going on."

"I can imagine." The innuendo was plain in his voice.

I rolled my eyes. "I know you think I'm good, but the girl was drugged, kidnapped, and married. She wasn't exactly in the mood when she woke up. Things have been ... complicated."

"Eh, she'll get over it. Have you talked with Alexander yet?"

"No, Pop. I haven't had time." My patience was wearing thin. "He's well aware of the situation. We can talk to him about the commissioner when I get back."

"The appointment is taking place soon, that's all. Otherwise, I wouldn't push you. I know you have a lot on your plate."

"Now that I'm married to Rowan, we'll have plenty of access to Alexander. And I'm aware of the deadline. I'll do what I can." If I didn't give him some sort of assurance, he'd hound me relentlessly.

"Good boy. I'm proud of you, son."

"Nothing to be proud of, but I appreciate it." It wasn't like I'd discovered a clean energy source or something of equal importance. That didn't matter to my father. In our world, family was everything, and a strategic marriage was the ultimate show of commitment.

"See you soon."

"Bye, Pops." I set down the phone and leaned back with a heavy sigh, my gaze lifting to where Rowan stood in the doorway across the living room. She was still wearing my T-shirt, which pleased the hell out of me, but instead of enjoying the sight, my body went rigid at the betrayal etched on her face. It was plain to read, even from across the large great room. She'd heard everything. Motherfucker.

"That's what this was from the beginning, wasn't it? How could I have been so stupid?" she said with a sneer, her eyes flitting around the room in disbelief.

"Rowan—"

"*No!* Don't call me that. It's Miss Alexander, remember? That's the important part, isn't it?" She marched forward, shoulders squared. "You know, I wasn't crazy about the fact that you'd married me just to keep me from getting killed, but knowing my safety wasn't even the main reason is pretty shitty. And I was ready to marry Stetson, so you know my standards aren't all that stellar." She was lashing out, every bit of hurt festering into cynicism and anger.

I had to fix this. We'd been moving in the right direction, but this would ruin everything. I moved closer, not as close as I would have liked, but I didn't want to antagonize her.

"This has nothing to do with your father."

"That's not how it sounded a few minutes ago."

"That was my father. For him, that *is* what this is about. For me, it's more complicated."

"Complicated is just another way of saying *I lied.* How could I have been so naive to think someone like *you* would marry me just to play the hero?" She waved her hands out wide with disgust, pacing back and forth. "And here we are playing house when that poor girl is being subjected to a living hell. What is wrong with me? My safety isn't worth letting her suffer like that." Her face hardened as she turned a steely green gaze back to me. "Take me home. *Now*."

"No." Iron clashed with iron.

Her eyes narrowed to angry slits. "No?" She squared her shoulders. "Fine, then I'll take myself home. I didn't need you then, and I don't need you now."

"You're not going back yet, Rowan, so calm the fuck down and listen."

"No, *you* listen." She pointed her finger at me, closing the distance between us. "I ran away once, and I won't do it again. That girl needs us. I don't fucking care how much danger I'm in because I don't want to live a life if it comes at the cost of someone else. You want access to my father? Fine, you got it. Now let's get home and save the girl before it's too late." She'd retreated into the skin of her warrior, locking up every ounce of the vulnerability she'd let surface the day before. Every bit of progress we'd made was erased in a flash.

Frustration scorched through the last of my patience. In a way, she had a right to be upset, but she wasn't the only one. I was doing my goddamn best in a difficult situation. Her father had played a role in my decisions over the past week, but it was more complicated than that, and I wasn't about to let her dismiss the other factors just because she was hurt.

"When I say it's complicated, that's because I mean it." I stalked closer, my words like knives shredding the air between us. "I have concerns that my family is tied up in the traffickers."

Rowan's eyes widened, and her lips parted with shock.

"When you came to ask for my help, I looked into Wellington. I even sat outside his goddamn house watching him, and that's when I saw men in possession of guns I'm confident were acquired from my family. Dangerous men with guns they shouldn't have going into Wellington's house like welcome guests. *That's* why I dragged you from class the next day to tell you I'd help. Because if this had all been about getting to your father, I would have seized the opportunity the second you walked into Moxy. You were easy pickings. But I didn't because I never wanted to put you in the middle. You think I would fucking marry just anyone to protect them? I did this for *you* because I fucking care—more than I should, it would appear." I shouldered past her to the bedroom and slammed the door behind me.

TWENTY-FIVE

How was it possible to fuck up so many goddamn times?

I was so concentrated on my problems and pain that I never even considered Keir might have his own. The stampeding herd of emotions unleashed inside me over the past week had compromised my ability to think clearly. After years of suppression, they were now running wild.

I felt so out of control. So goddamn lost.

And now, I'd hurt the one person trying to help. The man who'd seen my fractured truth beneath the glossy exterior and wanted me anyway.

The shame was too powerful to contain. I was a pulsing ball of pain, wrapped in the chains of my mistakes.

I'd said such hateful things. I didn't even recognize myself.

I only ever wanted was to do right by the people I cared about, yet I failed repeatedly.

All I could think as I stepped outside onto the deck was that it should have been me. I should have been the twin who died that day.

I deserved to die.

It was all my fault, after all.

All my fault.

EVERYTHING WAS ALL MY FAULT.

TWENTY-SIX

WALKING AWAY FROM ROWAN DIDN'T HELP THE situation, but I'd needed to cool down. The unfortunate part was that she wasn't the true source of my anger. I was upset with my cousin for getting involved in shit he shouldn't have. I was annoyed at my dad for thinking my actions revolved around the damn governor. I was furious that Rowan was in danger. And maybe worst of all, I was pissed at myself for lashing out when she'd already been through so much. I should have just been glad she was speaking to me at all, but her insinuation that I only wanted her for access to her father had struck a nerve. It made me wonder if she saw me at all.

I paced in the bedroom for a half hour before I worked through the emotions enough that I was ready to talk to her again and smooth things over. Only, when I went back to the living room, Rowan wasn't there.

I called her name with no answer.

Unease raised the hairs on the back of my neck just as I spotted her on the back deck.

Fucking hell.

The drizzle out had soaked her to the bone. I rushed outside to where she sat on her shins, eyes cast unseeing toward the ocean. Her entire body shook with cold.

"Rowan, baby. Shit, come here." I started to lift her, but she clasped my arms to stop me.

"N-n-n-no, you n-n-need to know ..." Her teeth chattered so badly she could hardly speak.

"You can tell me inside. I need to get you warm."

She shook her head insistently, but I ignored her, lifting her into my arms. The touch of her frigid skin against mine had my stomach plunging to my feet.

I ran a warm bath, making sure not to get it too hot. She was so cold, anything above lukewarm would feel like fire. While the tub filled, I stripped the soaked T-shirt and panties from her body. I left her bandaged hand. The bath wasn't going to get it any more wet than it already was.

Rowan stood shivering without protest throughout. She seemed to be in a trance, and it was freaking me the fuck out.

I never panicked about anything. Even when I was young, I had frustrated, angry outbursts, but fear and panic were never problems. That wasn't me. Yet this slip of a woman seemed to be rewriting my DNA—making me think and feel things I didn't know were possible.

My thoughts swarmed furiously, making it impossible to focus.

Why would she do this to herself? Would the bath raise her temperature fast enough? How the fuck did I know if hypothermia had already set in?

Urgency scraped beneath my skin, demanding I move faster.

I undressed, then situated us in the tub with her sitting in front of me, my body cocooning hers. I let the water fill to the brim to cover every possible inch of her. Then I held her. I absorbed her quivering shudders, wishing I could do the same with all the pain she carried with her.

Slowly, her body calmed and relaxed into mine.

"I'm so sorry," she whispered into the silence. "I didn't mean to scare you or be dramatic. Everything I thought I'd dealt with and packed away feels like it's resurfaced as fresh as the day it happened, making it hard to process everything."

"No need to apologize," I urged, my lips close to her ear.

"Yes, there is. I didn't mean what I said. I was angry and hurt."

I leaned back against the basin, bringing her with me and gently scooping water over her shoulders and chest. "Did you ever see a counselor or talk to anyone about her death?" I wanted to ask more detailed questions about what had happened, but that felt like too much too soon.

"No. I think my parents were so lost in their own grief that they weren't capable of addressing mine. They could hardly look at me without cringing or tearing up."

Jesus, that would fuck up a kid. I listened raptly as she continued.

"Mom sort of disappeared for a while. Self-medicated. She slept a lot. Dad threw himself into work. Sometimes I didn't mind, though, because when I was alone, I could hear her. Talk to her. I suppose that's why I've never had any close friends. I only ever wanted Ivy."

"That makes sense."

"Maybe, but it also sounds messed up." Despite their meaning, her words were spoken without judgment.

"Everyone has a touch of crazy in them."

"Right," she said defeatedly. "I'm supposed to believe that from Mr. Cool, Calm, and Collected."

"Believe it or not, I was expelled from three different elementary schools."

She twisted enough to look back at me. "Are you serious?"

"God's truth." I held up my right hand.

"Why?" she breathed, wide-eyed.

I coaxed her back against me before continuing. "I told you that getting upset made me tongue-tied. It used to be bad. I would get so frustrated that I'd throw chairs or hit other kids. The tantrums I threw didn't help my situation. I started to get bullied. Kids called me a freak and other delightful names. That's when the fights started. By fifth grade, I'd developed quite a reputation for myself. Enough that kids finally left me alone, and I had fewer outbursts. I figured out that the less I said, the better, and that when I did speak, I absolutely had to remain calm, no matter what, so I didn't lose my words."

"What about your siblings and cousins? They didn't give you a hard time, did they?"

"Nah." A smile teased my lips. "If anything, I was sort of a legend to them." I opened the drain to let some water out, then started the tap with warmer water to raise the temperature.

"Yeah?" she asked with a touch of amusement that did more to warm me than the water ever could.

"Yeah. My cousin Oran and I were closer back then. That's what makes this Wellington business so damn hard. Oran was responsible for those guns, and now I'm left wondering if they were really stolen, or if he made a deal behind our backs."

"Do you genuinely believe he could do something like that?"

I sighed deeply. "I'd already been struggling with suspicions that he'd played a role in his father's death."

"Oh, Keir. That's awful."

"Yeah." The single syllable was saturated with the weight of my worries.

"What are you gonna do?"

"When we get back, I'm going to talk to my pops. It's more his place than anyone's to decide how to proceed. I just didn't want to say anything unless I was sure, but now that the guns have resurfaced, I know in my gut that something's not right."

Quiet filtered in around us until she spoke again.

"What are we going to do about the girl?"

I took Rowan's hand and wove my fingers with hers. "We're going to get her out of there," I assured her softly.

"When I see her, I see my sister. I know they aren't the same, but it feels like it. Like this is my chance to do it right. To save her."

Fuck, how had I not made that connection?

I was learning how her sister's death had affected her, but I hadn't thought about how she might associate the two. That was why she'd been so hell-bent on helping the woman, even at the risk of endangering herself.

"We'll get her out of there, I promise." I had no business making such an assurance when the girl might not even be alive at this point, yet I couldn't stop myself. The deep-seated need to give Rowan the world was a compulsion I couldn't contain.

She lifted our hands, untangling our fingers to get a closer look at my hand. At the matching tattoo on my ring finger. She gently touched the marking. "Why did you do this? Is it some kind of family tradition?"

"Not that I know of."

"It's going to make divorce awfully complicated."

"Good thing I have no plans of ever divorcing." My words hung like steam in the air.

She wiggled around to look back at me. "You didn't just do this for the short term?"

I held up my hand. "Does this look short term to you?"

"But you hardly know me."

"I know enough."

Electricity heated the air around us as Rowan's eyes dropped to my lips. Slowly, she turned her body all the way around until her front was pressed against mine. My cock was instantly rock hard.

I cupped her waist, my hips arching to press my dick against her belly, a voracious hunger demanding more of her. When her lips met mine, my head spun with relief. I devoured her kiss like a man surfacing for air after being rolled by the tide.

I'd tried to be patient. I'd given her time to process and kept my hands to myself—in the shower and when her body lay next to mine in our bed. I'd done everything I could to be honorable, but that well had run dry. Her small offering was all the assurance I'd needed to claim what was mine.

Water was terrible lube, however, and my friend would be pissed if I flooded his house, so I forced myself to sever our connection and guided us to our feet. I was too drunk on her for towels, though. My lips were instantly drawn back to hers, my feet walking us blindly to the bed.

Rowan smiled through our kiss. "We're soaked, Keir. We'll get the bed all wet."

"It'll dry," I grumbled as I lay her back and spread her legs wide. "Fuck, you're beautiful."

TWENTY-SEVEN

I HADN'T SEEN A RAZOR IN DAYS, LET ALONE USED ONE, SO I started to panic when Keir spread me wide.

If he saw something he didn't like, it sure didn't show. His mouth was on me in an instant, licking and sucking at my center with such dedication, my brain short-circuited.

"You say you know me ..." I murmured distractedly. "Then you know ... I'm fucked up."

"Aren't we all?" He dragged his bottom teeth gently up my slit, then nipped at my clit with exquisite delicacy. "If you only knew the depraved things I wanted to do to you, you'd understand."

I opened my eyes, my stare colliding with his. "Show me," I breathed.

His eyes dilated until only a sliver of turquoise remained. "I'm not sure you're ready for that. You like to feel in control, Rowan. I want to take it from you."

My heart skittered in a frantic dance devoid of rhythm. "Show me," I repeated more firmly. Even though his proposition terrified me, I wanted it more than anything.

"Don't move." His words caressed my skin with their dark promise.

He was gone for several minutes, his absence stoking my anticipation to maddening heights. When he returned, he held a bundle of yellow utility cord in one hand and what looked like a spatula and a pair of scissors in the other. Nerves clamped down on my lungs, but just like the day I met him, I wasn't scared. I knew he wouldn't hurt me.

"Come here." Keir placed the scissors on the dresser and watched me inch forward with a predatory glint in his eye. "This nylon rope isn't ideal, so we'll have to be careful not to give you burns. Lift your arms." His voice grew ragged as freshly mined granite.

With deft hands, he slid sections of rope through his fingers until he was satisfied with the length. The cord was relatively new but still more abrasive than the silk variety would be. I sort of preferred it that way. This strange connection forming between us was raw and unrefined. It seemed only fitting the physical binds be the same.

Keir positioned himself behind me, bringing the rope around my ribs and securing it somehow at my back. "Turn to your left."

I did a small circle. Every nerve in my body focused on his touch as he guided the rope under my breasts. Once I'd performed a full turn, he worked the rope at my back, then nudged me to continue turning, this time guiding the cord to rest just above my breasts.

Everything about the process felt intimate and erotic. Even without the power dynamic driving up the intensity of this shared experience, the emotional vulnerability alone would give me pause if it were anyone but Keir standing before me. With him, I wasn't embarrassed or uncertain. How could I be when he watched me with such ardent concentration? The molten desire swirling in those turquoise depths made me feel priceless. The *Mona Lisa* come to life.

I completed several more turns, the rope wrapping around my body in different ways each time until my chest was a zigzag of yellow cord, save for my breasts. They were squeezed plump from their confinement like roses blooming from a vase, a centerpiece to be admired.

Being on display made my nipples almost painfully erect. Even more surprising was the thrum of pleasure I experienced from the coarse texture of the rope. It was abrasive. I probably shouldn't have liked it, but I did. A lot. The hint of burn stirred a heat deep in my belly.

"How does that feel?" Keir asked, pausing to meet my eyes.

I was so breathless with sensation, I struggled to speak. "Good ... it's good."

He hummed his approval, then wrapped my upper arms to secure them at my sides. Each of his movements was quick and confident in his technique, which made me endlessly curious as well as jealous. This wasn't his first time wielding a rope. I abhorred thinking of him doing anything so intimate with anyone else.

"You're doing so well, Rowan." He came to my front, admiring his work. Every inch of my skin flushed from his praise. "Lie back on the bed."

I did as I was told, somewhat awkwardly since my arms had limited use. Once I was situated, my breath hitched in my throat to see him kneeling above me.

"Bring your hands to your ankles."

The movement opened me to his sight. He took full advantage, unapologetically staring. One scalding hand slid down my shin. "What we're about to do is all about trust. Your control lies in your trust of me to respect your limits and take care of you."

"And what do you get from this?" I asked curiously.

"I told you. Your trust." He began to tie my hand to my ankle, avoiding my wet bandage, then did the same for the other side until I was rendered completely immobile.

If a heart attack could result from sheer exertion, my whirring organ was dangerously close to that limit. I took a slow breath through my mouth.

Keir's guttural rumble of approval kissed my ears and warmed my insides. "You're stunning, little lamb."

He sat back and admired his work before easing off the bed and coming back with the spatula. He assessed the black plastic, rolling it around in his hands. "Again, not ideal, but it will serve its purpose."

"Which is?" I breathed.

A wicked glint flashed in his eyes. He didn't answer, not verbally. Instead, he turned the utensil around and holding the spatula part, brought the rounded handle to rest in the middle of my chest between sections of rope. Slowly, he dragged it down and over to my right breast, circling the rounded mound in a spiral, inching closer to the taut peak.

I couldn't explain it, but something about his use of an object rather than his own hands was even more electrifying. An uncertain edginess that heightened the anticipation.

I arched as best I could in my confines, silently begging him to ease the ache in my nipples. He understood. His hand cupped my breast, enveloping all but the tip. Then he pulled his hand away, fingers cinching around my nipple at the last second. He gave it a sharp tug that had me seeing stars.

A mewl clawed its way past my lips. I'd never made a more wanton sound in my life.

Keir's mouth lapped at my nipple, soothing the pebbled flesh with his tongue. "When we get home, we can try out clamps for these." His teeth grazed over the sensitive skin, sending another bolt of desire to my throbbing clit.

Moisture dripped from my entrance. "I need more, Keir. *Please.*"

His lips curved up with satisfaction as he brought the spatula handle back to my middle, dragging it down until he reached the top of my slit. I quit breathing entirely when he dipped the cool plastic lower.

"I'm going to give you everything you need, Rowan. Will you trust me to do that?"

I nodded eagerly, no hesitation.

"Such a good little lamb."

The spatula handle crested my entrance. Watching him fondle me with something not meant for that use felt so damn taboo and erotic. I'd never experienced anything like it. When he started to stroke himself, I thought I'd lose my mind with desire.

Was it possible to come without a single touch to my clit? The sight of his tattooed arm, muscle flexing with each pump of his thick shaft, was about to test the theory. I was so perilously close to release that I could hardly believe it.

My inner muscles spasmed angrily. I gasped. "Keir, *please!*" I whimpered.

Then the handle was inside me. It felt foreign yet satisfying, easing the aching need I had to be filled. Keir fucked me with the plastic spatula, his other hand stroking the sides of my clit between his fingers. He used my body in the most delicious way, and I was helpless to stop him. Not that I wanted to. The powerlessness allowed me to let go of my objections and simply receive the pleasure he gave.

He took me to the brink, then moved his focus to my aching breasts, giving my core time to cool before lowering himself to lick at my entrance. Again, he teased me to the point of excruciation but stopped just as my legs began to twitch and tremble.

"*No!* Please, I need to come."

"And you will ... with my cock inside you." Finally, he aligned his body with mine, waiting until our eyes were locked before rocking himself deep into my sensitive channel.

Something profound was happening between us, and it had nothing to do with the delicious way his cock filled me. This was something intangible. Something transformative.

"Fuck, you squeeze me so good." He kept his body low so that each increasingly urgent thrust brought him in contact with my clit.

I was back on that cliff's edge in an instant, tears leaking from the corners of my eyes in anticipation of falling off. "*Yes*, Keir. Yes, *just like that.*"

"Milk my cock, Rowan," he commanded. "Show me this body is mine."

A scream tore past my lips.

My body ignited, every cell filling with radiant light.

"That's my girl. My *wife*. You're mine, Rowan Byrne. All. Fucking. Mine." He growled those last words through clenched teeth as his body coiled tight. At the last second, he pulled out and stroked himself as warm jets of cum decorated my breasts and belly. I fought for awareness through my orgasmic haze, enthralled with his show of possession and devotion. I couldn't ever recall feeling so acutely desired.

With our shuddering breaths filling the silence, Keir leaned forward and placed a reverent kiss on each of my kneecaps, then swiped a finger gently through his cum on my stomach. His gaze briefly cut to mine before he lowered his hand and rolled the digit around the inside of my entrance. Marking me.

As if I wasn't already his in every way that mattered.

I wasn't sure how it had happened, but it was true. Keir Byrne had captured what remained of my heart and held it captive in the palm of his hand. And the scariest part was, I wanted him to have it.

♦

"I'm famished, and if I don't get some coffee soon, I'll get a headache later." I put on a clean shirt and dug through my suitcase. We'd taken a quick shower, replaced my bandages, and were now approaching late morning.

"Should we do breakfast or go find lunch somewhere?"

"Either works, but after that ..." I paused, not sure how he'd feel about what I was going to say next. "I think it's time for us to go home. I know you aren't a fan of Stetson, but I feel like I owe him an apology. And most importantly, that woman desperately needs our help. We need to deal with all this. We can't hide forever." And I had intentionally ignored the fact that I'd been missing school. I could only worry about so much at once.

Keir appeared in the doorframe to the bedroom. "Technically, we could. I could make us both disappear, but I know that's not what either of us wants." He stepped closer and opened a small canister of ointment. "Your hand," he murmured. He coated my tattoo with salve, but I'd swear it was my heart he was healing. "I'll make the arrangements to fly home tomorrow."

I nodded, my throat impossibly tight. "Thank you."

As if I needed more evidence that I was falling for Keir Byrne. He stirred to life feelings I hadn't even known were possible. I'd thought what I felt for Stetson was love—maybe not deeply romantic love, but still a form of affection. Now, I couldn't imagine how that was possible when my feelings for him were faded, pastel versions of the vibrant hues I felt developing for Keir.

He was so much more than I ever expected. Passionate. Loyal. And even tender when he wanted to be. But what would that mean for my family and me? He was still a criminal.

Is that really how you see him? Because I think he's a hell of a lot more than that.

Damn, even Ivy sounded disappointed in me.

Of course not, V. But no matter how gallant he is beneath the surface, it doesn't erase the ugly truth of his profession and the dangers involved.

Stetson isn't a criminal, and you still ended up in danger. Sometimes the scariest monsters hide in plain sight.

She was right.

This world was drawn in shades of gray. All I could do was look at my priorities and decide how dark I was willing to go.

For Keir, I might erase the scale entirely.

TWENTY-EIGHT

We flew back to the city first thing the following morning. I spent the entire time biting my cuticles until my fingers bled. What would my father say when I saw him?

We had texted briefly over the past couple of days, but seeing my parents in person would be different. Would their eyes convey disappointment and heartbreak that texted words left unsaid? If the emotions were present, I'd see it in their eyes. They wouldn't be able to hide it from me because I knew them too well.

Hurting the people I loved was my greatest fear in life.

I knew how easy it was to cause utter devastation in the flippant passing of a single careless moment.

Keir insisted on walking me to my parents' door rather than dropping me off out front. In an almost ironic reversal of tradition, Keir walked me up the steps and handed off his new bride to her father. I was probably more nervous this way than had it been the other way around.

"Rowan, honey. I'm so glad you're home." Dad wrapped me in a relieved embrace.

Out of the corner of my eye, I could see Keir's stare locked with my father's. Their silent conversation saturated the air with testosterone and tension.

I pulled back to draw my father's attention, hoping to neutralize the situation. "I'm so sorry to worry you, Daddy."

"I'm just glad you're safe. That's all that matters." He caught sight of my bandaged hand, his brow furrowing. "What happened here?"

"Just a silly accident." I waved off his worry, not wanting to explain.

Keir interjected a welcome distraction. "I have a meeting I need to get to, but I'll return as soon as I finish. We'll have plenty to discuss."

My father stared at him with me still tucked at his side before eventually extending his hand to shake. Keir accepted, gave me a small nod, then left us alone.

My knees almost buckled with relief that it was over. The first big hurdle.

Dad must have felt the same. He let loose a breath laden with weariness. "I want you to know, sweetie, that we'll fix this. As soon as I know you're safe, I will do everything in my power to help you sever ties with the Byrnes."

My right hand curled protectively over my left to keep Dad from seeing my tattoo.

Nice try, sis. You didn't like the idea of erasing Keir from your life. Admit it.

I internally grimaced.

"Is that what you want?" I asked him, sounding smaller than I would have liked.

Dad stilled to study me. "Isn't that what you want?"

I suddenly had trouble meeting my father's gaze. "I guess I don't know what I want. I know you don't like Keir—"

"It's not that I don't *like* him; he's just part of a different world than us."

"I know, but I've gotten to know him over the past couple of weeks, and … he's different than I expected."

Dad stiffened, then ran a hand through his thinning hair. "He assured me you were on board with the marriage, but that's not really what I thought he meant. Are you telling me you *want* to be married to him?"

Oh God. Why was this so hard?

I chewed my bottom lip, trying to find the right words. "I guess what I'm saying is that I don't *not* want to be married to him, but I know how upsetting it would be for you and Mom ..."

Dad stepped closer, his brows narrowed. His eyes trailed over my face with the precision of a laser. "Something's different about you," he said softly.

I shrugged a shoulder. "A lot has happened recently."

His features softened. "Maybe more than I realized," he murmured, then placed his hands on my arms and brought his gaze back to mine. "I don't dislike him, Ro. I've only ever wanted you to be happy, and if he gives that to you by some strange twist of fate, then I won't complain."

"But what about your image? The next election is only a year away."

He held up his hand to stop me. "Let me worry about that. You've always taken on more than you should ever since ..." He dropped his eyes briefly to the floor. "Well, you know."

"Actually, I wanted to talk to you about that, too."

He pulled me into his side. "Maybe we can do that later. I really should check on your mom." He placed a loving kiss on my forehead. "I'm so glad you were able to be home for today." Emotion gave his voice a tremor. Dad wasn't one to get choked up, so I was instantly on alert.

"Is Mom okay?" I asked, suddenly realizing how odd it was that she hadn't been present for my return.

Dad's answering smile was wrought with sadness. It reached a fist between my ribs and squeezed my battered heart.

"You know how hard today is for her, but she'll be good as new tomorrow. Like I said, it helps to have you here." He turned toward the hall to the master bedroom, leaving me slack-jawed and reeling.

Today.

Dear God, I'd lost track of the days.

Grabbing my cell phone, I touched the screen and saw the date glaring shamefully at me. October 13th— the anniversary of Ivy's death.

How could I have overlooked it? Mom always locked herself in her room and spent the day crying. I'd been avoiding my phone, but I knew we were approaching mid-October. How could I have possibly forgotten what that meant?

You've had a lot going on, Ro. The gentle voice drifted through my head. *Don't be so hard on yourself.*

I squeezed my now burning eyes shut.

I'm so sorry, V. I will never, ever *let this happen again.*

I walked purposely to the drawer in the kitchen where keys to the family car were kept. On the way, my gaze snagged on the liquor cabinet. I fished out the car keys, then grabbed a small bottle of expensive tequila before hustling out the front door. Yes, it was reckless. Yes, I was putting my life in danger. And yes, I hated when women in stories did stupid shit like that, but I did it anyway.

This was for Ivy.

I'd gone to her grave on the anniversary of her death every single year, and I didn't plan to abandon her now. Not when I was the reason she was dead.

When I was little, my father would take me to see her. The cemetery was outside the city, so it wasn't a trip we took often. Dad probably preferred doing that to suffering through my mother's tormented cries. It was the one day a year she let herself fall apart, and aside from Ivy's death, listening to her wail was the most terrifying thing I'd ever endured. I could have been seven or seventy-seven, and those sounds would still haunt my nightmares. Hearing a parent come undone like that messes with a child. I was no exception.

Early on, I made it my life's mission to do anything and everything I could to be the perfect daughter. To ensure they felt nothing but joy 364 days a year.

October 13th, however, was the one day that grief was unavoidable for all of us.

I made the drive in silence. No music. Just me and my guilt as it should be.

I rarely drove anywhere, so it felt odd behind the wheel. I got my driver's license specifically for this purpose. I didn't need it in the city, but I didn't want anything to get in the way of me seeing my sister.

The day was unusually sunny for fall in New England. I was glad. I liked to think of Ivy basking in the sun. She was buried on a hillside. Not a large hill, just a gentle slope. Mom and Dad had purchased a plot for all four of us at the time. I doubted they would have thought so far ahead about their own deaths, but with Ivy gone, it made sense to secure a final resting place for the family to reunite. That meant her gravestone was easy to find because a halo of empty grass surrounded it.

. . .

Ivy Ophelia Alexander
August 5, 2000 - October 13, 2006
Loved with a love beyond telling.
Missed with a grief beyond all tears.

THE STONE WAS A BEAUTIFULLY CARVED slab of white marble. It was eerily peaceful in the cemetery. Some people can't stand them—a reminder of their own mortality. I could only imagine that those people had never lost someone they loved.

For me, the cemetery was solace. When I sat cross-legged in the grass next to Ivy's plot, I'd swear I could feel her there with me. She was always present in my thoughts, but this was different. Visits with my sister in the cemetery were precious bubbles of time beyond the reach of the world. I cherished each one.

This one was harder than most, however. The guilt I'd felt so many years ago resurfaced with a vengeance this time.

I lay my palm flat on the ground, tears welling in my eyes. "I'm here, V. And I have so much to tell you."

In theory, if Ivy's spirit was that gentle voice in my head, she'd see what I saw, and I wouldn't have to tell her about my life. A part of me genuinely believed that was the truth. That my sister was still with me. But on the off chance I was just batshit crazy, I always ran through recent events out loud when I visited to cover all my bases.

Usually, I would have started where I left off at my last visit. This visit was different. Nothing before Keir's arrival seemed of any relevance. Anything and everything that mattered had happened since he first appeared in my parents' kitchen.

I ran through every minute detail of events, sipping from the tequila bottle as I went. I told her about how Keir made me feel, about the girl in the attic and how she made me think of her. I explained my mixed emotions about Stetson and how bad I felt about hurting him.

"You know I don't want to hurt anyone. All I've ever wanted was to make people happy. But for the first time, V, I started to ask myself what I wanted. And the answer wasn't as clear as I thought it would be. Or maybe, the answer *is* clear, but I've choosen to black it out. Either way, the one thing I can say for sure is that my path wasn't taking me where I wanted to go. So where does that leave me, V?" I spread my hands wide, liquid sloshing from the bottle in one fist.

I peered at it and noticed it was lower than I'd expected. Had I spilled a bunch, or had I had that much to drink? Did I care either way?

I looked up at the trees in the distance, my head spinning from the movement.

TWENTY-NINE

I ONLY MADE IT TO NOON BEFORE I WAS PRACTICALLY twitching to get back to Rowan. Her father was home with her, and I was confident his security detail could manage one morning. No one even knew we were back in the city. Yet the need to be near her sank its claws in deep and wouldn't let go.

When I finally caved and returned to the Alexander home, a haggard Evan answered the door. I hoped he and Rowan hadn't fought. I suspected me beating the shit out of him would stunt the progress I'd begun to make with my new bride.

Rowan wasn't anywhere to be seen, so I decided to

seize the opportunity and have a private word with her father.

"Rowan told me about her sister." I decided to dive right in. No reason to dance around the matter. "I had no idea she had a twin."

He froze briefly midway through bolting the door. "It's not easy to talk about. I'm surprised she mentioned Ivy at all." His voice was laden with a profound weariness.

"She didn't mention her so much as have a breakdown." I wanted him to know that Rowan was suffering. It was about damn time they faced that fact.

Alexander placed a hand on the entry console to brace himself. "What happened?"

"Finding that girl over at the Wellingtons' seems to have brought her grief and fears to the surface. How bad did she struggle after it first happened?"

"Rowan's a tough one. We'd hear her cry at night, but otherwise, she handled it with such strength."

I'd been afraid of that.

Anger pricked under my skin. "No six-year-old is that strong, *Evan*. Did you talk to her about it? See how she was coping?"

His eyes narrowed. "Talking about it wasn't easy. I lost a daughter, too, you know," he shot back at me. "And besides, Rowan coped just fine. She grew into an incredible young woman."

"No, she crammed herself into a mold to suit your expectations in a desperate attempt not to disappoint you. There's a fucking difference." My tone edged on hostile. I took a slow breath to calm myself. "Tell me you at least sent her to a grief counselor."

His defiant glare was his only response.

"Jesus, Alexander. Don't tell me you have no clue how much pain your daughter lives with every goddamn day. Why do you think she was even dating Wellington's son? Because she loved that asswipe? Not a chance. She was doing it for *you*. She's so messed up that she doesn't even know who she is. She's only ever let herself be who she thinks she's supposed to be." It was harsh, but someone needed to quit sugar-coating the truth.

His entire body flinched. "That can't be. I would have known ..."

"Would you? Or did you see what you wanted to see? That is, when your ambitions occupied your complete focus."

His gaze lifted. I expected to feel the stab of an angry glare but saw only contrition in his mournful brown eyes. He studied me for a moment, head tilting to the side. "You care about her, don't you?"

The wonder in his voice pissed me off. I held up my hand to display the ring tattooed on my finger. "I don't marry just anyone, regardless of what you may think of me," I growled. "I don't know what you thought this was, but I take my oaths seriously."

His shoulders deflated further until he began to look like a husk of the man I'd first met. "I tried my best, you know. It wasn't easy," he said softly.

I could understand those early weeks and months

had to have been hell, but over fifteen years had gone by since then. I had trouble overlooking the fact that he'd never once during those years taken a deep enough look at his daughter to see how badly she was suffering.

"I'm not the one who's owed an explanation," I said grimly.

Alexander lifted his eyes to mine and gave a single nod. "Are you taking her with you now?"

"I am."

He nodded again. "I assume she's up in her room."

He didn't need to say any more. Our conversation was over.

I walked past him to the stairs, taking them two at a time. To the left of the landing, I could see into a large masculine office. To the right, a bathroom and two closed doors. Choosing randomly, I opened the door on the left to discover a little girl's room painted green and left perfectly intact as though waiting for her return.

My stomach twisted with revulsion.

Christ, it was no wonder they hadn't moved on. The loss was still there, a gaping wound to remind them of their pain every damn day. And right across from the morbid memorial had to be Rowan's room. She was forced to see that permanently abandoned shrine every day she'd lived in this house.

Shaking my head, I closed the door and walked across the hall. I knocked gently on the door, then opened it when I got no answer. Her room was a pale gray. Tidy. It had been left alone as well, and unlike other rooms occupied by teenage girls, hers held no corkboard full of photos with friends, no ticket stubs or band posters. The room was an empty shell, just like the girl who'd occupied it.

Not anymore.

I'd find a way to breathe so much life back into her that sorrow had no place left to linger.

I closed the door behind me and went back downstairs, finding Alexander with his head in his hands at the kitchen bar.

"She's not in her room. Where else could she be?"

His head shot up, brows knitting together. "Not there? I don't know where else …" His eyes clenched shut with realization, sending a jolt of trepidation shooting down my spine.

"What is it?"

"Today is the anniversary of Ivy's passing." When he opened his eyes, they were bloodshot and glassy. "She goes to the cemetery every year on this day. I completely forgot …" He paused, eyes lifting to mine as though hearing my accusations again for the first time. He nodded, lips pursed firmly together with dawning acceptance of his shortcomings. "I can take you."

"No. I'll go myself," I snapped. His time to play protector was over. "Just tell me where I can find her."

◆

THE DAMN CEMETERY was almost an hour outside the city, though I made the drive in under forty-five minutes. I swerved through traffic like a lunatic. I'd probably been flipped off a dozen times but didn't care enough to check the rearview mirror.

Not until I spotted the Alexanders' navy sedan parked on a narrow cemetery drive did my heart calm its erratic rhythm. Not far from the car, a lone auburn-haired figure sat among the orchard of marble memorials.

I parked behind her car. She had to have heard me approach but didn't look my way, staring at the ground with a bottle of alcohol cradled in her lap.

"You here to fuss at me?" She didn't sound totally wasted, which was a relief, but I had no doubt alcohol thrummed in her veins.

"Why, you want me to?"

"You probably should. I deserve it."

I slid my hands into my pockets, remaining on my feet across from her. "And why is that?"

"Because I'm a selfish, horrible human being." She met my eyes, undiluted shame staring back at me. She took a swig from her bottle, then rose to her feet. "You, Mr. Keir Byrne, are married to a murderer. Bet you didn't expect that, did you?" She lifted her hands out wide as if daring me to be shocked.

I slowly stepped around the grave. "Somehow, I doubt that very much, little lamb."

"Well, it's true. Your wife killed her own twin sister. We'd only taken the training wheels off our bikes two weeks earlier. I got cocky and went off the curb, then dared her to do the same. She was *so* nervous. I knew she didn't want to do it, but I kept at her, taunting her, telling her she would be a baby if she didn't do it. I might have only been six, but I knew better. I knew we didn't have our helmets on and that it was dangerous, but I did it anyway. The second her front tire went over, the bike went crashing to the ground. She went motionless, her head resting on that damn curb. I was so scared, I ran back down the street to get Mom from our front steps, but by the time we got back to Ivy, it was too late. She died alone on the street, all because of me."

I knew we'd finally plucked away the last of her layers. This was what truly haunted Rowan. The festering wound eating away at her heart.

She'd carried that burden like a noose around her neck since she was six.

My fingers clenched with the need to ram my fist in her father's face. I'd have bet every penny to my name that Alexander had no clue his daughter blamed herself.

As angry as I was, I had to force back the emotions. This was about Rowan, not me. When I didn't comment, she continued.

"That's why I couldn't leave that girl alone in the attic. I'd already been responsible for one person's death. I couldn't live with myself if it happened again." Her voice hitched on the last word.

I reached out and cupped her chin, lifting her face toward mine. "And you think I'm some kind of saint?" I spoke without emotion. Rowan was beyond coddling. If I had any chance of getting through, I sensed the only way would be through sheer force of will.

I took a step forward, and she a step back.

"I've killed people, and not even by accident. I ended lives intentionally without a shred of guilt." We took another step together. "You think I or anyone else would look down on you for an accident that happened when you were a child?"

Her back finally met with a tall obelisk memorial behind her.

"You're letting this go right fucking now." I towered over her, a wall of menacing authority.

Her face crumpled. "Don't you see? That's what I'm afraid of," she whispered. "That I'm finally letting it go. Today, for the first time in sixteen years, I forgot. Not until Dad reminded me did I realize it was the anniversary of her death."

"Life moves on, Rowan. That's a good thing. She'd want you to move on—and that means living your life. *Your* life. Not the life you think your parents want for you."

"But I owe them."

"Bullshit." I clamped my hand around her throat, pinning her harshly against the stone.

Shock widened her eyes. I squeezed. Not enough to leave a mark, but enough to minimize her air flow. Her hands held my wrist, but she didn't struggle.

"Is this what you want?" I hissed. "What you think you deserve? Death?"

Her hands tightened around mine.

"If that's the case, I can give it to you. Just a few more minutes, and it would all be over."

Her nostrils flared, panic filling her wide eyes.

My cold stare bore into her, watching as a myriad of emotions flashed behind wide hazel eyes. I saw the precise moment when her grief gave way to desperation and a rabid desire to live.

Every muscle in her body seized in preparation of a fight. But instead, I loosened my grip, bringing my face inches from hers.

"You want to live, Rowan, so do it," I growled. "Live your life in a way that Ivy would have been proud of."

She heaved for breath, her eyes wild as though seeing me for the first time. She launched herself at me, clinging to my body and kissing me as if my lungs contained the very last oxygen on earth.

I slid my hand down her leggings to her slick and swollen center.

"Keir!" she gasped. "We're in a cemetery." Undermining her objection, she tilted her hips to give me better access.

Two fingers found their way deep inside her. "They're dead. They'll be grateful for any action at all." Lust grated away at my voice, leaving my words harsh and raw.

Rowan didn't care. Her eyes rolled back as she allowed pleasure to sweep through her. I grazed my teeth against her earlobe, then kissed a path down the column of her neck.

"You're so fucking incredible, little lamb. So wet for me. Such a greedy little pussy." I felt her inner muscles squeeze my fingers. My dick lurched against my zipper, a reminder that it would very much like to be the one pumping in and out of her.

My girl was too greedy for that, though. In no time at all, her lips parted on a silent gasp as her body seized in a fit of ecstatic tremors. Her orgasm careened through her like a storm ravaging the plains. I had to help support her weight to keep her on her feet as her body recovered.

I removed my hand from her pants and lifted my fingers to my lips, waiting until her eyes cracked open before I sucked them into my mouth. Her taste did strange, intoxicating things to my body. It sent a flood of endorphins into my bloodstream and awakened a primitive urge to make her pregnant with my child. To claim her in every damn way possible.

"It's time to think about what *you* want, Rowan," I rasped through my lusty haze. "Not what's expected of you or what you think you *should* want. Figure out what makes you feel good, and seize it. Life's too fucking short for anything less."

Rowan slowly nodded, a spark of clarity shining in her eyes.

"Good, now let's get you home before I get arrested for fucking you on someone's tombstone."

She bit back a grin. "We wouldn't want that." Suddenly, her steps faltered. "Keir, I'm not sure I should be driving."

"I'm positive you shouldn't be driving." I urged her forward with my hand at her back. "I'll have someone get the car. You're coming with me."

Appeased, she continued but paused again after I opened the passenger side door. "Where are you taking me?"

"Home. You live with me now."

She nodded, but her brows remained knitted tightly together. I got the sense she wasn't convinced, and it grated under my skin. She still didn't grasp that I was in her life for good.

Rowan was mine, and I'd prove it to her every damn day if I had to until she finally understood.

THIRTY

That night while Rowan slept, I lay in bed and thought about my next moves. I had two big fucking problems—Oran's treachery and the danger surrounding Rowan.

Damyon had earned his nickname for good reason. The man was literally a shadow—no last name and no solid business or personal associations. He appeared on the scene from nowhere, making a savage reputation for himself in a matter of weeks.

When I first heard whispers about him, I half wondered if he was an urban legend. How could a man garner notoriety in such a short time while maintaining his anonymity? How was he still alive with no organization to back him? I figured he'd been made up as a scare tactic, the story morphing as it made the rounds. Then I saw him with my own eyes.

It was about six months ago, around a month after the rumors started circulating. I'd gone to watch one of Torin's fights. The location of our fight nights changed regularly to reduce the chance of being shut down. It was a pain in the ass, but the money was phenomenal.

That night, we were at a warehouse in Brooklyn. We preferred basement locations for better privacy, but this place was set near the shipyard on a rare, isolated strip of land. Knowing now what I'd learned about Damyon's association with Wellington, it likely explained his appearance that night.

Tor was the last fight on the schedule and the only one I was interested in, so I didn't show up until late. Anyone who had come for the fights was already inside. I was on my way in when I heard a strange sound around the side of the building. A mewling like an injured animal would make.

It was probably nothing, but I decided to take a peek because Tor was usually in charge at these things, and he would be occupied getting ready for his fight. And if for some reason the cops had surrounded the place, I wanted to get the drop on them and sound the alarm. I quietly approached the corner of the building and listened. Again, I heard a high-pitched keening.

Slowly, I peered around the metal siding.

Three men stood over a fourth who lay on the

ground. He was moving but in a disjoined, sickly way. I'd only taken them in for a handful of seconds when one of the three turned to look directly at me as though he somehow knew I was there. I didn't slink away. I wasn't in the habit of cowering. That was how I found myself staring into the most arctic, merciless set of ice-blue eyes I'd ever seen with the scar I'd heard so much about running from temple to lips.

Eventually, the two other men looked my way as well. I cut my eyes to each of them in turn, then briefly to the man on the ground before casually turning and walking away. I left them alone, and they seemed to do the same for me. Nothing ever came of the encounter. The morning after, however, when our men went to the warehouse to ensure it was free of all evidence leading back to us, they found the man who'd been writhing on the ground. His tongue had been cut out then shoved back down his throat, and at least half the bones in his body were shattered.

We weren't kind to our enemies. It would be a lie to claim otherwise. However, it took a special kind of ruthlessness to do that sort of damage in public. I realized that day that the rumors were true.

Damyon was a psychopath and practically untouchable with so little known about him. And now, he might or might not have wanted Rowan dead. I had no idea what to do about that or where to even start. For the moment, the best I could do was broadcast my claim on Rowan and hope that kept the wolves at bay.

The Oran situation, on the other hand, was much

more straightforward. I knew the steps that needed to be taken; I just hated to do it. But it made sense to deal with Oran first. If he *was* connected to Damyon, he might have information to help me get to the man.

God help us both if Oran didn't want to talk.

I'd do whatever necessary to keep Rowan and my family safe, but I hated to think about what that might mean.

I rolled to my side and watched my sleeping wife. She faced away from me, giving me a perfect view of the ivy inked along her spine. She was so goddamn strong. But even the sturdiest trees needed solid foundation for their roots. I wanted to give that to her—to see her thrive—and I'd cut out the heart of any man who posed a threat to her, even if that man was family.

◊

I TOOK ROWAN TO HER PARENTS' house again the following morning so she wouldn't be left alone while I met with my family. Her father had to work, but he made arrangements for security to stay at the house with Rowan and her mother. I would have preferred to leave her in the hands of one of my cousins, but I needed them all present for this conversation. It was time to bring them into the loop and decide what to do about Oran.

The Moxy had a short window of time each day from six to ten o'clock in the morning when the club was closed for cleaning. I'd set up our meeting for nine and arrived ten minutes early. Torin was already inside, sitting at the bar and scrolling through his phone.

"Thanks for being here," I said as I approached. "I know it's probably early for you."

"No fights last night, so I wasn't out late."

Late was relative. Most of the time, his nights and days were swapped. I wasn't sure if it was that or simply his personality, but the guy seemed to be in a perpetually bad mood. He was reliable and loyal—I had no problems with him—but I didn't fully understand him either. I had a feeling he liked it that way. He'd always been sort of a loner.

"You in the ring anytime soon?" I would have thought at twenty-eight he'd be done with that shit, but the chip on his shoulder kept him in the game. His choice.

"Nothing on the books right now. We're showcasing a new guy tonight in from Cuba. Figured I'd see what he's got. If he looks like a good fit, I might set up a match with him."

"Let me know if you do. I'll come watch."

"Don't encourage him, sir," Stormy chided in her soft Southern twang as she rounded the corner from behind the bar. "No reason for him to be doing that. He'll just end up hurt."

The corner of my mouth twitched upward. "Nothing like a little pain to make a man feel alive."

Torin grunted.

Stormy set the stack of glasses she was carrying on the counter and rolled her eyes. "You need to feel alive, go bungee jumpin' or run a marathon—no need to risk brain damage just for a little adrenaline."

I rapped my knuckles against Torin's head. "Nothing there to risk, Stormy."

"Fuck you," Tor said wryly. And if I wasn't mistaken, I think he might have even smirked.

The front door swung open, letting in a blinding shaft of light while Conner, Pops, and Nana filed inside.

What the fuck was Nana Byrne doing here? I glared at my father.

He raised his hands in annoyance. "Don't start with me. She has a doctor's appointment in an hour. You needed to meet? This was the only way it worked."

Christ.

Nana continued toward the bar, leaning heavily on her walker.

Stormy grinned. "I'm happy to have Nana's company while you boys talk."

"That's sweet o' ye lass," Nana said. "But for now, just hit me with a quick shot o' whiskey, then I'll listen in on the current state of affairs."

"Ma, it's nine o'clock," Pop fussed. "And we're about to go to your cardiologist's office. You really want to show up stinking of whiskey?"

She scowled back at him. "And what's he goin' to do te me, Jimmy Byrne? Put me in time-out? I'm eighty-five, and I'll have a nip if I feel like it." She turned back and nodded at Stormy, who bit back a smile and poured a respectable shot of whiskey.

Nana downed the liquid as though it was apple juice,

then turned herself around. "All right, let's get this show started."

No one was willing to argue. I gave a nod to Stormy, telling her to make herself scarce, and we selected a table large enough to fit our group and pulled up chairs.

"We not waiting for Oran?" Conner asked.

My father looked at me expectantly, his curiosity piqued. Family meetings generally involved the heads of each branch of the family. Of the three original Byrne brothers, Brody was now deceased, and Tully, who was the least involved of the three, rarely participated anymore. Torin, though he was the youngest of Tully's children, had assumed leadership of that line. Conner had stepped up as representative for the single Byrne sister, Mirren, and my father and I often worked together as he wasn't ready to pass the torch just yet. That left Brody's line unaccounted for at our meeting.

"I didn't invite Oran because he's the subject of our meeting, and for the same reason, I didn't think it wise to call in Shae either." As the one and only female Byrne heavily involved in the family business, she was also Oran's younger sister.

My father sat back, eyes narrowing. "What exactly is this about, son?"

Four sets of blue eyes bore into me. I forged ahead.

"My concerns started the day of Uncle Brody's death."

Pop grunted. "Not this shit again."

My hackles raised, and in an uncharacteristic show of temper, I slammed my hand on the table. "I don't like this any more than you do, but it needs to be said, and you're going to fucking listen."

Tension filled the room with a raging flood.

I took a slow, even breath and told my family everything I'd learned in recent weeks. How Oran had been the only person to know where Brody would be the night of his death. About the woman I'd seen him with and her disappearance. And finally, the stolen guns that had reappeared in the hands of the Russian.

I shouldn't have been surprised when Nana was the first to respond, her pruned lips pursed tightly together. "These are some very serious accusations, Keir."

"Agreed, that's why I wanted to discuss it as a family before making any decisions."

"Aye, and that's exactly what should be done," she said, nodding and crossing her arms over her chest. "Oran is family, just as much as any of us, and he should be given an opportunity to explain. You'd want at least as much if it were you in his seat."

"I planned to do just that," I told her. "But I think we should all be on the same page about how we approach him."

"Sooner rather than later," Torin said with an edge to his normally dry tone. "If there's reason to be concerned, I wouldn't want him getting wind of our suspicions."

"I agree," Conner chimed in. "I say we do it this morning. Wait for him upstairs. That's our best shot of getting honest answers."

My father frowned. "I can't join you, but I suppose

it's best you three handle the situation. He's your cousin," he said reluctantly. It wasn't easy for Pop to let go. If Nana hadn't been there, I wasn't sure what he'd have done.

"What are we going to tell Shae when she asks why she wasn't informed about her brother?" Conner asked. "I'm the one who has to work with her, and I don't want to spend the next six weeks having to watch my back in my own damn office."

I'd thought about that and had an answer. "Dad's got her babysitting Devlin, the guy sent over from Dublin."

"What guy from Dublin?" Conner challenged, sitting taller.

I exchanged looks with my father. "Didn't anyone tell you?"

Conner had just returned from his honeymoon days earlier and was spending most of his time with his new wife.

Pop shrugged. "It wasn't worth disturbing the honeymooners."

I gave a brief explanation. "It's not really relevant at the moment, but the guy just showed up out of the blue. Says he was sent over by Dublin to check on the Albanian issues."

Conner sneered. "That's been resolved for weeks."

"Exactly. That's why Shae's been assigned to keep tabs on the guy. Just in case."

"In case of what?" Conner looked from me to my father.

Pop shrugged again. "Who knows. Folks from the old

country do things a little differently. We're mostly independent of them, but some old rivalries are still alive."

"Just what we need," Conner muttered.

Torin grunted.

Nana grinned. "Just like the old days. This has been a real treat, fellas." She stood, effectively dismissing our meeting. "Now, go talk to your cousin and get this sorted. I never did tolerate my boys fightin', and I don't plan to start now." She banged her walker into the nearby chairs, shuffling her way toward the door.

Pop just watched, shaking his head in defeat. "Call me when it's over," he added quietly.

I tipped my chin. Nana might have been unbothered by what she'd learned, but I wasn't so optimistic. I had also intentionally avoided mentioning the connection between Oran and Rowan because I didn't want to discuss the possible implications in front of Nana. She was a tough old woman, but it would hurt her heart to know what I planned to do if Oran tried to hold back information. I never did buy into the prodigal son. People were either friend or foe, and there was no going back once that line was crossed.

◆

ORAN KEPT an office across from mine above the Moxy, though he had little to do with the club itself. Like his father before him, he had assumed the role of the face of our organization. Where my father was the mastermind,

Uncle Brody had been the front. He schmoozed with powerful people in all walks of life. Oran had followed in his footsteps, making sure he had an in with everyone who was anyone.

The setup had always worked for me. The last thing I wanted was to talk to anyone, let alone be friendly. However, with much of my time being eaten up running the strip club, and Conner handling our Bastion club, oversight of the family empire as a whole had slowly been transitioning from my father to Oran. I hadn't thought the power trip would go to my cousin's head, but it appeared I was wrong.

The three of us made ourselves comfortable in the large corner office. Conner sat on the leather sofa while Torin and I each took a chair. We were quiet on the way up, but Conner started conversation once we were seated.

"Seems I missed quite a bit on my honeymoon. I hear you managed to squeeze in a wedding while I was gone." Conner's stare demanded an explanation.

I tipped my chin, acknowledging his underlying jab. "I'm glad you brought that up because we need to talk about that as well."

"I knew Uncle Jimmy wanted in with the governor. That was the last I heard."

"He did, but that wasn't a part of my reason for marrying Rowan. It's complicated, but the reason we moved so fast was because Rowan's in danger. Damyon is somehow connected to a family friend. Rowan discovered that friend had a woman chained in his house, and he and Damyon are now aware that she saw the woman."

"Jesus Christ, she'll have a target the size of Rhode Island on her back."

Tor grunted his agreement.

"I'm aware," I bit out. "Like I said, it's been a complicated couple of weeks."

Conner was silent for a second, but judging by the way his eyes remained trained on me, he wasn't done. "Marriage—it's a bold move. Must be some girl to warrant that sort of protection." He was prodding for information. Fine by me. I had no need to hide how I felt about Rowan.

"She's mine, and now everyone knows it." I met his stare straight on.

Conner grinned. "Well, I'll be damned. Congrats, man." He turned to Torin and smirked. "Looks like you're next."

"Oh, fuck no."

Conner and I laughed, though it died quickly as the reality of our present situation filtered back into our minds. We weren't certain when Oran would arrive, but luck was on our side. Not ten minutes later, our cousin filled his office doorway, steely gaze meeting each of ours.

"Isn't this a cozy family reunion? To what do I owe the pleasure?" His voice was edged in wariness, as it should have been. We didn't show up unannounced like this without cause. Grave cause.

I stood as Oran strolled to take his seat behind the

desk. I kept my body language casual, but I was keenly aware of my holstered gun, loaded and ready. Men were nothing but animals when cornered. I didn't want to think my cousin was capable of shooting at us, but his back was firmly against the wall. Figuratively and literally.

"We'd like to talk to you about some issues that have come to light."

"I see. And what would those be?"

"Most recently, I happened to see a couple of SIG 550s in the possession of someone who shouldn't have had them."

"Who?" His stare hardened.

"Men working for Damyon. The Shadow." I didn't give him more information. I found my interrogations more productive when I let my subject squirm.

"Could the guns have been sourced elsewhere?" he asked, not overly nervous.

"Doubtful. You know that. Not military grade, like ours were."

He rubbed his chin absently. "I suppose they could have been behind the theft, but how could they have known about the shipment?"

The room was silent, our stares three sets of deadly daggers pointed at Oran.

"That's what we'd like to know," I finally said.

He snapped from his thoughts, his eyes slowly roving from one of us to the next. "You don't seriously think I had something to do with that?"

"You tell us. You've been the one pushing to keep gun

operations running. You took lead on the deal. You were the only one with full knowledge of the details."

"This is fucking insane," he growled, flashing his teeth. "You can't possibly believe I'd betray my family like that."

"I don't know, Oran. Maybe betrayal comes easy to you. I saw you talking multiple times with that young server from downstairs as though you two knew each other well. *Very* well. I wouldn't have thought you'd disrespect your new wife like that, either. Our father's taught us better. Yet, oddly enough, she disappeared not long after I noticed you two together. Just never showed up for work one day. But I don't suppose you'd happen to know anything about that either."

Oran pointed his finger at me, fury flashing in his eyes. "I was trying to help her. And I don't know anything about her disappearing." His adamant denials made my anger blister.

"Then how the fuck do you explain the fact that you were the only one who knew your father had decided to stop by Moxy the night he died?" I shot back at him. "It wasn't part of his routine. You expect us to believe it was a coincidence?"

Oran shot to his feet, slamming his hands on the desk on his way up. In the same heartbeat, Torin, Conner, and I drew our guns.

"I did *NOT* set my father up to die. Losing him fucking *gutted* me, and if taking a bullet is what I have to do to prove that, then *pull the goddamn trigger*." Oran's eyes blazed.

Seconds ticked by. Five. Ten. Fifteen.

I slowly lowered my gun, though my cousins kept theirs raised. "Then how do you explain it all, Oran? Because we need some fucking answers."

His anger flickered and faded to something that resembled dread. He placed his hands flat on the desk, leaning as though weary from the weight of his burden. "I hadn't said anything because I couldn't ever get proof, and I hated to make allegations I couldn't support. Not allegations like this." He slowly lifted his head until his tormented gaze met mine. "Caitlin knew. She was the one who made the call to Dad asking him to stop by the club for me. I had a splitting headache and asked her to call him while I lay down."

The room exploded into a deafening silence.

Caitlin? Sweet, demure Caitlin? Was he trying to blame everything on her? I peered at my cousins on either side of me, trying to understand what was happening, but they wore confused expressions that matched my own.

"What exactly are you implying?" I demanded.

Conner lowered his gun but took a menacing step forward. "You throwing your own fucking wife to the wolves just to save yourself?"

"You three truly think I'm capable of that?" Oran sneered, his eyes cutting to each of us.

My hackles raised. "You'd be forced to come to the same conclusions as us if you were in our position. Now, tell us whatever the fuck it is you have to say."

He took a deep, weary breath, his shoulders sagging.

"Something didn't sit right after Dad's death. I couldn't shake this uneasy feeling that it was all too coincidental, but I didn't know how else to explain it. Then the guns were stolen." He ran a hand through his hair. "My notes about the exchange were at my home office, thinking it was safer than here at the club. No one else knew anything about the drop. I hadn't even told our guys about the shipment when I normally would have, but Dad's death had me paranoid. A day later, the guns were gone. Another baffling coincidence—how unlucky was it that someone just happened to come across the shipment and steal it? But again, I had no direct evidence implicating Caitlin or anyone else. How the fuck was I supposed to accuse my wife of that shit without a stitch of evidence? We might not have been childhood sweethearts, but she's my fucking *wife*. I didn't know what to do except start watching her like a hawk."

"You keep your home office locked?" I asked.

Oran grimaced. "No. I considered starting to lock it after the guns disappeared, but I decided that would tip her off to my suspicions."

"And you haven't been able to find anything on her since then?"

"I've searched our house top to bottom, looked through her phone, and even fucking followed her when I could. She's so damn clean, I've questioned my own sanity."

"She was at Moxy," Tor interjected tonelessly. All

238

eyes turned to him. "I didn't think anything of it, but I saw her there having words with that girl."

"That girl?" I asked.

Torin finally lowered his gun. "Yeah, Darina, the server who disappeared. Caitlin was talking to her out back one day. I thought it was weird, but not my business."

A cocktail of emotions stirred under my skin— disbelief, wariness, relief. Could that be our answer? Had sweet Caitlin been guilty of these unforgivable crimes against our family?

"She said you've been working with her brother," I said to Oran, recalling my conversation with her outside Paddy and Nana's place.

Oran's face creased with disdain. "Seriously? Flynn's an asshole with a chip on his shoulder big enough to sink the *Titanic*. I steer clear of him at all costs."

Motherfucker.

I'd never even considered Flynn Donovan. "Could he be using her? Manipulating her into giving him information?" I wasn't sure what leverage he might have, but it would explain a lot.

"It's the only thing that makes sense," Oran answered gravely.

Before the meeting, I'd prepared myself mentally not to be swayed by denials just because Oran was my cousin. I had shut out all emotion and tried to view him as I would any other man I suspected of fucking us over. Even using my most unbiased filter, every fiber of my being agreed. He was telling the truth. Oran hadn't betrayed the family.

I was so goddamn relieved.

I slid my gun back into its holster, leading my cousins to do the same. All four of us sat as we processed the implications of this new information. I was the first to vocalize my thoughts.

"Could Flynn have actually believed he'd get away with this?" The whole thing dumbfounded me. "What could he possibly have hoped to achieve?"

Conner shook his head with incredulity. "The Donovan family crumbled years ago. There's no reviving it at this point."

"I'm done wondering why," Oran said with lethal calm. "The question is, what are we gonna do about it?"

I looked back at Conner. "You still have that stash of sodium pentothal from when we needed info out of that Albanian?"

He nodded. "After seeing how well it worked, I stocked up."

Good. "Then I say we head to your house, Oran, and get some answers." I held his tormented stare, my chest tightening. "I'm sorry to have doubted you. I hope you can understand."

His gray eyes sharpened to polished steel. "That's the thing. I *do* understand because the trail led directly to my door. That's the worst part. I think she set me up to take the fall."

That was fucked up.

How could she have sworn an oath, stood by Oran,

and let him inside her body, all while forging his death warrant?

That was some cold shit. I couldn't even imagine how my cousin must have felt.

"Come on, let's get this over with. This shit ends today."

THIRTY-ONE

SECURITY LET ME INSIDE WHEN I GOT TO MY PARENTS'
house. I peeked around the downstairs and didn't see
Mom, so I decided to chill in my room. When I reached
the upstairs landing, I immediately noticed the door to
Ivy's room was cracked open. That door was always
kept closed. Always.

It had been years since I'd gone inside. I didn't like
the swell of memories that hit me when I did, but I
knew in my gut that Mom was in there and that I
needed to follow her.

Each step I took felt heavier than the last, but
eventually, I reached the door. I'd been right. Mom was

inside, sitting on the bed with Ivy's pink teddy bear hugged to her chest. In all the years since my sister's death, I'd never seen my Mom go into this room. It had always seemed strange that she'd insisted on keeping everything unchanged if no one saw the room, but when my eyes met hers, I knew I'd been wrong. Mom was at home in here. This was her portal to the daughter she'd lost.

I half expected her to jump up and usher me out, but that didn't happen. Instead, she smiled and patted the bed next to her. Feeling like I was walking into a time warp, I entered the shadowed room and joined her.

"You okay?" I asked quietly.

"Yeah, sweetie. Just thinking. I've been doing a lot of that lately."

"Oh yeah?" I wasn't sure if that was a good thing or not. Mom and I had never had a super close relationship —I was more of a Daddy's girl—and we certainly didn't do heart-to-hearts, so I had no idea where she was going with this.

"I think it's time for a change. It probably seemed crazy that I never touched this room, but … I just couldn't. It's still not easy, but even if Ivy were here, she wouldn't want her room so childish. I thought we could freshen things up—give it a bit of a makeover. We could make it into an Ivy-inspired guest room." She looked at me with such hope that my chest grew tight. "You think … you might want to work on it … with me? I thought maybe we could do it together."

I had to swallow twice before I could get words past

the lump in my throat. "Yeah, Mom. I think that sounds great."

She nodded, dropping her gaze with a small sniffle before looking back at me and smiling. She lifted her hand and smoothed a stray lock of hair back with the rest. "You aren't wearing makeup today."

"Yeah ... I didn't wear any while Keir and I were away, and it was kind of nice. Just let my skin breathe."

Her eyes softened. "I'm glad. You're perfect just the way you are."

A torrent of emotions ripped through my chest, but before it could overcome me, Mom stood and grinned.

"Have you had breakfast? I could whip up some eggs."

"I already had a little something, but thank you."

"Okay, I'm going to throw together something for myself." She gently touched my hair again, then turned. I followed her out of the room, pausing to watch her disappear down the stairs. Losing Ivy had broken her. While I'd struggled, my twin connection always made me feel like I still retained a piece of my sister. Mom reminded me of the Lost Boy in Peter Pan who never could find his marbles. She did the best she could, but the loss had left her adrift, and she'd never found her way back.

With a heavy sigh, I crossed the hall to my room. I needed a minute alone to process.

I lay back on my bed, absently studying the chandelier fixture above. I must have drifted off because the next thing I knew, my phone buzzing in my pocket startled me awake.

Stetson: Can we talk?

A sticky shower of guilt rained down on me.

I'd been avoiding him, and that wasn't my style. I liked to address things head-on, but I felt so clueless about how to explain what had happened. Stetson and I had been together for a year and had known each other far longer. We weren't as in love as I'd thought, but that didn't mean what I'd done hadn't been a harsh betrayal. As difficult as it was, giving him closure was the least I could do.

Me: Of course. I'm at my parents' house, though.

Stetson: I'm at Dad's. Could you stop by here?

Keir would murder me himself if I stepped foot from this house again. No matter how much guilt I carried, I wouldn't even entertain the option.

Me: I can't. Could you stop by here instead? I'm sorry. It's complicated.

Stetson: Yeah, I'll be by soon.

It looked like my day would be filled with uncomfortable conversations. Joy.

I took a deep breath and tried to focus on the fact that at least it would soon be over.

THIRTY-TWO

Oran, Conner, Torin, and I piled in my car to go confront Caitlin. We made a quick stop at the Bastion club on the way to retrieve the items we'd need, then arrived just before noon at Oran's apartment building.

I texted Rowan to check on her while I waited for Conner to run inside Bastion. She assured me all was well. I hated that I had to worry about her, but dealing with Caitlin helped. At least I was moving toward a solution on one front. Once this was over, my cousins and I would find a way to deal with Wellington and Damyon.

"You ready for this?" I asked Oran quietly as we walked to the elevator.

"Don't worry about me." He'd been silent on the way over, nothing but resolute determination etched on his face, but I knew this had to be difficult.

"You don't have to do this, you know. We can take care of it without you."

"If she answers to anyone, it'll be me. It's my goddamn father she stole."

Fair enough.

None of us said another word on the way up or even as we entered the apartment. Caitlin greeted us in the living room, her smile faltering at the cutting stares she received in return.

"What's going on?" she asked hesitantly.

"Why don't you have a seat?" Oran nodded toward the sofa. "We need to talk."

Her eyes drifted down the line of us before she complied. Torin, Conner, and I stationed ourselves around the perimeter of the room.

"You're kind of freaking me out."

No one said a word.

Oran slowly stalked toward his wife. "How far back have you been planning this, Caitlin?" His voice was the menacing rumble of an angry panther.

Her brow furrowed. "What?"

"Was our marriage all a part of your plan to strike at us, or did you simply use the opportunity to your advantage?"

"Strike at you? Oran, I have no idea what you're talking about." Her wide eyes followed him intently as he began to pace.

"You made the call to my dad that night. You and I were the only ones who knew he'd be there."

Her jaw dropped as though ready to dispute him, but he continued.

"I didn't want to believe it, but when the guns went missing, I knew something was wrong. We had a mole at best and a fucking *traitor* at worst. You did a good job making it look like me. Fooled my cousins." He reached behind his back and pulled out a black 9 mm. Stepping forward, he casually placed the barrel against her temple.

Caitlin's body shuddered with a sob, tears filling her eyes. "Please, Oran. I didn't want to do any of it. *Please*, he gave me no choice."

"Flynn?" She gave a jerky nod.

Oran lowered the gun, still staring at her with ruthless calm. "You better pray that's the truth." He shot a look at Conner, who pushed off the wall and joined them with a small black box in his hands.

"Wha-what's that?" she stuttered.

Conner lay the case on the coffee table and took out a syringe and small glass vial.

"Oran, what's he doing? Please, baby. You're scaring me."

His patience thinning, he snatched her chin in his hand, squeezing her cheeks between thumb and fingers.

"You should be scared, Caitlin. You're about to tell us everything we ask, and if I judge you even the tiniest bit guilty, I'll kill you my fucking self."

Three yawning seconds passed in poignant silence before Caitlin jerked out of his hold and scurried away from him.

"Don't you fucking touch me," she hissed, eyes blazing. "You're fucking cowards, all of you. You deserve everything that's come to you and worse."

Oran lunged for her, snagging her wrist, then clamped his other hand around her throat. Torin and I rushed over to restrain her arms behind her back. She thrashed against us like a feral animal.

Jesus Christ.

A part of me had still felt certain there'd been a misunderstanding. She couldn't have possibly been responsible. But there was no refuting the vicious hate spewing from her eyes. Her deception had been so extreme, I wondered if there weren't somehow two of her because I'd never met the woman in front of us.

Once Torin and I had her secured, Oran released his hold, allowing breath back into her lungs. She coughed and wheezed. Her body vibrated with hate and fury when she finally lifted her stare back to her husband.

"I won't tell you *shit.* I don't care what you inject me with."

Conner flicked the full syringe. "Why don't we test that theory, huh?"

Torin and I held tight as Conner plunged the needle

into her arm. Caitlin winced, clamping her mouth shut. We'd seen the drug in action, so we knew it was only a matter of time. Fifteen minutes later, her eyes rolled back as her lids drifted shut. Her entire body almost liquefied until we had to sit her down onto the couch.

"Caitlin, can you hear me?" Oran asked.

"Yes." The single word was eerily toneless.

"Did you tell someone where Brody Byrne would be on the night of his death?"

None of us took a breath as we waited for her response.

"Yesss," she slurred. "It was too perfect to pass up. Flynn was so excited when I called." Pride lit her face.

A muscle twitched in Oran's jaw—the only sign he gave that what she'd said had bothered him. "Why did Flynn want Brody dead?"

"He killed Daddy, of course." Her voice grew disturbingly childlike. "And to weaken the Byrnes. If the Byrnes are weak, the Donovans can rise." Her arms floated upward.

Oran slowly shook his head. "And the guns? Did Flynn take the guns?"

"He needed them."

"Why?"

"For the scarred man." She now had every ounce of my attention. This confirmed that Flynn was a link to Damyon.

"What was his name?" Oran continued, likely wanting to confirm we were talking about the same scarred man.

Caitlin shrugged. "Don't know. Flynn never said and wouldn't let me join him at the meetings."

Before Oran could continue, I held up my hand. "How did you know he had a scar, Caitlin?"

Her lips quirked up in the corners. "Because I snuck a peek once. Flynn wouldn't tell me anything, and I was curious." Her eyes remained shut, but her hand lifted as though touching something before her. "He was unlike anyone I'd ever seen. Like Jack Frost had come to life, carved from pure ice."

"Do you know anything else about him like where to find him?" I pushed.

Caitlin shook her head. "He's no one. Just a shadow, and shadows can't be found."

I sat back against the couch cushion, disappointment a boulder on my chest.

"What about Darina, the young server at Moxy?" Oran continued the interrogation. "Did you have something to do with her disappearance?"

"Your slut girlfriend?" She scoffed. "I got rid of her."

"Why? What did it matter to you?"

"You had no right," she said, a sneer teasing at her lips.

"To cheat? That's rather hypocritical coming from a traitor."

"No." Her dilated eyes slowly opened and met his. "No right to happiness." The emptiness in her voice made my blood run cold.

Oran, however, was somewhere beyond reach. As though nothing she said could touch him. "All you did was damn yourself," he responded in an equally hollow tone. "Because I never touched that girl."

Caitlin gave a limp shrug and closed her eyes again.

Oran peered around the room for a second, then walked to the kitchen and returned with a phone in his hand. "Is this your only phone, Caitlin?"

A devious grin slithered across her face. "No."

"Where do you keep the other?"

"Inside my box of tampons." She half chuckled, entertained by her own cleverness.

Oran disappeared for a minute, then returned with a second phone. He lifted his wife's head upright. "Open your eyes." She obeyed. He swiped once the facial recognition had unlocked the phone.

He tapped several times, then slowly scrolled, his forehead creasing angrily. "The *fuck*? What is it? Some kind of *Game of Thrones* shit? Are you fucking kidding me?" Oran shot a look of incredulous disgust at his wife. "Tell me you are not in love with your own brother."

"Of course, I love my brother," she said with saccharine innocence.

"Have you fucked him?" Each word dripped disdain.

"No," she shot back, a touch of emotion resurfacing.

"Do you want to?"

She finally opened her eyes again, leveling him with a semi-lucid stare. "More than I ever wanted to fuck you."

Jesus. I shook my head. "Tor, go find something to tie her up with. Oran, think we can text and make him believe Caitlin wants to meet up?" We needed to focus, no matter how disturbing the degree of her dysfunction. Traveling down that road at the moment wasn't going to help.

Oran grimaced and returned to scrolling. "We could figure out where Flynn was living and go to him, but setting up an ambush in neutral territory gives us more of an advantage. Looks like they did meet up on occasion, so that might work."

He texted out a message and waited.

The phone buzzed.

"Says he's got a meeting in an hour and asked if she can wait until tonight."

I looked at Caitlin, coaxing her face toward mine. "Caitlin, look at me," I said softly.

Her eyes cracked open.

"You love Flynn, right?"

She nodded.

"All you've ever wanted was to be with him—to make him proud?"

Moisture pooled on her lashes. "Yes," she breathed.

"I bet that means you worry about him, don't you?"

Again, a nod.

"You've even followed him, wanting to be close. To protect him. That's how you saw the scarred man, am I right?" My heart thudded in my chest.

"The men he works with are so dangerous," she whispered.

"Where does he meet with them, Caitlin?"

"The warehouse."

"I need you to tell me where it is."

A tear broke free and trickled down her cheek. "On 30th across from the High Line."

I looked at Tor, who now stood behind her. "Secure her."

He bit off a section of duct tape and placed it over her mouth, then set about taping her hands.

I turned back to Oran. "An hour doesn't give us much time, but we have the element of surprise."

"Let's get that fucker."

♦

I'D NEVER SEEN this scale of operation come together so quickly. We summoned every man available and each were given a specific station in or around the warehouse. Luckily, only one warehouse was situated on 30th across from the High Line, so we knew we had the right place.

It was run-down and looked abandoned. So stereotypically perfect for a lowlife like Flynn. The interior was full of dust-covered shelves still loaded with inventory, which made for excellent cover. One portion of the building by a garage bay showed signs of recent activity—tracks in the dust-coated floors and several crates that were newer than anything else in the building. Six of us positioned ourselves inside, just out of sight. We only had minutes to wait before the side door opened, and Flynn entered.

The stupid motherfucker was alone. It was no wonder the Donovans had ceased to exist. No one survived in our world without people watching your back—that was why families stuck together, and men like the Russian were so rare. There was power in numbers.

Knowing Flynn was meeting with someone, we had all agreed not to make a move until both parties were present and we could assess the situation. We sat silently while Flynn remained glued to his phone.

A half hour passed, and just as I'd begun to think the meeting had fallen through, a knock sounded at the metal door. Flynn rushed to open it. When the scar-faced Russian walked in with two men flanking him, I couldn't believe our luck.

A calm certainty chilled the blood in my veins.

This was our chance—two birds, one stone. I wouldn't waste the opportunity.

"Mr. Donovan," Damyon said evenly in his Russian accent. "Thank you for meeting with me again."

"Of course, you know I'm always happy—"

Damyon held up his hand. "Before you continue, you should know that we aren't alone."

Flynn stiffened, his eyes darting to the sides.

"Please do join us, gentlemen."

Fuck. Fuck, fuck, fuck. Things were not supposed to go down like this.

Oran and I shared a wary look, then stepped from the shadows. We still outnumbered them, and I'd be damned if I ever showed an ounce of fear to a man like the Russian, advantage or not.

"What the fuck are you doing here?" Flynn spat, his face contorting in anger.

"If anyone here is answering questions, it's you, Donovan, so shut the fuck up until you're spoken to." Oran's command sliced through the room with lethal calm. He then turned to Damyon. "I'm surprised someone with your reputation willingly deals with this sort of incompetence."

He raised his palms in an acquiescent gesture. "Normally, I wouldn't. But you see, I didn't come to the city for business and have no plans to stay long-term."

A shocked silence echoed in the air.

"Is that so?" I cut in. "Because it looks like you've been establishing connections between Flynn here and your time at the Wellington house."

Damyon raised a brow. Seems we managed to surprise him as well. "Tell me, Keir. Were you interested in my activities or those of my associate when you were watching the house?" His use of my name was intentional—a display of his knowledge and power.

"Your associate. You were just an unlucky coincidence."

Flynn began to fidget. "What the fuck are you talking about?"

"Your Russian friend here works with Lawrence Wellington, the shipping mogul. Apparently, the two are in the skin trade together," I explained.

"Not exactly," Damyon said. "We have a mutually beneficial arrangement for the moment."

"You're telling me you weren't the source of the woman he has chained up in his house." A tendril of anger snuck its way into my voice.

"Lawrence is too focused on financial gains to mess with keeping a pet. Now, his son, on the other hand..."

Adrenaline surged through my veins, sending my heart rate into orbit.

Stetson? The fucking runt? He'd been responsible for the girl in the attic? Surely not. If that was the case, he was infinitely more dangerous than I'd ever suspected.

I clenched my fists to keep from pulling my gun. An overwhelming need to get the fuck out of there jackhammered inside my head, demanding I do whatever was necessary to get to Rowan.

"Yes," Damyon continued. "I was a little surprised as well. Though, I shouldn't have been. Young Stetson fits the mold perfectly—spoiled yet neglected—makes for a nasty combination." He tsked. "But that is not why I'm here. It has come to my attention that the items I acquired from Mr. Donovan were not his to distribute. As I said before, I'm only in town briefly and have no interest in making enemies." He dropped his chin in a gentlemanly nod. "Please accept today as a sincere token of my apologies."

With the flick of his wrist, light and sound exploded outward. The effect was so intense, I had no choice but to clamp my eyes shut, cover my ears, and drop down to the ground in the hope of avoiding possible gunfire. The sensory assault didn't last long, though the smoke filling the room lingered.

"What *the fuck* was that?" Oran's words were almost inaudible over the ringing in my ears.

"A goddamn flash-bang?" I called back. "Who the hell walks around with that sort of thing in their pocket?"

Disoriented and choking on smoke, we searched the area, but Damyon and his men were gone. At first, I thought Flynn had escaped with him. Then I noticed a body on the ground. Caitlin's brother lay in a pool of his own blood, his throat slashed wide open. The Russian had killed him before escaping. An apology?

What the fucking hell?

I ran toward the door, hoping our men stationed outside had managed to stop him. They didn't. And worse, those we could see were gagged and bound.

"He must have had an army of his own men out here," I thought aloud. We'd thought he was working alone, but it looked like we'd been wrong.

"Yeah, but he didn't harm anyone except Flynn. What the fuck does it all mean?" Oran stood at my side, both of us baffled.

"No fucking clue." I took out my phone, and my heart thudded to a stop. Rowan had texted only minutes earlier. Her ex was on his way over to talk, and she had no idea he was a sociopath.

"*Fuck!*" The ragged curse exploded from my smoke-ravaged throat. I took one lurching step before a pair of hands wrenched me backward.

"Where are you going?" Oran barked. "He could still be out there."

I didn't even think. My fist was deep in his solar plexus before I realized what I'd done. "Don't fucking care. Rowan's in trouble, and if you get in my way again, I'll break your fucking jaw."

This time, no one tried to stop me.

THIRTY-THREE

I waited downstairs for Stetson, pacing from one side of the living room to the other. Nerves spiked my blood with adrenaline. My ex might have been in the dark about his father's activities, but that didn't make our conversation any less intimidating. In fact, if Stetson had known, he might at least begin to understand my perspective. Instead, I would have to explain to the man I'd been dating for a year why I'd broken his heart for seemingly no reason at all.

At some point while wearing a path in the wood floors, I texted Keir to let him know what was happening. I wasn't used to updating someone on my activities. Stetson and I had never had a relationship like that. But I knew Keir would want to know, and I enjoyed knowing it mattered to him. That *I* mattered.

I'm so happy for you, Ro. You deserve joy in your life.

Ivy's presence was a soothing balm to my nerves.

I stepped over to a mirror near the entry that I usually avoided and smiled softly at my reflection. Ivy *was* here with me. I'd always felt like my face reminded me of what I'd lost, but suddenly, I realized it was also a rare gift. My very DNA enabled me to keep her with me always.

I tilted my head down and studied the blond roots starting to show at my part. How would it feel to let it grow out? To let all the hurt and guilt and blame grow out until it no longer suited me, and I could start fresh with a new style. A new me.

That sounds awfully drawn out. Two-tone is so yesterday. How about we go to a hairdresser and just bleach it back to blond?

I snorted with a laugh. *I'll consider it.*

The doorbell chime wrenched me out of my lighthearted thoughts, dunking me back in a vat of oily dread.

I expected the security guard out front to let Stetson inside. When that didn't happen, I hurried to the door and opened it. Stetson stood on the other side, his face unusually solemn.

"Hey, come on in." I stepped back to allow him room, then peered around the landing, surprised to find the security guard unexpectedly absent. Had he run an errand or been called away? I would have asked Mom, but she was on the third floor in the library doing whatever Mom did to keep busy.

I closed the door and led us into the living room. "Stetson, I'm so, so sorry about everything. I never wanted to hurt you." I perched on the edge of a club chair, my hands clasped tightly together—partly out of worry and partly to keep my tattoo out of sight.

Stetson didn't sit. He stood several feet away, his arms crossed with one hand rubbing his jaw. "You know, Rowan, that's the thing. Your actions didn't just hurt me. You made me look fucking *pathetic* in front of the whole damn city." The malicious glint in his eyes shocked me.

I shot to my feet. "If you'll let me explain—" I had no idea how exactly I'd explain anything, but I never got the chance.

"*Sit. Down.*" His words were blades taking me out at the knees.

Something wasn't right. I felt like a stranger stood in my living room. Weeks earlier, when I'd found Keir in the house, I hadn't felt a lick of fear. I wasn't sure if I'd changed that drastically since then or if an innate sense of intuition had kept the emotion at bay, but either way, this was different.

Fear licked up my spine and sent waves of unease tingling down to my fingertips.

"You would have made a perfect wife," Stetson mused. "No questions. No opinions. Pretty enough and intelligent but undemanding. And the best part? You were utterly devoid of emotion. I didn't have to deal with you getting your feelings hurt over the slightest fucking thing like so many women do." He smirked and chuckled to himself. "It was a shame things didn't work, but I could have found someone else. There's always someone willing to play the desired role when enough money is on the line."

I kept my lips firmly sealed, afraid to say a word. This was insanity. I'd been locking away my emotions to protect myself, but Stetson's cool demeanor was sheer depravity. An inability to understand emotion at all. That sort of disconnect was unpredictable. Terrifying.

He tsked, continuing with his monologue. "But then, you had to grow a fucking conscience," he said slowly, prowling closer. "I hear someone crying, Stetson," he mimicked my statement weeks earlier, mocking me in a whiny, hapless voice.

Shock tore through me.

He knew that I'd found her, which meant … he knew about the girl. He'd known all along.

Sticky nausea curdled in my belly, clotting into a heavy mass as true fear set in. I had mistaken a frozen pond for an open field, and now I was stranded out on thin ice, the air filled with the creaking sound of my impending death.

"How could you?" It was all I could say, and in a whisper at that. Horror had scrambled my thoughts.

"You should have let it go, Rowan." The words were soft with a touch of remorse, not preparing me for his sudden attack. His hand whipped out and clamped around my throat, yanking me to my feet. "*You should have let it go!*" he screamed in my face, his features contorted in rage.

He was a psychopath. He knew about the girl, and he didn't care. How could I have been so blind?

You weren't in the right headspace, Ro. Don't blame yourself. Not again.

Ivy's words together with the stinging in my lungs brought tears to my eyes.

"I'm sorry," I rasped, clutching his hand at my throat, my stubby nails scraping for purchase. I wasn't even sure what I was sorry for, but I had to try to calm him.

"Sorry changes nothing, Rowan. When Dad told me you'd uncovered my little secret, I swore you wouldn't be stupid enough to make a fuss. Not my Rowan. She knows how to stay in her lane. Then you started to pull away. Not ideal, but whatever. I could have dealt with that. But no, you had to go and do something monumentally *stupid*. Everyone in the goddamn city saw the photos of you whoring it up with that thug. How do you think that made me look?"

I tried to shake my head. "Not you, me." I wanted to tell him they'd only think I'd gone crazy, not him, but I didn't have the air. Black dots danced in my peripheral vision. Dizziness clouded my thoughts.

I was about to pass out, but when I heard my mother's steps approaching, a renewed surge of adrenaline gave me the boost I needed to stay alert.

"Stetson! What's going on! Let go of her," she cried from across the room.

I used the distraction to plunge my knee up into his

groin, then shove him away. I coughed in a lungful of air and stumbled to the other side of the coffee table, but before I could make it to my mother, I heard the terrifying click of a gun cocking.

"Take another step," he rasped, still hunched with an arm hugging his middle. "I dare you."

I'd never heard more chilling words spoken. He meant it. He'd kill me where I stood.

I didn't want to die. Keir had helped me with that realization, and now, I felt the truth down to my bones. In the past, dying meant being with my sister again. Reunited and whole. How could I have feared that? But now ... I wasn't ready to go down that road yet.

Ever since meeting Keir, my world had changed, and for once, I'd started to feel true happiness again. I didn't want to lose it. I didn't want to lose Keir.

A month ago, I might have challenged him. Walked right up to the gun and dared him to do his worst. Now that things were different, I kept every muscle perfectly still.

"What's happened?" Mom asked in a thin, terrified voice. "Why are you doing this, Stetson?" She didn't know about his family's proclivities. I wasn't surprised. Dad would have wanted to protect her from worrying.

"It's okay, Mom," I assured her. "Just stay there. We'll work this out."

Stetson grimaced. "I'm afraid there's nothing to work out, Rowan. What's done is done. All that's left is punishment. You can't be allowed to walk away without any repercussions for your actions. Not when you're so damn unpredictable at this point." He lifted the gun, then swiveled his aim to my mother. The gunshot exploded in my ears the second the barrel pointed her direction.

I screamed, surging toward her as if I could somehow beat the bullet.

Mom's body jolted, sending her stumbling to the ground. He'd shot her in the side. Crimson blossomed across her blouse, her face scrunched in pain.

I dropped down to my knees beside her and pressed my hand to the wound. "Stay still, Mama. Don't move. I'll get you help." My heart practically vibrated in my chest it beat so frantically.

This can't be happening. Not again. I can't lose Mom, too.

Panic and desperation ignited like kerosene, my fury setting them ablaze. But before I could react to the emotions, a hand fisted in my hair, yanking me back to my feet.

"You're not doing anything except learning your place," Stetson spat in my face. "I hear American pussy goes for a premium in some countries, and I just happen to know someone in the business. It's time to make a deal." A malignant grin darkened his face before he tugged me toward the entry.

My eyes strained to keep sight of where my mother lay on the ground. She'd bleed out alone, just like Ivy, all because of me.

Something in my mind snapped. Civility. Humanity.

Everything that made me *me* faded away until I was nothing but primal rage.

A cry tore from my throat, so feral and unhinged that I didn't even recognize my own voice. I swung my body around and slammed both hands into his forearm, knocking the gun to the ground. It slid several feet away, but I hardly paid it any mind. All my focus was trained on Stetson.

He yanked on my hair to no avail. In my animalistic state, I felt no pain.

Baring my teeth, I turned and kicked him in the side with all my strength, then reached for a nearby ceramic candlestick thick as my fist and swung back around for his head.

Finally, he was forced to release me in an effort to protect himself. "What the *fuck?*" Stetson growled through gritted teeth.

I never paused, grabbing a table lamp next and launching it at him to give myself enough time to dive for the gun.

It wasn't enough.

He dodged the lamp while also surging toward the discarded weapon. I reached it first, but he was right behind me. My hands gripped the cold metal, his hands wrapped around mine.

"It's fucking cocked, Rowan. You're gonna shoot us both."

"Good," I growled. "So long as you fucking die, I don't care what happens to me."

We strained through grunts and labored breaths, fighting for control of the gun. Despite the extra strength my rage afforded me, I would be no match for his size the longer our struggle continued. I had to find a way to stop him.

Come on, Ro! Ivy urged me on. *You gotta fight dirty, or this asshole's gonna win.*

No. Fucking. Way.

My head dove forward until my teeth clamped down on his forearm. Stetson screamed as I gnawed through skin and flesh, a metallic tang flooding my tongue. The second his concentration wavered, I twisted us around, praying it was enough, and pulled the trigger.

THIRTY-FOUR

I'D NEVER DRIVEN SO GODDAMN FAST IN MY LIFE. I CALLED
Rowan three times on the way. No answer. By the time I
pulled up at her parents' house, my heart was ready to
explode out of my chest.

Despite my panic, the house exterior looked like it
had that morning when I dropped her off except for the
absence of the security guard Alexander had stationed
out front. Normally, the men stayed with him, but in
light of recent events, he'd instructed one to stay and
watch the house.

When I walked up the steps to the front door, I
discovered the reason for the guard's absence. He lay

motionless down below in the fenced concrete cutout for basement access.

Shit. I'd been right to be worried.

Gun in hand, I swung open the door, thanking God it was unlocked. I kept my back pressed against the stone exterior, waiting to determine whether it was safe to enter. I was met with a bottomless pit of silence.

Fear unlike any I'd ever known coated my insides with dread as thick as tar.

My pulse thundered in my ears.

I took a deep breath and swung around through the doorway into the house and was met with a scene straight out of a Quentin Tarantino movie. Broken bits of porcelain and blood splatter dotted the floor, and on top of it, Stetson sat against the wall at the far side of the entry bleeding from his left shoulder. The wound wasn't fatal, but he hadn't moved because Rowan sat a dozen feet away with a gun trained on him.

Her eyes were impossibly wide, face ghostly white, but her hand never wavered. She hadn't killed him, but she would in a heartbeat. It was written on every inch of her.

I was so relieved she hadn't. I didn't want that memory staining her conscience.

"Rowan, baby. I'm here," I said softly, not wanting to startle her. She should have heard the door, but she seemed to be in a sort of trance. Shock, most likely. While her one hand held a gun, the other was pressed firmly to her mother's middle, already stained with an alarming amount of blood.

Keeping my gun trained on Stetson as well, I took out my phone and dialed 911. "A woman's been shot, home invasion. She needs an ambulance immediately. 113 East 90th." I didn't stay on the line. They'd send help, and I didn't have time for asinine questions.

Rowan's eyes finally flicked to mine, triggering a shuttered gasp for air. She lowered the gun, her hand suddenly wrought with tremors. She'd held it together, but only just.

"Keir, my mom."

"I know, little lamb. Help is coming," I assured her, squatting next to her and placing a kiss on the top of her head.

She never let her eyes stray from Stetson.

"I didn't leave. I wouldn't leave her." The childlike innocence in her voice wrenched my heart wide open.

"You did so good."

Stetson groaned. "Jesus, you two are fucking disgusting. The pussy's not that good, man."

I slowly stood and turned my attention back to the man who had been at the center of all our trouble. "You've got some balls for a man with a gun pointed at him."

"Cops are on their way. What are you gonna do?" he quipped with cocky defiance, expecting Daddy to get him out of any legal mess. Only, the sort of trouble he'd brewed by pissing me off didn't involve lawyers.

Vile satisfaction carved a wicked grin across my face. "Your point?" I raised the gun and shot him right in the crotch. It was the least of what any man like him deserved.

A glimmer of satisfaction brightened my mood at the sound of his pained wailing. The evolutionary failure curled in on himself, attempting to protect what was left of his junk. I closed the distance between us and squatted near his grimacing face.

"It brings me great joy to inform you that you have sorely misjudged the situation," I explained quietly, my voice a menacing purr. "This is only the beginning of your suffering."

As if summoned by fate, two figures joined us in the room, casting an ominous shadow over my new toy.

"Fuck, man. Thought I'd never catch up with you." Oran and one of the younger guys from the warehouse stood in the doorway, assessing the situation. "Sounded like you could use some backup, though it looks like you have it handled."

"Yes and no. Cops are on their way, and this one's mine." I motioned to a weeping Stetson and handed Oran my gun. "Get him out of here for me; I'll deal with him later."

They didn't even flinch. Oran kicked Stetson in the head to knock him out, then hoisted his unconscious body over a shoulder in a fireman's hold. The two men weren't in the house for five minutes total.

I was finally able to join Rowan on the floor. Thank God.

Her mother was still breathing but unconscious. She'd need immediate surgery, and even then, I wasn't sure she'd make it. I pulled Rowan close, making sure she could keep pressure on her mother's wound. Her body shook uncontrollably in my arms as sirens rounded the corner and stopped out front. When the EMTs swarmed inside, I pulled Rowan away from her mother's side, sweeping her into my arms.

"Keir, I can't leave her." Her voice was shrill with growing panic.

I forced her eyes to mine. "You aren't leaving her; you're letting these folks do their jobs," I said in a soothing but firm voice.

"I have to stay with her. She'll be alone if I don't." Fat, heavy tears pooled on her lashes before tumbling down her cheeks.

"I'm about to call your dad. He'll meet her at the hospital so she won't be alone."

"I can ride with her, though. Until he gets to her."

I shook my head. "No, baby. You'll be in the way. The best thing you can do for her right now is to let the medics help her."

Her eyes clamped shut with frustration, but she nodded in short, jerky movements.

I asked the crew what hospital they'd go to and told them about the man who'd been injured out front. I had forgotten about him and had no clue if he was alive or dead, nor did I truly care.

Once that was addressed, I opened my phone and dialed Alexander.

"Keir?" he answered, worry plain in his voice.

"There's been a development. I need you to stay calm."

"What's happened?"

"Stetson came to your house. One of the guards is down, and your wife's been shot. An ambulance is here, and Rowan is fine, but you'll want to meet the paramedics at New York Presbyterian."

It took him several long seconds before he spoke. "Shot?" he asked in a wavering voice.

"I think she's going to be okay," I encouraged, maybe out of turn, but he needed to keep it together. "They're getting ready to take her over now."

"Right, okay. And Rowan?"

"She's fine. I'll keep her with me."

"Okay. Thank you."

The line went dead just as several police officers filtered inside and immediately honed in on us. "You two think you can step outside and tell us what happened?"

I stepped forward. "Just briefly, then I'm getting her out of here. If you need a more detailed statement, we can go to the station another day."

"And who exactly are you?" The cop eyed me.

"I'm her *husband*," I said in a low, menacing tone. "That's all you need to know."

The man's lips thinned, but he nodded. "All right. Let's step outside."

I pre-emptively explained how Stetson was holding a woman captive and had broken into the governor's house to stop Rowan from telling anyone. That way, all she had to do was relay today's portion of events, though I cut in before the end and explained how Stetson had escaped just before I'd arrived. I'd considered telling them the attacker was unknown but decided linking Stetson to the shooting would be a nice explanation for his disappearance.

By the time we'd covered the basics, tremors had taken control of Rowan's body. Shock had set in hardcore. I needed to get her warm and fed.

"That's all you're getting today, but it should be enough to do a search of the Wellington house, correct?"

The two officers exchanged a look. "Yeah, you said the woman is on the third floor?"

Rowan nodded. "Yes."

"What precinct did you guys say you're from?" I asked.

"The nineteenth. Why?"

"Just wanted to be sure." I tipped my head and stood, helping Rowan to her feet as well. "You have my number if you need to reach us." I didn't wait for them to reply. My patience had run out. If I didn't get Rowan away from there soon, I was going to lose my shit.

Just getting her in my car eased the tension knotting my shoulders. Thank God traffic cooperated. It took fifteen minutes to get back to my place. I used the time to call Conner and instructed him to ensure our guys on the force followed up on the girl at Wellington's.

Rowan sat motionless in the passenger seat. She didn't make a sound. She hardly even blinked.

It gutted me to see her like that when I knew how

strong she was. My tough girl could have handled anything, but seeing her mother shot like that was more than even she could take.

Fucking Stetson was in for a world of pain.

Once home, I led Rowan straight to the bathroom and stripped us down. We were about to step into the shower when she suddenly stopped and turned to me.

"My mom! I need to check on my mom." Whatever haze she'd been in was starting to thaw, allowing her thoughts to process.

I cupped her face in my hands and placed a kiss on her forehead. "Your father is with her, and he'll call as soon as anything changes. We can't do anything at the moment, so let's get you cleaned up and warm." I stared deep into her green and gold eyes, mine fixed with assurance. "She's safe. She's going to be just fine."

And that was when it hit. All the emotion careened into her at once, wrenching a sob from her shuttering lungs. Heaving, cathartic sobs wracked her body.

I pulled her against me, wrapping her in my arms and moving us into the warm spray of the shower. We stood like that for a half hour. She clung to me and wept while I whispered soft words of reassurance. I wished I could do more.

That was when I realized there was nothing I *wouldn't* do for Rowan.

She'd become my wife out of impulse and necessity, but she'd won my heart with the purity of hers. For me, she existed in a place without rules or reason because without her, nothing else mattered.

I'd always thought binding myself to someone like that would equate to weakness, but that was the opposite of what I felt when I thought of her. With Rowan in my life giving me purpose, I could conquer the world. All she'd have to do was ask.

Rowan

THIRTY-FIVE

AFTER A SHOWER AND FOOD, WHICH KEIR INSISTED I EAT, I was overcome with exhaustion unlike any I'd ever felt. I lay down to rest my eyes for a few minutes, only to wake the following morning in a panic.

"I can't believe I slept so long," I berated myself, hopping on one leg while trying to slip on a pair of jeans. I'd jumped out of bed the second I realized what had happened and ran straight to the closet. "I have to get to the hospital and check on my mom. How could I have left them there alone?"

Two large hands gently clasped either side of my face, forcing me to still.

"Your mother is fine. She made it through surgery and is resting. I would have woken you if you needed to be there." He spoke in that preternatural calm he was so good at, almost hypnotizing me with the sound of his voice.

I nodded dazedly. "I need to see her, though."

"And we will. Let's get you some food, and we'll go."

I nodded again, but he didn't release me. His gaze did a lazy sweep of my face that felt as real as any physical touch.

"You were so fucking brave yesterday." His words were a warm blanket around my heart the same way his kiss heated my skin.

"I was terrified," I whispered, recalling the deranged glint in Stetson's eyes. "He wasn't at all who I thought he was."

"He's gone now, so you don't ever have to worry about him again."

"Gone?" I stiffened. "Did I kill him?" I'd been so worried about Mom that I hadn't even thought about what happened to Stetson. What would happen if I killed him? Would I be prosecuted? It was self-defense, but they might still charge me. And how would I feel knowing I'd ended his life?

A blur of emotions thickened in my chest until Keir shook his head.

"Stop, Rowan. You didn't kill him. I promise." He tried to lead me out of the closet. "Let's get you some food so you can see your mom."

I held my ground. "But he's gone?" What did that even mean?

When Keir's stare returned to mine, he allowed me to see beyond his mask to the merciless vengeance beneath—a blond-haired, blue-eyed archangel prepared to inflict God's wrath.

I shivered from head to toe.

I did a quick evaluation before speaking to determine how I felt about what Keir had just implied and discovered that I was glad he would handle the matter. Stetson and his father would have manipulated the justice system every way possible. I would have spent years looking over my shoulder. And after seeing how warped his mind had become, I was confident no amount of therapy or punishment would fix him. Better to end his worthless existence before he hurt anyone else.

"Breakfast sounds good."

A smirk teased at the corner of Keir's lips.

Over the next half an hour, I learned about the insanity Keir had faced the day before—about how his cousin's wife had betrayed them and the unexpected murder of her brother by the mysterious Russian. I felt like I was listening to a movie synopsis rather than a retelling of his day.

"That's so wild. And I feel so bad for Oran. What's going to happen to Caitlin?"

"As far as I know, that hasn't been decided yet."

"And what about the girl in the attic? Do we know if the police got her out of there?" I mentally cringed, afraid of his answer. It had been days since I'd last seen her, and if the Wellingtons knew I'd been up there, I wouldn't have been surprised if they moved her.

"They got her out last night, taking Lawrence into custody at the same time."

The mountain of worry I'd been carrying on my shoulders crumbled into dust. "Oh, thank *God.*"

"She confirmed that she was brought over in a container on a ship, but there's no way to prove it was Wellington's ship or that he was involved in any way. For now, it looks like he'll be charged as an accessory to Stetson's crimes but nothing major since he wasn't the primary perpetrator. It's not ideal, but at least it's something."

Yeah, it's definitely a good thing Keir took care of Stetson because that's some bullshit. Maybe he should take care of Lawrence, too.

"Ivy!" I blurted, then looked wide-eyed at Keir. "She hates to think of Mr. Wellington getting away."

He took a sip of coffee and peered at me over the rim of his cup. "I'm not sure if these little conversations you two have are endearing or disconcerting."

I would have been insulted if his eyes weren't brimming with amusement. "I suppose it's irrelevant. You married me, and now you're stuck with me." I infused extra snark in my tone.

Keir took my coffee from my hand and placed it on the table, then tugged me onto his lap. Oxygen fled from my lungs in a whoosh, first from the sudden movement, then from the blistering hunger in Keir's eyes. Our faces were inches apart, his large body enveloping me in warmth both inside and out.

"I knew exactly what I was getting into from our very first conversation. Maybe not the specifics, but I knew nothing with you would be dull or ordinary. I chose that—I chose *you*—and I'd do it again in a heartbeat."

I couldn't breathe. Every warm, gooey emotion I was capable of filled my chest so completely, there was no room for air.

If you don't kiss that man right this second, I will.

She didn't have to tell me twice. I slammed my lips on his. A part of me felt it was wrong to feel so much peace and happiness in the wake of such tragedy, but I couldn't help it. Being with Keir was an injection of liquid elation right to the heart, and I was quickly becoming a junkie.

"If you want to see your mom, you need to stop, or I'll have you naked in my bed instead." His strong hands kneaded my ass, his words coming out as thick and heavy as the cock pressing into my thigh.

I grinned and rested my forehead against his. "Thank you, Keir," I said softly.

"For wanting to fuck you?"

"No." I laughed, then sobered. "For helping me when I needed it. For not giving up on me and for accepting me the way I am. Maybe that most of all because I was too scared to do it myself."

We sat motionless for a pregnant moment. I was

about to pull back to see what he was thinking when he launched to his feet, keeping me tight in his arms.

"That's it. You're getting fucked."

I threw my head back and laughed as he marched toward the bedroom. "But what about my mom?"

"She can wait. I only need five minutes." He tossed me on the bed, his molten stare devouring me. "Maybe ten."

He took thirty. I didn't complain.

◊

I HATED HOSPITALS. I was in a hospital when Dad first told me Ivy was gone. Just walking through those sliding glass doors dropped a cinder block on my chest. I had to take slow, shallow breaths to keep from hyperventilating.

Having Keir at my side helped in more ways than one. Aside from the death grip I kept on his hand, he did all the talking to help us locate Mom in the intensive care unit. She was stable, but they didn't want to transfer her to recover yet.

Dad was with her when we finally found her room. I was relieved he didn't look as bad as I'd expected. He was tired, and Mom was pale, but otherwise, the two were in decent shape.

"Hey, Ro! I'm so glad you're okay." Daddy pulled me against his chest, hugging me close to the point of suffocation.

My grin nearly split my face in two. "I'm more than

okay. I hope your night wasn't too terrible." I pulled back to meet his eyes again before giving my mom a gentle hug.

"Sleep is hard to come by around here, but that didn't bother me so long as your mom was stable."

Mom gave me a groggy wink. "He's been hovering over my bed since they woke me up." Her gaze drifted over my face as though searing it into her memory, then she looked passed me to Keir in the back of the room. "Thank you, Keir. Thank you *so* much."

"It was all Rowan. I was just the cavalry showing up after the fact," he said quietly.

Dad extended a hand, and the two shook. "You did a hell of a lot more for us than that, and you know it."

Keir's eyes drifted to mine. "Can't say it wasn't worth it."

Something inscrutable yet profound passed behind my father's eyes. "Well, now that you two are here, I can make a quick run to the cafeteria. Keir, you willing to walk with me?"

"Happy to."

I watched them walk away, praying they were all right alone together, then sat on the edge of Mom's bed. "Are you in much pain?"

"Not at all, though I'm sure that will change once my meds wear off." Her speech was lazy, but she was present enough to talk, and I needed to get some things off my chest. So much time had already passed with a chasm between us that I hated letting even one more day go by without trying to fix it.

"I was so scared I would lose you." My words grew thin, sticking in my throat on their way out. "I love you so much, and I don't tell you that nearly enough. I'm so sorry."

She rolled her head from side to side. "When I saw Stetson pointing that gun at you, I realized how stupid I've been."

"Not stupid, Mom—"

She raised a hand. "I couldn't change anything about Ivy being gone, but losing you to my grief was my own fault. I didn't see it until that moment. I could have lost you before I ever truly got to know the woman you've become." Tears trickled down her cheeks, but she smiled, and for once, it glowed all the way to her gray-green eyes. Eyes that Ivy and I had both inherited. "I love you so much, baby girl."

This time, I leaned in and hugged her with more force than before. I couldn't help myself because what I was about to say might have made her look at me differently, and I hated for that to happen when we'd only just found one another.

"Mama? I have to tell you something," I said into her hair, not able to look her in the eye. "It's eaten at me all these years, and before we can move forward, I think you need to know what happened that day. The day Ivy died." I pulled back, my gaze dropping to my fingers as they worried at my sleeve. "It was my fault." The words were nothing but breath and guilt, yet they cleaved me in two.

"What?"

"I dared Ivy to jump the curb that day. I knew it was dangerous and did it anyway. I know I was only a kid, but she'd still be here if I hadn't done it. It was all my fault." Finally. I'd finally spoken the truth. And in a way, it was a relief.

Cleansing tears streamed down my cheeks, and my chin quivered, my body overcome with emotion.

Mom's brows knotted together. "Baby girl, nothing was your fault."

"I knew you'd say that because—"

"No." She cut me off. "I don't think you do know. Sweetie, your sister had an aneurysm. That's why she fell off the bike. She passed before she'd even hit the ground."

My ears began to ring as my brain attempted to process what she was saying.

"Don't you remember doing a brain scan not long after she died? With you two being identical, we had to have you checked, but they didn't find anything. All the doctors could say was that it was a fluke. One of those mysteries of nature."

My lips opened and shut like a fish stranded on shore. "I ... an aneurysm? I remember ... a loud machine."

"That's the one."

"But I didn't know what it was for."

Sorrow lined her already pale features. "I'm so sorry, Rowan. You were young, and we tried to explain, but communication was difficult between your age and our grief. As the years went by, it never occurred to us that you might have blamed yourself. I'm so incredibly sorry." She gripped my hand with all her limited strength.

"I—" A sob choked back my words. "I didn't ... It wasn't me..."

"No, baby. Not your fault at all."

I lost it. Every emotion I'd ever felt about Ivy's death poured out of me in a sobbing, heaving mess of tears and snot. My head bowed into the edge of Mom's mattress as I gave myself over to the cathartic release.

"That's why I wanted to be so perfect for you guys." I hiccupped once the worst of the sobs subsided. "If I'd taken Ivy, I felt like I owed it to you to be the perfect daughter."

"Rowan, you are and always will be perfect, just the way you are."

THIRTY-SIX

ROWAN HAD BEEN CRYING. I KNEW THAT THE SECOND I walked back into her mother's room, but the brilliant smile she flashed assured me that her tears were the best kind. I waited until we were alone in the car on the way home before satisfying my curiosity to know more.

"Feeling better?"

"I'm still in shock," she said dazedly.

"Shock?" I'd thought she'd started to process the whole Stetson incident even though it had only been twenty-four hours.

She looked at me with such raw vulnerability that she could have been six years old again. "For sixteen years, I believed I was responsible for my sister's death. Sixteen *years*. And I learned today that it wasn't my fault."

I'd told her that, but if it took talking to her mom to truly believe it, then I was glad. So long as she got the message. "I'm glad to hear it."

"No, you don't get it. It wasn't my fault," she said pointedly. "Ivy had an aneurysm, and that's why she fell from her bike—not because I dared her to jump. Mom and Dad tried to tell me when I was younger. I remember them telling me about blood in her head, but all I could see was the blood in her hair from hitting the ground. I never understood that she'd had a blood clot, and I felt so bad about what I thought I'd done that I never told them about daring her to go off the curb."

Fuck me.

I was so glad she knew the truth, but what a fucking tragedy for her to live with that misunderstanding for so long. No wonder she was shocked.

"That's one hell of a silver lining."

Rowan grinned. "It really is. And what about you? What did you and Dad talk about?"

"He wanted a rundown of what had happened."

"What did you tell him?"

"The same thing I told the authorities. No reason for him to know any more than that."

She nodded, gaze returning to the road ahead as my phone rang over the car speaker. I automatically selected privacy mode on the dash display and answered my phone directly. Tor was calling, and Rowan didn't need to hear every detail of our conversation.

"Yeah?"

"I need to know how long I'm dog-sitting. Do I need to give him food and water?" He was talking about Stetson. He wanted to know how long I planned to keep him alive.

"I'll head over there in a bit to check on things myself, but you can give him some water in the meantime."

"You sure? He already smells like piss," he groused.

"Suppose you could hose him off. Two birds, one stone."

"Fuck, yeah."

The line went dead. I set the phone back in the console and let a small smile grace my lips. Today was turning into a pretty fucking phenomenal day.

"That was about Stetson, wasn't it?" Rowan asked.

I peered at her from the corner of my eye. "I'm gonna take you home, but I have to go out for a bit. You think you'll be okay alone?"

She arched a blond brow. "I've lived alone since I was eighteen, you know."

"You went through a lot yesterday. That can change a person, and rightfully so. The Russian is still a question mark, and Wellington could have a vendetta. Besides, there's always a certain degree of danger present for people close to me."

"I've spent some time thinking about all that even before yesterday, and I decided life with you isn't all that different from having a politician in the family." She said it so matter-of-factly that I almost laughed.

"You really think so?" I asked skeptically.

"Well, you might involve a bit more danger, but you should see some of the whack jobs Dad deals with. You never know when one might go off the deep end. One time, this giant tattooed mobster broke into their house and held me at knifepoint. Can you believe that?" Her eyes gleamed with mirth.

"You don't say." My tone was drier than an AA birthday party.

"I do," she continued, unfazed. "So you don't have to worry about me staying at your place alone."

"Our place," I corrected automatically.

Silence.

"Our place," she finally said in a much more reserved tone. "You sure you want to do this? The danger's over now. No one would blame you if you wanted to walk away." My little lamb's voice shrank to no more than a mouse's squeak.

The car behind me blared its horn after I slammed on my brakes and pulled to the curb. I cupped the back of her neck and locked eyes with her, reinforcing our connection in every way possible.

"I know you have a lot of old scars to heal, and we didn't start down this road in the most conventional way, but the one thing in this world I never want you to doubt is me and my commitment to you. I don't care what you did or didn't do in the past. I don't give a fuck about what your father does or how you ended up in my club. All that matters is that I chose you, and I will continue to choose you so long as you'll let me."

She blinked back tears, her lip quivering. "Okay."

The hope in her voice was too much. I brought our lips together in a passionate kiss that filled both my dick and my heart with warmth.

"Jesus, you're so fucking wholesome," I mused, my lips still brushing against hers.

She bit back a grin, gaze lowering coyly. "I'm not so sure about that. You did see what you packed in my suitcase, right?" Then she gasped, her eyes popping wide. "Oh God. That was you who packed my bags, wasn't it?"

A booming laugh bubbled up from my chest and filled the air around us. It took a minute for me to compose myself, and when I did, Rowan stared back at me with an arched brow.

"I'm guessing you're referring to the toys, and yes, I'm the one who packed them. I wanted to make sure you had all the essentials with you." My deviant grin rivaled that of a Disney villain.

"I'm glad you think that's funny because I nearly had a heart attack."

I gently pinched her chin between my thumb and finger, then pulled the car back onto the road. "I'm surprised you care what anyone else would think."

"It's not that," she corrected almost too assuredly. "I just didn't want anyone else's grimy hands on my dildos. That's just gross." She brushed at the invisible lint on her lap. "Speaking of your family. How do they feel about all this—you and me? I'm not AKC registered Irish stock or anything."

"Are you kidding? You know my father is thrilled, and I think everyone else is just happy to focus on something other than Caitlin's betrayal."

AKC registered. I swear, the things that come out of my wife's mouth.

"That's good to know. I mean, that they'll be accepting, not the part about Caitlin. That really sucks. What will happen to her?"

I sighed deeply. "It was Oran's call to make. He's decided to punish her in a way that would deeply wound her. She's been arrested for her brother's death. And while she wasn't the one who technically ended his life, she helped make it happen, and now she'll have to live the rest of her life with that fact." I snuck a glance at Rowan. "As you know, something like that eats at a person's soul."

"That had to have been a tough call for Oran. I feel bad for him," she said softly.

"He's not in a great place, that's for sure. But our family has united again and is stronger than ever. He'll get past it eventually."

"It's great that you have each other. I used to wonder how things might have been different if I'd had cousins to fill that void." Her tone was wistful, but when I peered over, a guilty grin flashed on her face, her eyes unfocused out the window. It was the same every time she had one of those silent conversations with her sister.

I had no clue if a shrink would say they were

unhealthy, but I didn't care. That had been Rowan's way of coping with the loss, and the connection, even if imaginary, brought her peace. Sometimes a little crazy was a good thing.

"Tell Ivy hi for me."

Rowan's answering grin lit my entire fucking soul on fire.

♦

TWO DAYS LATER, the governor's office summoned me. I was curious how my presence would be received. The first time I'd gone to his office, I was brushed off with hardly a word. I knew this would be different, but I didn't expect what unfolded.

Evan Alexander introduced me to his staff as his new son-in-law. I couldn't have cared less about his opinion of me except for how it would affect Rowan. In that regard, I truly appreciated his willingness to have an open mind.

Once he'd made the introductions and I'd received an update on his wife's condition, we retreated to his office for a private word. Rather than sit behind his large executive desk, Evan sat in a visitor's chair next to me.

"I wanted to talk to you because I've been very worried these last couple of days with Stetson on the run." His haunted gaze drifted to the window. "I hate that the police haven't been able to bring him in."

"Don't be worried. He's not coming back." My softly spoken words were intentionally ominous.

I watched the rule-abiding governor intently, curious how he'd respond. The moral high ground didn't always look so appealing when your family was on the line.

Sure enough, Evan Alexander nodded, his relief palpable.

"There's not much I wouldn't do for your daughter," I informed him.

"I'm starting to understand that, and I'm glad. She deserves the best in life."

I dipped my chin. "Agreed, and I plan to give it to her every damn day I walk this earth."

"That's all I've ever wanted for her, despite my failures in helping her achieve it." His lips thinned. "I've severed all ties with Lawrence Wellington as best as I could. The newspapers will talk, but something else will catch their interest before long. I just hope he pays for his crimes."

"Chances aren't great. The charges against him are minimal, as you know, and there's no evidence he had anything to do with the girl. He can blame everything on his son and play the grieving father."

"I know," he glowered. "It's so frustrating to think I could have been so wrong about them."

"Corruption can hide anywhere, especially in positions of power." My own hands weren't exactly clean, but at least I had some form of moral compass, albeit a rusty one. Men like the Wellingtons had no such measure to guide them.

"Speaking of ..." Alexander leaned forward and retrieved a document off the desk, handing it to me.

It was a press release slated to go out later that day announcing the mayor's new appointment for police commissioner.

I lifted my gaze to him. "It seems the mayor had a change of heart."

"He did. You aren't the only one who can be persuasive when needed. I did a little digging into the candidates and found a man who'd somehow been overlooked despite his exemplary record. I figured a compromise in this situation would benefit us all."

My lips twitched in the corners. "You're a wise man, Mr. Governor."

He stood, extending his hand. "And a grateful one. Just don't make me regret it."

"My wife would skin me alive."

He harrumphed. "Tell my baby girl I said hello."

I grinned all the way home.

THIRTY-SEVEN

Three Weeks Later

"How was your session?" Mom was in the living room reading when I arrived at their house.

My new therapist was located not far from my parents' house, so I had my driver take me over for a quick visit. Keir had insisted on hiring a driver to be on call for me. I felt like it was a little excessive but didn't argue. Life was too short. If using a driver gave him peace of mind, I could do that.

"It was good. I clicked well with Evie. She's young, so

I feel like we relate well to one another. I think we'll be a great fit."

"That's wonderful! How did you find her? I wouldn't even know where to begin."

I joined Mom on the sofa, angling myself toward where she sat with a blanket on her lap. "Friend of a friend. Conner gave us her name. I guess she's somehow connected to some of his Italian family. She recently opened her own practice, and the office is super cute. It feels more like stopping at a friend's house than counseling."

"If that's the case, maybe I might have to check her out."

"I'm happy to share her info anytime." I appreciate Mom's enthusiasm, but I wouldn't hold my breath. Chances were, she wouldn't make the call. And to be honest, I'd seen such a remarkable improvement in her since the incident with Stetson that, for once, I wasn't worried. Mom was coping with life just fine on her own.

"You sticking around for dinner?"

"No, Keir should be here soon to pick me up. I just wanted to stop in and see how you were doing."

She tossed the blanket off her lap and stood with only a small degree of stiffness. "I'm doing beautifully, according to the doctor. No need to worry there, but I want you to come upstairs while you're here. I almost forgot that the painters finished up yesterday." Mom's joy was infectious. Seeing her renewed enthusiasm for life filled me with energy and optimism.

"I'd love to see it, but I thought you weren't supposed to be climbing stairs yet."

"That's just silly." She scoffed. "My legs are fine. Now, come on."

I was a little wary after watching Mom nearly bleed to death, but she took each step one at a time without any obvious difficulty. At the top of the stairs, the door to Ivy's old room was wide open—something I was still not used to seeing.

"Oh, Mom. It's perfect." I walked inside, warmth and happiness enveloping me. The walls were a cheery pale yellow without being obnoxious. We'd spent ages looking at color swatches and debating, but I was so happy with our decision. "Ivy would have loved this."

"I think so, too," she said softly.

I put my arm around her shoulders for a side hug, and we gently rested our heads against one another as we took in the new room. Afterward, we spent a few minutes discussing new curtains and possibly painting the headboard before I helped her back down the stairs.

A half hour later, Keir picked me up at the house. We were supposed to go to dinner, but he had to stop by the office first. I decided to have a drink at Moxy rather than follow him upstairs. He wasn't thrilled with my plan but begrudgingly relented after confirming Torin was there.

"Someone forgot the sugar in their sweet tea," Stormy teased as I walked up to the bar.

I peered over my shoulder to watch Keir push through the front entrance with more force than necessary. "He's just being dramatic." I turned back and slid into a seat at the bar. "I wear a little pleather, and he thinks every guy in the bar is gonna hit on me." I winked, and Stormy bent over in a fit of laughter.

"Girl, I have to say. You do look smokin' today. The man's not totally wrong."

"Why, thank you. I was feeling a little extra saucy today." I'd chosen skintight black pleather leggings and a short but baggy off-the-shoulder sweater with white sneakers. It was the perfect mix of carefree chic with a touch of sexy.

"Mission accomplished. I've wanted to get some of those leggings myself. Maybe I'll wander the mall for a bit tomorrow." She towel dried the last of a set of glasses and started stacking them upside down.

I watched her work and realized that I really liked Stormy. She was sweet but sassy and fun to talk with. She was the type of girl I wouldn't mind being friends with, if I knew how to make friends.

Seriously, Ro. It's time. Put your big girl panties on and ask.

Pushy much?

I cleared my throat. "Um, a trip to the mall sounds fun. You ... uh ... interested in any company?"

Stormy beamed. "I'd love some company. I haven't been in the city long, so I haven't made many friends."

I wished my reasons for being friendless were so benign. But regardless of the past, I was doing things differently now.

"Where did you move from? Somewhere in the South, I take it?"

"I'm originally from Savannah but lived in Chicago before moving here. What about you?" She leaned against the bar, all her attention fixed on me.

"I'm a city girl, born and raised. What brought you to Manhattan?"

Her gaze lowered before she picked up a towel and wiped at a spotless bar top. "Just needed a change of scenery." She stilled, her eyes cutting over to either side with a smirk. "And I mean, you can't hardly beat the Moxy in terms of scenery."

We both burst into a fit of giggles, which drew Torin's attention. He sauntered over, lighting a cigarette while he walked.

"You shouldn't encourage her, Rowan. She'll never get any work done if she can talk instead."

"It's six in the evening," I shot back at him, giving a pointed look around at the mostly empty club. "Surely a few minutes isn't going to set you behind for the night."

Tor glared while Stormy snickered.

"Don't mind him, Rowan. His bark is worse than his bite." She locked eyes with Tor, and something odd happened in the air around us, like maybe Stormy had somehow summoned the sultry air of a Georgia night in the middle of our New York winter.

"Pretty sure you don't know what you're talkin' about, Storm." Torin's words had a new edge to them.

She arched a perfectly manicured brow, not bowing

to him an inch. "If memory serves, I know better than most."

Hot damn! Something had definitely gone on between these two, and I needed all the details.

I pulled my phone out. "What's your number? You can text me your address, and I'll pick you up tomorrow."

"Pick her up? For what?" Torin barked.

Stormy ignored him and called out her number.

"The mall," I said snidely as I typed. "You want to shop, too?"

He grimaced and stalked away, grumbling something under his breath about women and misery. I could hardly keep my laughter contained. Stormy was right there with me.

"Oh, man. That was priceless," she said as her laughter calmed.

"He'll learn better than to rile me up. I can get a little feisty sometimes."

"Don't I remember! I saw you up on that stage. You owned the whole dang club."

I grinned, an idea forming. "Keir wasn't so thrilled. But you guys have rooms for private dances, right?"

Her chestnut eyes sparked with excitement. "Wouldn't be a proper strip joint if we didn't. *And* they're all still freshly cleaned for the night."

Ew. I wasn't going to think about that part.

"Do me a favor. When Keir comes down, let him know I'm back there waiting for him."

"Yes, ma'am. But first …" She grabbed a bottle off the

second shelf and poured two shots. "I'd say this calls for a drink."

My smile couldn't get any wider. "Bottoms up."

We clinked glasses, tapped the bottoms to the wood bar, then downed the fiery tequila. It burned all the way down in the very best way.

I slid my glass toward her and winked. "Wish me luck."

"Oh, I think you're about to be plenty lucky."

I wasn't sure I'd laughed so freely and often in years. It felt amazing.

After I ducked into the first of the private rooms, I took off my shoes, socks, and leggings, leaving only my panties and top. The room was dark with a soft red glow and even had an elegant chandelier overhead. The Moxy was classy, all things considered, so I shouldn't have been surprised that its back rooms were nicer than I'd expected. Simple yet clean and modern. Shiny glass tile walls gave the small space an edge, and the only other accouterments were a leather armchair and a pole.

I ensured my sweater exposed plenty of shoulder, then leaned against the pole. Keir opened the door not two minutes later. His entire body went rigid at the sight of me. All but his eyes. Those shards of blue glass melted to twin pools of liquid azure.

"I need your help," I told him from across the room, my voice pitched low and husky.

"Is that so?" He crossed his arms over his chest. "I'm working right now. Don't have time to help little girls."

I bit down on my bottom lip and peered up at him

through my lashes in the most demure, cliché way possible. I started to feel a little silly until I saw the way his cock tented in his pants.

"What if … I gave you something for your time?"

"Like what?" His voice, so soft yet so heady, resonated through time and space like the rumble of distant thunder.

"I could dance for you." My breath hitched, lifting my chest skyward. I was reenacting my first visit to the club, and even though I knew Keir so much better now, I still felt that same intoxicating spike of adrenaline I had weeks earlier.

He pulled out his phone and lifted it to his ear. "Turn off the cameras in room 1." He slid the device back into his pocket and finally closed the door behind him. "I'm not making any promises."

"All I'm asking is for a few minutes of your time."

My heart skittered and whirred as he stalked closer, then lowered himself into the chair. I began to sway and roll with the music. Soon, I was fully emersed, teasing and seducing with every move of my body.

"You dance professionally?" Restraint grated away until his voice was almost unrecognizable.

"No." I peered over my shoulder, my gaze colliding with his. "I only dance for my husband."

His eyes flared. It was my only warning before he lunged forward and yanked me onto his lap, my legs straddling his. My center pressed against his hard length perfectly. If we sat like that for long, I would leave a wet mark on his pants, but I couldn't bring myself to care. It felt too damn good.

"Say it again," he demanded roughly.

I considered playing dumb but thought better of it. This was the first time I'd used the term. I hadn't avoided it intentionally. Not really. I just hadn't had a reason to say it.

From the looks of it, Keir had noticed, and he was hungry for more.

"My *husband*," I breathed, my mouth inches from his.

His answering kiss was nothing short of savage possession. He tattooed his claim onto my lips, sealing it with an oath of forever. And I made him a vow of my own with the offering of my body and soul.

It was no great sacrifice.

They'd been his almost from the moment we met when something deep inside me recognized him as safe and familiar. Being with Keir felt like coming home, and I never wanted to leave.

EPILOGUE

Two Weeks Later

"YOU HAVE PLANS TOMORROW?" I HAD WRAPPED UP SOME
phone calls in my home office and came out to find
Rowan at the dining table with her laptop. It didn't seem
like the most comfortable spot to work, but she swore
the view was better there than anywhere in the
apartment.

"I'm just trying to get as much done on this term
paper today and tomorrow. I doubt I'll get much done
the rest of break, and after Thanksgiving, it's only a

couple of weeks until finals." Her hair was piled on her head in a messy bun, and she was wearing sweats at least two sizes too big. She wasn't even trying, yet she was so damn cute.

"If you think you can make some time, I have a designer coming by tomorrow morning."

"Designer?"

I pulled out a chair and joined her at the table. "Yeah, she comes highly recommended. She's agreed to help us turn one of the spare bedrooms into a dance studio."

Rowan's eyes rounded. "Really?" she breathed.

I couldn't hold back my smile any longer. "Really, if that's what you'd like."

"I hadn't said anything, but I've been thinking a lot about what to do after graduation. At this point, it would have been silly not to get my degree, but we both know politics doesn't suit me." She tugged nervously at her sleeves. "I've been thinking about getting back into dance. I know it's been a while since I trained, but I love it so much. I was thinking maybe … I could even teach."

"If there's one thing in this world I have absolute confidence in, it's your ability to accomplish whatever it is you set out to do."

"So you don't think it's a silly idea?"

"When it comes to you dancing, silly is the last thing on my mind." My dick throbbed as if seconding my opinion. "Why do you think I want a studio here in the house? You may think it's thoughtful, but I assure you, it's one hundred percent selfish."

Her bottom lip scraped between her teeth as her smile spread wide. "I'm good with that." She closed her laptop and looked back at me excitedly. "Which room were you thinking?"

"Doesn't much matter to me."

"The gray room," she shot back. "If you don't care, the windows in that room are perfect."

I dipped my head once in acquiescence. "The gray room it is. Shall we have a look?"

She was up and out of her chair like a rocket. We walked back to the gray bedroom and talked about the changes that would be needed. The flooring would be the most impactful and intensive part of the remodel. The rest was relatively cosmetic once the furniture was gone.

"And this wall would be perfect for mirrors and a ballet bar." Rowan surveyed the only wall in the room without a window or door.

"Regular or frosted?"

She no longer cringed when confronted with a mirror, but I wasn't sure if she was ready to commit to a full wall of them.

"Regular." She smiled, her eyes softening as they met mine. "I hadn't realized how much I missed having a studio until now. I'm so excited, Keir. Thank you."

I snagged her fingers and pulled her close, taking long seconds to admire the splashes of green and gold pigment battling for dominance in her eyes.

"Kiss me," I ordered in a soft rasp.

She lifted onto her toes and brought her lips to mine. Reverently. Passionately. Perfection.

Her arms came over my shoulders before the kiss waned and her eyes drifted open to stare into mine. "I love you, Keir Byrne."

It was the first time she'd said the words. The first time either of us had. I'd known for weeks that I was hopelessly in love with her, but I'd been reluctant to say it. The fact that I'd forced her into the relationship at the beginning made me want to hear her take that next step on her own, not out of some need to reciprocate.

Hearing her finally say those three little words made my ribs feel inadequate to contain the rapid expansion of my heart. It pressed on the confines of my chest and filled my throat, strangling my voice to a thick, garbled growl.

"Show me."

Rowan swiveled us around, and in one sweeping motion, pushed me back onto the bed. Where I went, she followed, straddling my body and bringing her lips back to mine. I inched us farther onto the bed, wrenching the baggie sweatshirt over her head. She was bare underneath, and it made my cock impossibly hard.

One article of clothing at a time, we stripped away the barriers between us. I waited until the head of my cock teased at her entrance before my hands clasped tight on her hips to halt her movement. Her gaze locked with mine.

"My love for you, little lamb, is endless. I love you so

goddamn much it hurts." I thrust upward while holding her in place, sheathing my cock deep inside her.

Rowan threw her head back, her long two-toned hair reaching all the way down to her ass, giving me an eyeful of her perfect breasts. My hands drifted up her sides to cup the rounded mounds, then pinch her pebbled nipples. So rosy and pert, I could almost feel them on my tongue.

My touch summoned her gaze back to mine. She placed her hands on my chest and began to rock herself, rolling her hips to glide along my cock.

"*So goddamn much,*" I breathed again.

I let my wife establish the pace as long as I could. When my insatiable hunger for her demanded more, I flipped her onto her back and took the lead. I'd told myself I wouldn't, but where Rowan was concerned, my self-restraint had never measured up. I needed her just as much as air in my lungs and blood in my veins. And should I need to, I would defend all three with equal savagery.

My wife. My love. My life.

♦

"YOU HAVEN'T SNUCK out the back once tonight," Nana pointed out quietly after signaling for me to join her.

"Well, it didn't seem very fair to abandon Rowan at her first family dinner, and on Thanksgiving, no less."

Nana grinned mischievously, peering at me from the side of her eye. "I know that's right," she agreed in an exaggerated tone that plainly stated she didn't think that was the only reason. "Ye can't be leavin' the lass alone in all this chaos. It might be overwhelmin' for the poor thing."

We both glanced over to where Rowan sat on the floor playing a surprisingly rambunctious game of Candy Land with Pippa and Noemi, each with a squirming kid in their lap. She wasn't remotely at risk of being overwhelmed.

I shot Nana a wry look.

She puffed out her chest and preened with delight. "I don't blame ye in the least. In fact, I'm pleased as punch yer so happy together. I wish all my grans could be in such a good place as you." Her lips thinned as she shot a quick look at where Oran stood at a window with a whiskey in hand. He'd come for dinner but hardly said a dozen words.

"He'll get over it, Nana. It'll just take some time."

"Of course, it's just a shame because he's gettin' older, and that doesn't make it any easier."

I wasn't crazy about discussing Oran's mental health with my grandmother, so I was relieved when the Candy Land group burst into spontaneous cheers and boos. The game was over. Time to check on my wife.

I leaned down to kiss Nana on the cheek and moseyed to the group. The three women were breaking the difficult news to the kids that game time was over. They started to argue but took one look at me and scattered.

"You beat them when no one's around?" Pippa

teased, looking from me to the smoke trails left by the children.

"Use a belt one time, and they think you're a monster."

Her head swiveled back to me *Exorcist* style.

"Kidding, Pip." I raised a brow.

Rowan and Noemi burst out laughing. I caved and freed a small smirk of my own as I pulled over a dining chair and sat next to them.

"Game time over?"

"Yeah," Rowan replied. "Three rounds was enough." She was collecting the cards printed with colorful squares when Pippa clasped her hand to study Rowan's tattoo.

"You and Noemi both have badass tattoos with your husbands. Why is it I suddenly feel like I should have one?"

Noemi grinned. "We both got them when we got married. Maybe that's at least *one* thing you could save until marriage." Noemi was relatively quiet, at least compared to other women in the family, so when she hit a zinger like that, it was all the more entertaining.

I had to cough to hide my laughter.

Rowan clamped a hand over her mouth while Pippa's eyes nearly fell out of their sockets. I expected a scathing yet playful reply, but she surprised me with a single-word response.

"Touché."

All three laughed so hard they started crying, and Noemi had to run to the restroom wailing about peeing in her pants. That only made the other two laugh harder.

I didn't anticipate my intense pride at seeing Rowan fit in so well with my family. Yeah, I wanted her to like them, and vice versa, but I hadn't realized how important it was to me until I watched her blend in like a natural part of the group.

I caught my wife's eye and leaned forward. "I was thinking of calling it a night. Did you want to stick around a while longer?" I loved seeing her so happy, but that didn't make me any more of an extrovert. I'd peopled for hours and was ready to escape home.

"We can head out. I'm pretty wiped out myself."

Thank God.

I was about to stand when my phone vibrated in my pocket. Everything in the city was shut down, and everyone who was important to me was in this room. Who the fuck was calling?

"Yeah?"

"Mr. Byrne? This is Aaron with Precision Security. We're showing sensor activity at 126 W. 38th Street. Would you like me to send the police over to investigate?"

The alarm had gone off at Moxy? What the hell was that all about?

"No. I'll head over and check it out. I'm sure it's nothing." I wasn't so sure, but the last thing I wanted was the cops snooping in my club. If there was a problem, we'd handle it on our own.

"Thank you. Have a nice night," said the monotone voice before the line went dead.

"What was that all about?" Rowan asked as Torin joined us. He'd noticed me take a call.

"Alarm went off at the club."

"I'll go check it out," Tor quickly offered.

"We were about to head out anyway," I told him. "I'll run in with you on our way home, just to be safe."

He gave a curt nod, and Rowan jumped to her feet. We said a quick goodbye to everyone and were on the road in a matter of minutes. Torin was on his bike behind us. I liked a good bike as much as the next guy, but I'd never understood his refusal to drive anything else. Stubborn asshole had to be freezing. Between the fights and his bike, sometimes I wondered if his mother hadn't dropped him as a baby.

Thirty minutes later, we parked out front of the Moxy. Everything looked as it should. I preferred to prepare for the worst, but the alarm might have been a fluke.

"I'm going to check things out with Tor. I want you to stay here, doors locked. Understood?"

"Yes, Sir, Colonel Sir." She saluted, hand at her forehead.

"Smart-ass." I smirked. "Spare gun's under the seat, just in case."

"In case of what?" She balked.

I shrugged. "Hell if I know." I stepped out of the car, turning and waiting for the doors to lock behind me before joining Torin at the Moxy entrance.

"It's locked. If someone got in, they went in through the back."

"I seriously doubt anyone's in there," I told him, inserting my key into the lock. "It's Thanksgiving. Even the Albanians aren't out tonight. If I had a guess, I'd say it's those damn rats that keep multiplying in the back alley." I opened the door and stepped inside, flipping on the light switch, which only turned on a set of fluorescents at the front. The main switchboard was in the back.

Gun in hand, Torin started making his way through the club. I kept mine holstered and followed him. Everything looked fine until we got to the lady's locker room. A light shone from under the door.

Tor and I exchanged a look. We moved to either side of the door, and I finally took out my gun, clicking the safety off. After listening for a minute and not hearing anything, he flung open the door to reveal the very last thing I expected to see.

Stormy sat against the lockers, her knees curled protectively to her chest, shaking like a leaf. And that wasn't all. Her left eye was swelling shut, and her lip was bleeding. When we burst inside, she flinched, then brought her arm around her middle and winced.

"Storm, what the *fuck!*" Torin roared.

"*Easy,*" I barked at him.

"I'm so sorry, guys," Storm pleaded. Her voice was brittle—unlike the sassy Southern belle we were used to hearing. "I wondered if coming here might trip the alarm, but I didn't have anywhere else to go."

My cousin and I walked over to her and squatted down to take a closer look.

"What's goin' on, Stormy?" I asked. If she had a guy at home who had done this, he was about to get seriously fucked up.

"It was my own damn fault. I had a feeling someone was following me on my way home, and I should have listened to my instincts." Her eyes stayed focused on her knees as she spoke, refusing to look at either of us. I wasn't sure if she was embarrassed or hiding the truth.

"You need a place to stay?" I asked.

She slowly nodded, lifting her gaze to mine. "I can't go back there right now."

Torin shot to his feet. "Here's the key to the bike. She's coming with me." He held out his hand, presumably for the key to my car.

I slowly stood, surprised at his vehemence. "Keys are still in the car, and I'm not taking Rowan on the damn bike. We'll call an Uber."

Torin started to drop back to the ground, but I put an arm out to stop him.

"You sure you're okay to handle this? She's not up for an interrogation." I wasn't sure what had gotten into him. He wasn't the caretaker sort, but I felt like I'd be coming between a dog and its bone if I stopped him.

"I'm not a total asshole, Keir," he shot back at me.

That was debatable.

My lips curved with a frown. "I want an update tomorrow."

He gave a curt nod, then lowered to gingerly lift Storm into his arms.

This was *not* how I'd expected my night to end, but that seemed to be my world, anymore. A month of peace followed by all hell breaking loose. We'd had our month. It was time for the chaos.

♦

Thank you so much for reading CORRUPTED UNION! The Byrne Brothers is a series of interconnected standalone novels, and the next book in the lineup is Ruthless Salvation, which you can read more about below.

Bonus Epilogue

Before you move on to the next book, make sure you grab your FREE bonus epilogue for Corrupted Union. You won't want to miss the incredible way Keir and Rowan celebrate their one-year anniversary!

Scan the QR code below or head to my website listed below for your free download.
www.jillramsower.com/bonus-content/

Bonus Epilogue

Ruthless Salvation (The Byrne Brothers #3)

Torin battles relentlessly to keep his obsession for Stormy at bay. Watching her from the shadows is the only concession he allows himself … until the southern beauty is savagely attacked. His possessive nature unleashed, Torin is compelled to claim Stormy for her own protection, whether she wants him to or not.

Ruthless Salvation

Missed the first Byrne Brothers novel?

In Silent Vows, Conner chose his arranged marriage bride because she was mute, thinking he wouldn't ever have to talk to her. But when he learns Noemi was silent to protect herself from an abusive father, he becomes obsessed with his new wife and vengeance on her behalf.

Silent Vows

Stay in touch!!!

Make sure to join my newsletter and be the first to hear about new releases, sales, and other exciting book news! Head to www.jillramsower.com or scan the code below.

ABOUT THE AUTHOR

Jill Ramsower is a life-long Texan—born in Houston, raised in Austin, and currently residing in West Texas. She attended Baylor University and subsequently Baylor Law School to obtain her BA and JD degrees. She spent the next fourteen years practicing law and raising her three children until one fateful day, she strayed from the well-trod path she had been walking and sat down to write a book. An addict with a pen, she set to writing like a woman possessed and discovered that telling stories is her passion in life.

SOCIAL MEDIA & WEBSITE

Release Day Alerts, Sneak Peak, and Newsletter
To be the first to know about upcoming releases, please join Jill's Newsletter. (No spam or frequent pointless emails.)
Jill's Newsletter

Official Website: www.jillramsower.com
Jill's Facebook Page: www.facebook.com/
jillramsowerauthor
Reader Group: Jill's Ravenous Readers
Follow Jill on Instagram: @jillramsowerauthor
Follow Jill on TikTok: @JillRamsowerauthor

Made in the USA
Columbia, SC
02 December 2023

27572078R00198